THE FOURTH OPTION

Matt Hilton worked for twenty-two years in private security and the police force. He is a 4th Dan black-belt in Ju-Jitsu. He lives in Cumbria with his wife and two dogs.
www.matthiltonbooks.com

Praise for Matt Hilton's JOE HUNTER thrillers

"Matt Hilton delivers a thrill a minute. Awesome!"
Chris Ryan

"Vicious, witty and noir…a sparkling new talent."
Peter James

"Check the edge of your seat – it's where you are going to spend most of the time when in the company of Joe Hunter."
www.thrillers4u.com

"Roars along at a ferocious pace."
Observer

"Action-packed from start to finish."
Heat

"Electrifying."
Daily Mail

THE FOURTH OPTION

A Joe Hunter Thriller
By
Matt Hilton

THE FOURTH OPTION

MATT HILTON

First published 2020
Copyright © 2020 Matt Hilton

This is a work of fiction. Names, characters, places and incidents are either the product of the author's imagination or are used fictitiously, and any resemblance to actual persons, living or dead, or to actual events or locales is entirely coincidental.

Matt Hilton has exerted his right to be identified as the author of this work.

Cover images used under standard license from Pixabay.com/AlemCoksa
Cover design © 2020 Matt Hilton

The Fourth Option

<u>1</u>

'It's good to have you back, brother,' said Jared 'Rink' Rington as I dragged my suitcase towards him. Having crossed the Atlantic, I'd just disembarked a connecting flight from Orlando at Tampa International Airport. I'd been on the move for almost fifteen hours. I was stiff, tired, and hot, but seeing my friend brought a grin to my face.

Rink was a man of contradictions. Sometimes he was as still and centred as a Zen master, on others he was magnanimous with his affection. On this occasion he was the latter; he caught me up in an unashamed bear hug that almost had me on tiptoes as he squeezed the breath out of me.

'It's good to see you too, Rink,' I wheezed.

He set me down, held me at arm's length and said, 'Let me have a look at you.'

'I'm still as ugly as ever,' I reassured him.

'Uglier,' he decided. 'You need to get a bit of colour back in your cheeks, Hunter. You're lookin' kinda grey.'

'Grey's the colour of my homeland,' I said.

He held out his hands, a question in his eyes.

'OK,' I said, acknowledging that I was back in sunny Tampa, 'this is home.'

'Darn tootin',' he said. 'You've no option other than to stay here now. There's less for you in the Panhandle than there was back in the Old Country.'

'It's that bad?'

'Didn't you check out the photos I sent ya?'

'I couldn't bear to look.'

I was lying.

It wasn't long ago that armed mercenaries made an incursion of my home. Luckily my beach house had withstood the ensuing battle, and it had only taken minor repairs and a lick or two of paint to make it habitable once more. But from Rink's photographs I'd seen my house was now no more than a pile of sticks.

Hurricane Michael had made landfall and devastated the small Florida Panhandle city I called home. The category four hurricane hit Mexico Beach with winds of one hundred and fifty-five miles per hour, wiping out all but the most sturdily built beachfront structures, including the house in which I'd dwelt these past few years. Since the armed attack, I'd been contemplating a move closer to Tampa, the base from which I worked, but hadn't yet committed to the idea. It'd be egotistical to suggest Mother Nature was giving me a motivational kick in the arse or think she cared a jot about me when she'd ripped the homes and livelihoods away from my neighbours as well: I was truly gutted for their losses.

I'd avoided the devastation wreaked by the hurricane, because I was thousands of miles away in northern England at the time. It'd been years since I'd returned home to Manchester, and a visit with my mother had been long overdue. Ours had never been a close relationship. After my dad died young, and my mother remarried, I'd always felt like a loose end tagged onto her new family, but that isn't to say I didn't love her. I'd also dropped in on Diane, my first and greatest love

The Fourth Option

— and now ex-wife — because although our marriage had ended we'd stayed friends. Besides, she still looked after my dogs, Hector and Paris. At fourteen years old, Hector had already outlasted the life expectancy of most German shepherd dogs, and Paris wasn't far behind him, and I wanted to hug them before it was too late.

The visit with my mother had lasted longer than anticipated. I'd stuck around a few days more until I felt we'd made our peace. My mother and stepfather didn't blame me for the loss of my half-brother John, but I sensed that they thought I could have tried harder to save him. Apparently it wasn't enough for them that I'd fought tooth and nail to protect him, or that I'd stopped the demented murderer hunting him. That I later also saved his wife — the mother of their grandchildren — after the same killer resumed his mission to end John's life, won me slight gratitude but I still felt they'd rather it was me who'd perished and not their favourite son. When the news arrived that the hurricane had wrecked my home in Florida it earned me some sympathy. My mother had tears in her eyes when I announced I should return to Mexico Beach to assist with the clean up but she gave me her blessing to leave. I'd wondered if she was glad of the excuse to get shot of me, but I think she was being genuine when she reminded me that I still had a bedroom there to come back to if I needed it.

Rink kind of echoed her sentiment. '*Mi casa es tu casa*, brother,' he said. 'Or if you prefer your own space you can set up in back of the office.'

'I'll avail you of your couch for a day or two, if that's OK?'

He didn't answer. It was a done deal.

Rink has an office in downtown Tampa, an official shop front for Rington Investigations. Behind the office he has a room equipped for when his workload keeps him late. There was a time when an armed incursion took place there too, and a woman I felt strong feelings towards died in that room. I'm not suggesting her restless spirit haunts the place, but the memory of her death troubles me to this day, so I doubted I could sleep there without suffering nightmares.

Rink had left his Porsche at home, choosing instead to collect me in a cab. The driver had kept it running at the curb in the queue of other taxis and vans collecting the holidaymakers that'd accompanied me from Orlando and beyond on my flight. Rink grabbed my suitcase off me and slung it in the back, and we climbed inside. The air-con was on, and welcome. I'd only been over in the cool of Blighty a fortnight or so, but would need to reacclimatize to the blistering heat currently pounding Florida in the wake of the storms. The cab took us out onto the interstate, and then East Busch Boulevard past the famous theme park and on to Rink's condominium in Temple Terrace. Sweating my arse off, I lugged my suitcase inside, and Rink didn't pause before heading for the refrigerator and grabbing a couple of cold beers. We took them out onto his balcony where I unbuttoned my shirt and kicked back on a comfortable chair. The birds were singing and when the gentle breeze blew in the right direction I could hear the distant, delighted shrieks as people rode the rollercoasters at Busch Gardens. We sat in companionable silence for a while. Making the pilgrimage to England had been a necessary distraction, because the last time I'd sat there on Rink's deck I'd struggled with where I really belonged: I concluded that it was good to be back, because Rink was as much my family as any of my loved ones across the Atlantic.

2

Sometimes the old saying "seeing is believing" is true. Other times you doubt what your eyes are telling you, especially when you know they must be lying. Your eyes can be deceived: fact. But then there are times when you simply must trust your gut and go against everything your other senses are telling you.

It happened to me three days after returning to Florida. I'd been back in Mexico Beach a day and a night. In that time I'd barely rested, first working hard to sift through the wreckage of my beach house to salvage the few personal belongings I could find, and then helping some of my neighbours to do the same. I'd booked into a hotel spared from the storm, slept like the dead for a few hours, and then got back to the task of clearing up. Sweating and powdered with dust, I'd taken a break at one of my favourite oyster bars on Highway 98, where you could buy T-shirts emblazoned with the legend "I Got Shucked!". It had been beaten up by the storm, but the owner had got it back in decent shape again and opened for business. I'd eaten a breakfast of eggs and bacon and then nursed a large black coffee as I gathered myself for more toil. I was seated in the shade of a porch out of reach of the glaring sun but not the stifling atmosphere. I kept gazing out to sea, or observing the vehicles passing by on the highway, or the customers coming and going to the adjacent parking lot. I should have paid more attention to my coffee and I would have missed that fleeting glance I took at a man getting into the front passenger seat of a steel-grey Mercedes Benz SUV. I saw him for no more than two seconds, and from an angle where he didn't even present his full profile. I caught a glimpse of the curve of his jawline, his deformed right ear, and the silvery hair curling on the back of his head that failed to conceal a crescent-shaped scar. But I knew him. Recognition sent a slither of ice knifing through my guts, and the breath hitched in my chest.

A driver already had the SUV's engine running, and I saw the reverse lights glow. I stood, craning for a better look, but the windows were tinted and denied me a clear look at the passenger. The SUV swung out of the parking bay, presenting a view of the driver's side, and this time the window was open a few inches. I could make out the vibrant red hair of a woman, swept up and back into a ponytail. I dodged around my table, taking a few steps along the porch, but already the Mercedes was moving for the exit and I could see nothing of either of the car's occupants.

I disbelieved what my eyes told me, and should have shaken off the uneasy feeling in my gut, let them go and have done. But it wasn't in my nature. I threw a handful of dollar bills down on my vacated table, and rushed for my Audi that I'd parked within spitting distance of where the Merc had previously sat. By the time I'd clambered inside and got it moving the SUV had gone right towards Mexico Beach. I went after it.

As I drove through the post-apocalyptic scenes of town, I kept telling myself it couldn't be him.

It couldn't be.

But I had to make certain.

I was tempted to put my foot down, maybe even force the SUV off the road and pull the passenger out so I could stare him in the face. But what if I was wrong? In fact, I had to be wrong, so I denied my natural instincts and fell in a few cars behind the Merc and followed through Mexico Beach and on towards Panama City. As we forged on adjacent to the Sound I contemplated ringing Rink on my cell phone, but again decided against it. I had to confirm an identity before bringing Rink on board; otherwise my friend would think I'd finally lost it.

Bypassing Tyndall Air Force Base we got on to Dupont Bridge where it spanned the eastern wing of Saint Andrew Bay, and then entered the outlying neighbourhoods adjoining Panama City. For all I knew I could have a long journey ahead, but I doubted it. I trusted that they called somewhere in or near Panama City home. My assumption was rewarded a short time later when the Merc pulled into a residential neighbourhood, driving only a couple more blocks before it pulled up at the foot of a short driveway. I parked about fifty yards shy of them, watching while the woman hopped out of the driver's door and went up the drive. She was pretty, and a flowery dress floated about her shapely legs as she strode for the house. I expected the man to follow, but he didn't.

I was itching to confirm that my eyes hadn't deceived me, and almost got out of my Audi, but if the passenger was who I thought then I'd have to do something. This sunlit residential street wasn't the right place for a confrontation. So I waited instead and after a few minutes watched the woman come back down the drive and climb in the SUV. For all I knew she'd only made a brief visit to an acquaintance's home, but I doubted it, because before she got in the car I noticed she'd changed out of her summer dress into jeans and a T-shirt and was now carrying a large tapestry bag. She'd made a brief stop to change and the way I saw it the house had to be hers. I committed the address to my memory, the way I'd already subconsciously done with the SUV's license tag.

When she drove away, I followed again, and this time was led into downtown Panama City. At a red light the Merc drew to a halt, and I was tempted to pull up alongside them in the next lane, maybe get a clearer look at the face of her passenger. But the tinted window would foil me, and allow the passenger a clear look at my face if he happened to glance down. If it was the person I believed, I didn't want our first reunion to be on those terms. I held back, and again played tail. When the woman pointed the SUV towards a subterranean parking lot beneath a glass- and steel-fronted office block I pulled into the curb and watched as the SUV slipped for the first time out of sight. Following them down the ramp would be a mistake, because it might be unavoidable that I'd be spotted and identified.

I mentioned earlier that if I fronted him I'd have to do something about it. The same could be said for if he recognised me in the parking garage, and again it wasn't the right place. There was a security guard at the barrier, and most likely CCTV cameras inside. But my need to confirm my eyes weren't playing tricks was too much to ignore. I left my Audi illegally parked, and jogged across the portico to the front of the office block. There were various plaques on the wall, denoting that the office building was used by a number of companies. Good and bad. Good because it offered me the anonymity to enter unchallenged, but bad that it didn't tell me whom those in the SUV were visiting. I entered a foyer area, and ignoring the reception counter I went to the right where I'd spotted a number of chairs and sat down. Some magazines had been supplied to keep visitors entertained while they waited to be collected for appointments, or to be called forward to the elevators and sent on up. I picked up a well-thumbed magazine and made like a bored appointee, despite the fact I was still dressed in dusty work clothes.

Luck was on my side. At least it was partly favouring my decision to sequester myself in the lobby, because I had a good angle on the elevator doors when they slid open to allow access to another visitor heading up. The couple I'd followed here was standing inside, and the man moved aside to allow the visitor to join them in the car. He was partially hidden by the man stepping aboard, but he was that much taller so that I got a look at him from the bridge of his nose to the top of his head. His gaze lighted for the briefest second on me, before slipping away. But in the next instant his eyes snapped back on me, and recognition lit them up. That was all the confirmation I required. I quickly dipped my face as if squinting at the magazine, and before he could get a better look at me the doors slid shut. I got up, ready to move away, half expecting him to hit the button to open the doors. But the indicator panel above the elevator showed the car was in motion.

I chucked down the magazine, and hurried back to my car. Thankfully it hadn't been towed or ticketed. Getting in, I allowed myself a moment's reflection, sinking low in the seat, exhaling deeply. Then I reached for my cell phone and hit Rink's number.

'You aren't going to believe who I just seen,' I said once Rink picked up.

'Kim Kardashian?' he asked hopefully. 'Tell me, brother, is her butt as deliciously curvy as it looks on TV?'

I ignored his question, and he must have sensed that this wasn't a time for jokes.

'C'mon, Hunter. Just tell me.'

'Jason Mercer,' I said, and if I hadn't seen him with my own two eyes I wouldn't have believed me either.

'Can't have been.'

'Trust me, Rink. It was Mercer.'

'It couldn't have been,' Rink said, stating exactly the same as my own mind had been telling me. 'You were there when I put two rounds in that frog-gigger's skull.'

3

Rink drove up to Mexico Beach in record time. If he'd come in his Porsche he might have cut his journey time by a few more minutes, but it was negligible. He pulled up on the packed sand that served as my driveway in the company Ford we used when requiring a less conspicuous vehicle. He couldn't immediately see me for the piles of debris. I was waiting for him on the raised decking at beachside that gives an incredible view over the Gulf, the only recognisable part of my house to survive. For a tall guy built like a pro-wrestler, Rink is usually graceful and smooth in motion, so I could tell he was jittery with nervous tension when he clipped his way towards the foot of the stairs to the deck. He was unshaven, and his thick black hair was finger-combed back off his brow. An old scar on his chin was vivid against his deep saffron skin; it was pulled taut as he gnawed at his bottom lip.

'It couldn't have been him,' he announced by way of greeting.

'Trust me, Rink, I've told myself the same thing a thousand times, but it was him. I saw Jason Mercer. No doubt about it.'

Rink climbed the short stairs to the deck.

We stood side by side, looking out at the sun as it dipped towards the distant horizon.

'Couldn't be...'

Rink was in denial. But seeing as he was the one who'd shot Jason Mercer it was more difficult for him to accept the truth. He possibly wouldn't believe until he too laid eyes on Mercer, and maybe not even then.

'I got two looks at him,' I said, 'and to be fair neither were full on, but I know it was him.'

'I put two bullets in his head, Hunter.'

'I know. And I saw his scars.' I touched my head at the back of my right ear. 'The second time I saw him he was in an elevator and he looked me dead in the face, Rink. He recognised me, too.'

Rink exhaled through his nostrils. 'If by some miracle he survived, why wait until now to show himself?'

'That's the thing; he wasn't exactly showing himself.' I told him about Mercer being with the woman at the oyster bar where I first spotted him. 'To me it looked like he was on a lunch date or something, maybe an illicit one. Why drive all the way here from Panama City when there are plenty of restaurants nearer by, especially when half of this town has been blown away? I think they were keeping their rendezvous a secret.' In the next second I made a reassessment. 'Then again, Mercer was with the woman when she went home, and he accompanied her to a meeting in the city. So I guess they weren't trying too hard to hide.'

Rink faced me. 'You think they knew you were there and wanted you to follow them?'

'No. I arrived at the bar after they did. Their Merc was already parked when I pulled up. I remember. I never went inside, just ordered at my table on the porch. I never got a hint that they'd spotted me as they left, and Mercer looked surprised to see me when our eyes met when he was in the elevator.'

'So he's not here on some revenge gig.'

'If he were he could easily look you up in the telephone directory,' I said. 'No. I think it was pure chance that I happened to be in the right place at the right time.'

'I don't usually believe in coincidence.'

'Fate? Karma? Maybe there's something in it.' I'm an advocate of the old saying: what goes around comes around. This wouldn't be the first time that a ghost from our past had come back to haunt us.

'If it was Mercer, what are we gonna do about it?'

'Maybe we should do nothing,' I said.

Rink grunted.

He crossed his arms, leaned on the deck rail, and stared out to sea, but his gaze roamed further distant. I wondered what pictures were in his mind, and if they included dead women and children, murdered in a village in Sierra Leone.

'Here,' I said, handing him a Coke from a cooler box I'd brought. 'Sorry I've nothing stronger.'

He knocked the base of his bottle against mine.

I chugged down half my cola in one long draught. Rink allowed his to swing from his hand by its neck. Condensation dripped off the bottle to the sand below.

'As much as I hate to admit it, we're gonna have to call Walter,' Rink finally said.

I'd come to the same conclusion, but was waiting for Rink to make the suggestion first. My pal held no love for our old controller and might have gone ballistic if I'd gone ahead with the call before consulting him.

The Fourth Option

'Before we do that, I'm up for another look at him. Just to make certain.'

'We should,' Rink said. 'But I'm afraid of what I might do if I see him.'

'Whatever you do, the bastard will deserve it.'

'There's a law in this country, Hunter. Double jeopardy. You can't be tried for the same crime twice.'

'When did we ever observe the laws of the land?' I offered a sly grin. 'And don't forget: the same goes both ways. Who's going to blame you if you have to put another couple of bullets through his skull?'

'That's what I'm afraid of.'

'So we just forget about him. Let him go.'

Rink didn't reply.

He didn't have to. He knew as well as I did that if Jason Mercer had escaped death then others wouldn't — and perhaps hadn't during the intervening years. I seriously doubted that his near death experience had changed Mercer for the better.

'I vote we take a run up to Panama City. You have to see him for yourself; whatever happens after that depends on it.'

'You know where to find him?'

'I know where the woman lives. I take it Mercer won't be far from her side.'

'You expect her to point us at him?'

'I'm not going to twist her arm if that's what you're worried about. But where's the harm in asking about an old friend?'

Rink snorted. 'That's stretching the definition.'

At the end, it was, but not in the beginning. I looked my friend fully in the face, adding weight to my next words. 'We were all Arrowsake once.'

'I hear you, brother,' Rink said, understanding exactly what I meant. 'Loud and clear.'

Evening was on its way.

'You want to head on up there now?' I asked.

Rink took a cursory sip of his Coke, but he'd no intention of finishing it. I took it from him and placed it on the deck. 'Now's as good a time as any.'

'Yeah,' said Rink. Neither of us would rest until we were sure that Jason Mercer had genuinely resurrected.

Without discussion we went to the Ford.

'Want me to drive?' I asked. Rink had just driven the three hundred and fifty-plus miles from Tampa.

'I'm good.' It was probably best that he drive, because he'd be a fidgety passenger all the way. I got in the other seat, and Rink reversed off my drive and onto the short lane that led back to Highway 98. He turned left, following the same route I had earlier when chasing the SUV. He didn't need directions to the red-haired woman's home until we were in the city proper.

When we arrived on the suburban street, I indicated the house where the SUV had stopped earlier, and we did a slow drive-by. There were no lights on in the house and the Mercedes-Benz wasn't on the driveway. It was too early for the woman to have retired for the evening, and best bet was that she was yet to return home. Whether she'd do so with Mercer or not was still to be seen.

The Fourth Option

Rink turned the Ford at the end of the street and we came back for a second look. Nothing had changed in the past minute. Rink turned the car again then parked beneath the boughs of a spreading oak. The extra shadows would help our car blend with the deepening night while we waited.

'So we just sit tight?' I asked.

'Yup.'

'What if they don't come back tonight?'

'Then we wait til they do.'

I glanced over at my friend. Rink is Asian American. His hooded eyes were inherited from his Japanese mother, Yukiko, as surely as his large build came from his Scottish-Canadian father. The epicanthic folds were more pronounced than normal, setting his eyes deeper; I hadn't seen my friend this intense since we'd hunted the murderer of his dad a few years ago.

'I've all the time in the world,' I reassured him, 'but I could spend some of it being more productive than getting a numb arse.'

'You want to go in and take a look around?'

No. Entering the home of a woman who could be totally ignorant of whom she was associating with was firmly off the cards. I was more inclined to check her out without having to sneak about like a thief. I took out my phone and rang Raul Velasquez, an employee of Rink's and a good friend. First I made an apology for disturbing him at home.

'Whassup?' he asked, shrugging off the inconvenience.

'I need an address checked, and any details on the homeowners.'

'Easy enough,' he said. 'Beats watching reruns of *Storage Wars* on TV.'

'Cheers, buddy,' I said, and gave him the address of the house we were currently watching.

'How soon do you need this?'

'Soon as,' I said.

'Rink with you?'

'He is.'

'We got a job on?' Velasquez was hopeful.

'Too early to say, Val,' I said. 'But if anything comes of this, we'll let you know, okay?'

I hung up, looked over at Rink. His hands were on the steering wheel, the skin taut over his large karate-calloused knuckles. I didn't require a warning from him, because his body language spoke volumes. A silver grey Mercedes-Benz GL450 had just entered the street from the far end and was already slowing as it approached the target house. Even without being able to read the tag, I knew it was the same SUV I'd tailed earlier. The tinted windows and the glow of its headlights thwarted any view of how many people were inside.

The SUV pulled on to the drive this time, but we were in a good position to see the same red-haired woman get out. She wore the same jeans and T-shirt from earlier, and still toted the large tapestry bag. Unfortunately, that was as far as the similarities went, because this time there was no passenger along for the ride. She walked up the drive fast, her legs scissoring, and up onto the porch steps. She already had her house keys in hand, and before going indoors she took a quick glance around, ensuring that nobody was about to rush her and bear her inside. Nervous? That wasn't it; it was more like precaution. Before she unlocked the door she looked directly at our Ford. From the distance, and hidden in the shadows from the oak tree we wouldn't be apparent, but I'm sure that the woman sensed our observation. Her gaze lingered a moment, then her head shifted subtly, apparently writing us off. She unlocked the door and went inside. Lights went on in the downstairs windows, but no shadows shifted behind the blinds. I looked higher up and after half a minute I thought I caught a shifting of the darkness in one of the bedrooms. She was up there, surreptitiously watching us as we watched her.

'Interesting,' Rink said, and he was more pensive than I'd ever seen him.

It was interesting. The woman wasn't exactly acting counter surveillance savvy; otherwise she wouldn't have been so obvious as to look directly at our car. But she was more aware of her surroundings than most civilians, and pointedly checked out anything unusual, which was enough to suggest she had a reason to be wary.

'You said that Mercer met your gaze when he was in the elevator,' Rink said. 'Maybe he mentioned seeing you and she's on the look out for us.'

'That'd suggest she knows who Mercer really is, and how he knows me, and why that should concern them.'

'He could have lied to her. He was good at lying.'

'He certainly fooled us for years,' I concurred.

'Fooled me when the frog-gigger played possum too.' Rink shook his head, sighed again. 'I should've made sure the sumbitch was dead.'

I didn't reply. Recrimination wouldn't help.

The front door of the house opened and the woman stepped out. She'd pulled a jacket on over her T-shirt and jeans, and was still lugging her large bag: it looked heavier now. Purposefully she stared at our Ford again, but instead of going back inside, or even striding towards us she got back into the SUV and backed it down the drive. Rink started our engine but didn't turn on the lights, maybe anticipating following. But the SUV drove towards us.

The Mercedes came to a halt, its driver's window adjacent to Rink's. We were being studied from beyond the tinted window.

'Some stake out,' I admonished under my breath.

Rink didn't reply, he just sat there looking up at the elevated window of the SUV. It powered down, and Rink also hit his window button.

I had a poor view of her from where I sat, and could only see the bottom edge of her window and the shape of one shoulder. Rink observed her in silence.

'Jared Rington,' the woman said, and it was the subtle accusation in her tone that made my pulse leap.

Rink still didn't reply. He didn't have to. It was apparent that she'd positively identified him. And exactly what the consequences were.

The Fourth Option

A tubular object appeared above the window frame, and even from my poor angle I recognised it as a suppressor screwed onto the barrel of a handgun.

'Bastard!' the woman snapped and the gun aimed for Rink's head.

Rink hit the gas and the Ford lurched forward, just as the woman squeezed the trigger. Even with a silencer, this close the report of the gun was a harsh *crack!* The round striking was a dull thud. Thankfully it had impacted the headrest of Rink's seat and not his skull. In the next second or two we were a full car's length out of range, and to fire on us again the woman would have to lean out of the window. She didn't. She also hit the gas and tore away, and the distance between us lengthened rapidly.

Rink hit the brake and we came to a halt.

Rink, I could tell, was tempted to chase her down. And I'd've been with him. But he didn't.

He looked across at me, surprisingly calm for having come so close to death.

'I guess you were right, brother,' he said. 'Mercer is back from hell, and he's brought somebody equally as mysterious with him.'

4

Rink dug the spent slug out of the headrest, held it up for my appraisal. We'd driven away from the scene, found some waste ground overlooking a stretch of water the colour of burnished brass, and now stood alongside the Ford. The floodlights from a nearby factory stained everything the same amber hue.

'It's nine millimetre,' I said, though he already knew that.

It was a calibre of round big enough to have addled his brain if the woman had gotten a clean shot at him.

'Good job you hit the throttle,' I said.

Rink grunted, bouncing the barely misshapen bullet on his palm. 'Not sure she would've hit me even if I didn't.'

'Warning shot?'

'If she wanted to she could've killed me, no problem.'

'So she didn't want to kill you?'

I waited.

Rink pulled his bottom lip over his teeth, thinking hard. The scar on his chin was vivid again. Then he looked at me, and I knew what was coming.

'I knew her.'

'Yeah, I guessed.' I thought about his enigmatic statement from earlier. 'You identified her the second she got out of the SUV.'

'Suzanne Bouchard,' Rink said. 'At least that's what she was called back then. It's been a few years.'

The name didn't mean anything to me.

Rink stared up at the sky. The light pollution from the nearby factory washed out the stars, but the moon presented a fingernail clipping of radiance for him to concentrate on.

'So,' I said.

Rink exhaled, but didn't elucidate.

I waited.

'I dated her,' he finally said.

'No wonder she tried to shoot you in the head.' I smiled to punctuate the joke, but he wasn't looking at me. I shut up.

'You don't remember her?'

I shrugged.

'She was younger — obviously — didn't have that dyed red hair back then. She'd a short dark crop? Canadian girl?'

'Ah,' I said. Back in 1989 a Canadian Human Rights Act appointed the full integration of women into the Canadian Armed Forces. It took some years afterwards but Suzanne Bouchard — though the name still didn't mean much to me — had been put through for selection with Arrowsake. She hadn't completed the course. As I recalled, she was deemed physically incapable of the rigours male recruits were subject to and the Arrowsake command would not allow a significant lowering of the physical performance requirements — but that was just bureaucratical, misogynistic bullshit. The truth was, they'd vetoed the intake of women into front-line military combat, choosing instead to use them as their own undercover operatives, the way that the CIA and MI6 did. If women were going to get killed in combat, it wouldn't be while wearing a recognisable uniform. When female operatives had worked alongside us on missions they'd proved themselves every bit as capable as any of the men, sometimes more so. I could vaguely remember the young woman from Toronto, though she looked nothing like she did now and back then went by the shortened name of Sue. She was tough and resourceful, and now that I thought back, as hot as hell. Rink had spent some downtime with her, but I'd have been a third wheel on their dates. Anyway, back then I was still loved-up and when off duty I'd returned home to England and my wife, Diane, so I never got to know Rink's girlfriend. Now that I thought about it, their relationship had cooled after the death of Jason Mercer.

'She wasn't there when Mercer caught it.'

'No. But Mercer was.' Rink ruminated a little more. 'From the look of things he's kind of skewed the version of events he's told her. Like I said: he's a good liar.'

'He's convinced her he was badly done to and you were the one in the wrong.'

'Maybe she didn't take too much convincing. She already thought I was the one in the wrong before we said goodbye.' Rink shook his head, rueful that things had ended badly with Sue. 'I wanted to see Mercer for myself; now it's not as important. That was definitely Sue, so there's no reason to doubt it was Mercer you saw with her.'

I waited for clarity.

The Fourth Option

'Suzanne Bouchard also died.' He scowled at the wrongness of his statement. 'According to Arrowsake she died,' he corrected himself.

'It wouldn't be the first time those bastards have lied to us,' I said. Our old masters had played with the mortality of no less than three people in the past few years, and two of them had done a Lazarus. Of the trio only my brother John was truly dead, except the cabal behind Arrowsake had lied to me by swearing he was alive and in hiding, until I'd done their bidding and the truth finally came out. As absurd as it sounded, I wasn't shocked to learn that another two dead people had been resurrected without the aid of supernatural intervention. 'What was the line of bullshit they used with Sue?'

'Drowning. Allegedly she was scuba diving off one of the Canary Islands and didn't resurface.' Rink shrugged. 'I bought that line, because I knew she was into diving. Even experienced divers can easily get into trouble.'

'Has it occurred to you that maybe Arrowsake also bought the line? What if they had nothing to do with the cover up this time? They were the ones who ordered Mercer's death, maybe they have nothing to do with him resurfacing either.'

'They're a lot of "maybes" to consider, Hunter. We won't know until we talk to Walter.'

'Maybe not even then,' I said, and finally elicited the faintest smile from him. I took out my phone. 'Want me to do the honours?'

'Not sure he'd answer if he sees my number,' said Rink, which wasn't exactly true.

There were few contacts in my list, and I hit the number for Walter Hayes Conrad's personal cell phone. Before it ever reached him, my call would be bounced via various servers and encryption devices. Walter was that secretive. But under the circumstances, it was probably best that our conversation wasn't open to eavesdroppers. Still, despite the nature of my call, I put the phone on speaker so Rink could listen in.

'Joe? I wasn't expecting to hear from you.' As soon as Walter made the announcement I knew that he was lying.

'It's been a while, Walt, thought it was high time I got in touch,' I said, making out a social call had been on my agenda for a while. But he would know I was lying too. Our conversations often took similar shape, half-truths and out-right lies on his part, gruff acceptance that I'd never get a straight answer on mine. Occasionally though, I could get what I wanted from him if I persevered and dug through the deliberate obfuscation. I'd gone beyond a point where I found his lies offensive, because it was simply in his job description to be deceptive. He was after all a CIA subdivision controller, whose secret went even deeper. He was also a direct conduit to Arrowsake, perhaps even one of the shadowy figures behind the recently re-established counterterrorism group Rink and I once worked for. This new incarnation of Arrowsake was a different beast than the one we'd belonged to, and there was nothing about it that appealed to my morality, while Rink passionately hated it.

'Where are you?' Walt asked.

'I'm surprised you have to ask.'

'Despite what you think I don't keep tabs on your movements.' Walter snorted out a laugh. 'Not all of the time.'

'I'm near Panama City.' If he wanted to it would be a simple task for Walter to identify the source of my call.

'Is Rink with you?'

'I'm here,' Rink growled.

'Of course you are.'

I looked at Rink and raised my eyebrows in question.

'Go for it, brother,' he said, urging I make a point and get the call over as quickly as possible.

'Jason Mercer,' I said into the phone.

'Who?'

'You heard me, Walt. But I'll repeat the name incase your hearing is failing in your old age. Jason Mercer.'

'I heard you fine, son, I'm just unsure why you mention *that* name.'

'So you do remember it?'

'Of course.' Walter was the one who'd sanctioned Mercer's death. It was probably one name among hundreds, but I believed that he knew the name of every person whose execution he'd personally ordered. Perhaps their faces even plagued his dreams the way they did mine some nights. 'I only question why you bring it up now.'

'He's alive, Walt, and I think you already know that.'

I waited for his response, but Walter was silent for a moment. I wondered what lies he was trying to come up with. When his answer came it wasn't what I expected. 'I did suspect he'd survived.'

'It wouldn't be the first time you saved the life of an enemy. What did you do, Walt: have him taken away to some secret bunker where he was coaxed back to health, held there and reprogrammed until you could mobilise him again? It'd sound crazy if I didn't know it has happened before.'

'Martin Maxwell was different,' Walt said.

'Martin Maxwell was a psychopathic serial killer,' I corrected him. 'Mercer isn't that different. The only difference was he didn't keep trophies from his victims.'

Walter exhaled into the phone.

'You'll probably doubt what I say, but I had no part in saving Jason Mercer. Rink? You're the one who shot him, you're the one who reported him dead.'

'Don't put this back on me, you son of a bitch,' snapped Rink.

'That's not what I'm saying. I meant you were the one who carried out the sanction; was there ever any doubt in your mind that you'd failed?'

Rink stared up at the moon again.

'He's carrying the scars where he was shot,' I explained. 'There was no way Rink could have suspected he'd survived the wounds he did.'

'Rink reported positive confirmation of death,' Walter pointed out.

The Fourth Option

'Don't speak about me as if I'm not here, Walt,' Rink said without taking his eyes off the sky. 'As far as I was concerned, I'd put two bullets in Mercer's head. He was dead.'

'That's the point, son,' Walt said. 'You made a positive confirmation: so why would I send in a trauma team to pull Mercer out? How would I know that he'd survived when I had such trust in you?'

'Two things,' Rink said. 'Don't call me *son*, and don't mention trust. There's no trust between us. Never will be again.'

'I understand. But it still proves my point. You believe you'd killed him, and at the time I'd no reason to doubt you. Things might be different now, but not back then.'

I shook my head at Rink, stalling another angry retort. Argument would get us nowhere, particularly one where Walter's trustworthiness was in question. The concept was largely alien to one whose entire existence worked through the manipulation and machination of others. Rink pursed his lips. But then he held up a hand to catch my attention. I pressed the phone against my thigh, muffling it as Rink whispered: 'Don't mention Sue.'

I nodded, lifted the phone again.

Walter had apparently been deep in thought. I could hear him breathing.

'What happens now?' I asked.

'I'm unsure,' Walter admitted. 'There's much to learn. More importantly than that he survived, we need to find out who saved him, and why. What is he doing now, and for whom?'

Those were questions I also wanted answering, among others. I closed my eyes, understanding where this was going. Calling Walter as we had, both Rink and I knew that we were tugging on the threads that inevitably connected us to Walter and Arrowsake, and what that would ultimately mean for us. So his next words came as a complete surprise.

'I want you to stand down.'

'Sorry? Say that again.'

'So mine isn't the only hearing that's failing,' Walter countered with a grunt of laughter. 'You heard me, son. I want you to stand down. That goes for both of you. Walk away and forget you saw him. Leave Mercer to me.'

'You're kidding, right?'

'Nope. I'm deadly serious. Forget Mercer, walk away, don't look back.'

I caught the squint of Rink's eyes, and took it as a greater warning than any that Walter made.

'If that's the way you want it, Walter, so be it,' I said, but again it wasn't the entire truth, and I knew Walter didn't buy it. I cancelled the call before he could push the issue one way or the other.

5

There was a missed call notification on my phone. It was from Raul Velasquez, so I hit the reply button even as we got back in the Ford and Rink pulled away. 'Hey, Val,' I said when he answered. 'What have you got?'

'The address you gave me? It isn't registered to an individual owner, but to a company.' He gave me the name of a real estate agency based in Panama City. 'I checked the local census records and it shows as being home to a single female by the name of Suzanne Carter. No husband, no significant other or dependents on the books, but that's saying nothing. It's dependent on whether or not the records are up to date, I guess.' He paused, ordering details in his mind. 'I dug a little deeper, to see what I could find out about Miss Carter. She's forty-two, born in St Petersburg, Florida. Worked as a kindergarten teacher in Tampa until four years ago. Apparently she began working for this company as a licensed realtor after moving to Panama City a short time after. Seems to me like a strange career change, but what do I know about anything?'

Velasquez was pushing for more information on what we'd gotten involved in, but I deemed it best that he was kept out of things for now. 'How'd you find out so much about Carter so quickly?' I asked him, more to divert his attention than anything. 'Have you been taking tips from Harvey?'

'Nu-uh. Wonderful thing called Social Media,' he said. 'Some people live out their lives on the social networks these days. I'm surprised you don't have your own page, Hunter.'

I ignored the suggestion. 'Any current pictures of Carter on there?'

'Yeah. I'm looking at one now. Shame: she'd be a good looking woman without the scars.'

I frowned.

'Can you send me a copy to my phone?'

'No problem, Hunter. Wait up.' I heard tapping from the other end, and thought Velasquez was juggling both his cell phone and computer at the same time. A chime from my mobile notified an incoming text message. I said my thanks and ended the call. Opened the text image.

'What's up?' said Rink.

'The house is registered to a private company, and it's supposedly let to a woman called Suzanne Carter. My first thought was that it was a cover name for Sue, but Val found some pictures of Carter on line. It isn't Sue.' The woman I was looking at had a round face and large brown eyes, a slightly turned up nose, and swarthy complexion. She'd suffered a burn at one time, and the skin was a pink and white patchwork of scar tissue that extended from below her right eye, beneath her nose, pulled at the corner of her mouth and then extended down and under her chin.

'Odd that they'd both have the same first name,' Rink said, as I offered him a look at Carter's photo. 'We both know that when some one takes a new identity they often choose to keep the same first name to avoid confusion. When I heard what Val said to you, I also thought Sue had established a false identity. But that isn't Sue, and she couldn't even pass for Carter at a glance.'

I gave a mental shrug. 'Maybe Sue shares the house with Carter.'

'Perhaps it isn't that important. That real estate agency, they're the ones we need to learn more about.'

Rink was correct. As soon as Velasquez mentioned the name of the company that owned the house, I'd mentally pictured the brass plaques on the wall of the office block I'd earlier followed Mercer and Sue to. One of those brass plates had carried the same company name. So Sue, via the house, had an association with the estate agency, and, through their earlier dual visit to the office, so did Mercer. It was possible that the connection was tenuous — Sue could have been visiting to pay her rent for all I knew, and Mercer had accompanied her — but I didn't think so.

'Walter told us to stand down,' I said.

'Walter can go screw himself,' said Rink.

'You know why he wants us out of the way, right?'

'Of course I do. He's going to send someone after Mercer.' Rink glanced across at me, and probably saw the seriousness in my expression. 'As far as I'm concerned, he can do what he likes with Mercer, but not at the expense of Sue getting hurt.'

'I didn't mention Sue, but I got the impression that Walter already knew about her.' Where Walter was concerned, whatever went unsaid was more important than anything he shared. It had struck me that he hadn't asked about where we'd seen Mercer, which meant he already had a good idea. And telling us to stand down was tantamount to admitting he was sending an assassination team there.

'He sounded downbeat about it all, but we both know how the old fart works. He was practically jumping up and down in reality. You ask me, brother, we just gave him a link in the chain he'd been missing. You can guarantee that a wet team is being mobilised as we speak.' Rink pulled the Ford into a gas station, but it wasn't for the purpose of filling the tank. He spun the car around on the forecourt. 'I have to warn Sue.'

'This is the same Sue who just shot at you.'

'The same Sue who shot to miss.'

'Fair enough,' I admitted. 'But that's not to say she'll be such a poor shot if you show your face a second time. Warning shots only work once, Rink.'

6

We returned to the house allegedly rented by Suzanne Carter, neither of us believing that Sue Bouchard has returned already. We were wrong. The big SUV was tucked up close to the house on the drive. The rear door on the driver's side stood open. Its interior light was on. There were also more lights on in the house than before, this time Sue having lit one of the bedrooms upstairs. She'd dropped the blinds, but we could see her shadow darting back and forth: she was in a hurry.

'Looks as if she might be getting ready to run,' I said.

'Wouldn't you, suspecting what's coming?'

'It'd be unwise to sit put,' I concurred. Except, for now Walter had no idea about this house. Undoubtedly he'd have pinpointed the source of my phone call to him, but that had been from the waste ground alongside the river. Our friend Harvey Lucas was a bit of a whiz with technology; he'd previously shown me how to disable the location device in my phone so it couldn't be tracked, unless it was in use. I'd switched off my phone after last speaking with Velasquez, as had Rink. There was no rush for Sue to abandon her home for now, but she couldn't know that. For all she knew we'd been purposefully hunting her and had called in a strike team. I wondered if she regretted not shooting Rink now, and me along with him.

In my line of work, I keep several grab bags ready for instances when I'm forced to move quickly. They contain cash, and fake ID, credit cards and burner phones, also weapons. If Sue Bouchard had returned home to grab a similar bag, she'd have been in and out of the house in half a minute. It suggested that she'd grown complacent, had never expected to be discovered living in this suburban neighbourhood, and was now reacting in a mild form of panic. I felt a little easier about her, because if she were still engaged in a similar nefarious game as Mercer used to be, then she'd have been prepared for an eventuality like this one. We had to consider if Mercer was still the monster he'd become in Sierra Leone — before Rink had halted his murderous rampage — or if having two bullets in his skull had changed him for the better. Determining Mercer's current nature, and what the hell he was up to here, could wait. For now Rink wanted to ensure that Sue didn't fall into the crosshairs of those coming to end things with Mercer.

'How do you want to play this?' I asked.

Rink had brought the Ford to a halt under the same tree as before. It hadn't hidden us then and wouldn't now, even as the night had grown darker. Sitting there, we were easy targets if Sue decided to come out with her gun blazing. This time I doubted we'd get a warning shot. Without answering, Rink set the car rolling, and he bumped up off the road and into Sue's drive, blocking in the Mercedes. I checked the bedroom, and Sue must have heard us arrive. She'd stuck a couple of fingers between the blinds, prying them apart to check who was outside. The blinds snapped shut. Our angle didn't give us a clear look at the shadow play as before. In fact I couldn't see her silhouette at all, meaning she'd retreated deeper into the room, beyond the source of the light.

'I'll cover the back door,' I said, even as I was slipping out. Rink went without comment towards the front door. Neither of us was armed, so we were risking our arses.

I jogged around the side of the house and set up next to the back door on the rear porch. Faintly, I heard Rink knock on the door and call Sue's name. There was a scuff of feet from inside, and suddenly the back door was yanked inward and Sue emerged. She clutched her tapestry bag, plus a bulging rucksack, in one hand, and her silenced pistol in the other. Silenced pistols, I reminded myself, were the tools of hitmen and assassins, and despite my reason for being there, I mustn't underestimate Sue's possible reaction. Rink knocked the front door again, and it grabbed Sue's attention for a fraction of a second longer than once she might have given the noise. As she made the decision to ignore him, and use the opportunity to flee across the rear yard, she bolted out of the house, swinging her gun around as she sought danger. Thankfully for me, her first move was to swing the barrel towards the rear garden — her immediate direction of travel — so I was already in the arc of its swing as she jerked it towards me. I struck into her wrist with the edge of my left hand, immediately stopping it, and followed up with both hands to grab the gun, and strip it from her grasp. I had to for my safety, and for hers.

Sue didn't understand that I was trying to help.

Her amateurish move with the gun told me that her combat skills were rusty, but nobody tried for selection with Arrowsake who wasn't at the top of their game. Her skills might not have been used for years but it's a bit like riding a bike. No sooner had I taken her pistol from her than she'd dropped her bags and snapped an elbow into my face. I dodged back, and the elbow missed, but then her follow up strike rapped her knuckles into the side of my head. If she'd caught me an inch or two lower on the neck, she would have dropped me cold, but as it were, my initial dodge had been accompanied by a dipping of my knees to retain balance. Her knuckles smacked my ear instead. It was sore, and I felt my ear swell in response, red hot, but it was preferable to being shot. I stepped away, keeping her gun out of reach, even as I stiff-armed her, palm planted on her upper chest, to make some distance.

'Sue, stop!' I hissed, but didn't get to add: "We're here to help."

Sue grasped my hand and twisted under it, flexing my wrist and elbow in some kind of Aikido lock. I didn't want to hurt her, but—

My wrist was in danger of breaking. So I kicked out with my heel, slamming it into her nearest thigh, and Sue buckled with a cry of agony. I wrenched out of her grasp, and spun on her, kicking her feet from under her. She slammed down on the porch floor with enough force that I'd swear the entire house shook. I aimed the gun at her, a visual threat only, but hopefully one she'd heed.

Sue kicked at me. But I didn't give ground. I dropped a knee onto her, and held her down. 'Stay put,' I growled, 'and stop trying to hurt me!'

She must have thought she was about to die, and resolved not to make it easy for me. She neither stayed put nor gave up the fight. She batted at the gun, even as she flexed up from her hips and tried to lock her heel around my throat to force me off her. It was a reckless do-or-die attempt at saving her life, and took a liberty with my reticence to shoot.

Rink appeared behind us. I tossed the pistol towards him, freeing both hands to control Sue. I'd to dodge to avoid her heel that was dropping like an axe at my shoulder, and I swept both her legs sideways so she was forced onto her side, facing away. Immediately I grappled her and squashed her flat under my body weight. 'Sue, for Christ's sake,' I snapped into her ear, 'stop struggling and listen to me.'

'Get off me, Joe!' I don't know if she recalled me from when she was Rink's girl, or Mercer had recently told her who I was.

'We aren't here to hurt you,' I tried again.

'Liar!' She struggled once more but was going nowhere. 'You're here to—'

'We aren't with Arrowsake, we haven't been for years.'

'I don't believe you.'

'If we were you'd be dead by now.'

Her struggles weakened as the truth set in. She exhaled, and all tension seeped from her body. I relaxed some of my weight too, but not enough for her to renew the fight. I glanced back at Rink. Ordinarily my struggles would have elicited a joke at my expense, but Rink looked grim. He'd collected the gun off the floor and held it down by his side.

To Sue, I said, 'If you behave, I'll let you up.'

'You've got me, and taken my gun. What else am I going to do?'

'Yeah,' I said. 'It will be good to remember that.'

I pushed up to a knee, but continued to hold her down until I'd got both feet under me. I helped Sue stand. Her red hair was awry. She glared at us both with seething green eyes. Then she purposefully rubbed at her thigh where I'd kicked her.

'What are you doing here?' she demanded, staring directly at Rink now.

'Believe it or not,' Rink said, 'we're here to help you. Acting ungrateful isn't your best idea.'

'Help me?' Her angry gaze switched to me. 'You just dumped me on my ass, Joe. If that's supposed to be helping me, *thanks for nothing*.'

'You were trying to break my arm at the time.'

'I should have broken it,' she growled.

'No. You should've given me a chance to explain. Instead you gave me a thick ear. I took you down to stop you hurting anyone, including you.' I nodded at the gun in Rink's hand. 'You seriously intended using that?'

The Fourth Option

She rolled her neck. 'We'll never know now. But if you're really here to help me, you can give it back.'

'I'll hold on to it for now.' Rink shoved the silenced pistol into the back of his belt, covering it with his shirttail.

She appraised her ex boyfriend. 'I could barely believe my eyes when I saw you earlier. I couldn't think of another reason for you and Joe to be skulking on my street, other than…' She shrugged an apology. 'I hope you're not going to hold shooting at you against me?'

'You missed. No harm, no foul, I guess.'

Sue was doing OK at trying to disarm us with her geniality. But I was watching the subtle shifts of her feet, and how she'd gained a few inches of space between us. She was preparing to run.

Before she could jerk away to leap inside, maybe with the idea of slamming the door on us, I too shifted. Without warning I grabbed her elbow, and drew her further outside. If she was going to run, it'd have to be through the garden, and we'd catch her before she could scale the far fence. Sue grumbled at me for spoiling her plan, but she settled her feet and faced Rink again. 'Why are you here, Rink? Don't give me that story about being here to help, because I don't buy it. When we laid eyes on each other earlier, you were as surprised as I was.'

'Having a gun pointed at me tends to do that,' he said. But she was owed an explanation of sorts. 'I didn't expect to find you here, Sue. But once I did, I knew you'd need help.'

I said, 'You must've been expecting us.'

'Why would I? It's been years since—'

'Since you supposedly died,' Rink finished for her.

She shook her head. An explanation why she'd faked her death wasn't forthcoming yet.

'Jason Mercer didn't warn you about us?' I asked.

'Jason? How would *he* know you were here?'

'We crossed paths earlier,' I said, 'in a building in downtown Panama City, after I followed you both from Mexico Beach.'

Her dumbfounded expression looked genuine.

'You guys were in the elevator,' I prompted, 'and I was in the lobby. Mercer met my gaze when the doors opened. He didn't tell you about me?'

'He didn't. No offence, Joe, but it's a long time since any of us saw each other. We've all aged. We are all different people these days.'

Rink studied her. He didn't comment on her looks, though I could tell he found her as attractive as ever, despite the passing years or maybe because of them. Sue had been a great looking girl, but she'd become a beautiful mature woman. He spoiled the moment by saying, 'Mercer shouldn't have aged.'

Her teeth were bared as Sue snapped, 'You have no idea the torment Jason has gone through since you shot him.'

Rink snorted. 'He deserved to suffer worse.'

'Why?'

'He was a murderer, Sue.'

'Says the man that shot him in cold blood.'

'Twice,' Rink corrected. 'I shot the bastard twice.'

The Fourth Option

Even I winced at his words.

Sue shook in anger. 'What makes what you did any different from what Jason was asked to do?'

'Asked to do?' Rink replied, incredulous. 'I was a soldier, I acted under orders; *Jason* killed for the hell of it.'

Sue turned away, shaking her head in disbelief. Arguing semantics was pointless; there really isn't a moral high ground when it comes to the role of an assassin, state-sanctioned or otherwise. I took her arm again, but this time to calm the situation.

'Sue,' I said softly. 'Let's leave the past behind us for now. What's more important is to get you somewhere safe from harm.'

She pulled out of my grasp. 'Thanks, but I can look after myself. I have done for years, and don't need either of you now.'

'No offence,' I said, to partially echo her words from earlier, 'but I'm guessing it's a long time since you were in the field. Don't deny it. There's no way I'd have taken you down as easily if you were still active. You do need us. Arrowsake are coming.'

'You told them where to find me?'

'No, but I did mention spotting Mercer. We had no other option. You understand what that probably means now.'

'I have to warn him.'

'No. It's too risky. For now, Arrowsake has no idea you're still alive, I'd prefer to keep things that way.'

'Then *you* must warn Jason.'

'Uh, no.' Rink had been acting on orders when trying to execute Mercer, but it had been a task he'd had no qualms about. He wasn't wrong when he'd said Mercer had killed for the hell of it. Shooting him had been a service to humanity. 'Mercer is fair game. You, on the other hand, are not.'

'I'm not deserting him—'

Rink frowned so hard that his nostrils flared. 'Don't tell me that you and him are—'

'What? Lovers? And what if were are, what the hell has our private lives got to do with you, Rink?'

He shrugged. 'Just thought you'd a better taste in men, Sue.'

'If that was true, then we'd never have gotten together.'

'Ouch,' I said to my friend, 'I bet that stings?'

Except it had the opposite effect. Rink's features softened, and a grin blossomed. At the same time, Sue turned away to hide a sly tightening of her lips.

'This thing with Jason,' she said, 'we are friends, colleagues…we work together.'

'Like you said, nothin' to do with me,' Rink said, 'but it doesn't change my opinion of him. I don't regret shootin' that frog-giggin' sumbitch, an' I'll do it again if I have to.'

'You don't have to. He's not the man he was. In fact,' she looked earnestly back at Rink, 'he was never the man you were told he was. That was lies, fed to you by evil men who wanted him dead.'

'I saw the proof of his crimes,' Rink countered.

The Fourth Option

'You saw what Arrowsake wanted you to see. Jason was following orders, exactly the same way as you did. He knew what he was doing was wrong, but was too afraid to disobey. He was afraid for his life. Ha! He was damned either way. I'm surprised that either of you has been allowed to live, knowing what you know about Arrowsake.'

She had a point. Walter Hayes Conrad had become a surrogate father to me, and it's only through his protection that I've never been on the wet end of a hit. Because Rink was more than a brother to me, Walter had extended his protective shield over him too, and that's despite Rink's obvious hatred for our old masters. But Walter couldn't protect us if we actively defied him and Arrowsake: we'd be making an enemy of the only man that could keep us alive, or out of prison.

7

Back in the day we were soldiers. I was 1-PARA, while Rink was a US Army Ranger. We were already near the pinnacle of our particular trees, special operatives in our right, and it might have been expected of us to aim next for selection with the British Special Air Service and US Navy SEALS respectively. Those weren't the obvious routes we followed. We were handpicked instead for the grueling selection process with an experimental coalition of allied Special Forces operatives, codenamed Arrowsake, and packed off to a secret base on the northwestern Scottish coastline — Arrowsake's codename was derived from a mispronunciation of Arisaig, the fabled home of the Special Operations Executive, the forerunner of the modern MI5. At its inception, and for many years, Arrowsake operated under noble intent. We fought terrorists and tyrants, destabilized cartels and international criminal networks. We were idealistic and blindly followed orders. Then the rot inevitably set in. Instead of soldiers we became something else entirely; we became assassins. The world changed following the terrorist attacks by al-Qaeda against the United States on the morning of September 11th 2001, and with it the face of modern counterterrorism. Rough men with big guns were out, superseded by tech nerds and drone strikes.

Post 9/11, Arrowsake was disbanded, and those of us that'd survived went our separate ways. It was a few years later before Rink and I hooked up again, and inescapably fell under the influence of our old controller, Walter Hayes Conrad. Asking for help from Walter was akin to selling our souls to the devil. He scratched our backs and we had to scratch his, but where we'd tried to sever the relationship the manipulative old bastard still had his claws buried deep. There'd been a few occasions in the latter years where he'd used us to accomplish his personal agenda, and one time where we were pawns of a re-emerged Arrowsake. This Arrowsake was different to the one we'd belonged to, led from the shadows by a cabal of influential and self-serving people, one of whom, it turned out, was Walter. Rink had sworn off any further dealings with them, and I echoed his sentiment, but what could we do when they were once again heading in our direction? Especially when, this time, we'd be deemed stumbling blocks in their way, ergo their enemies. It might sound as if the only way to save us was to leave Mercer to Walter, as instructed, but that would also mean sacrificing Sue, and that didn't sit well with either Rink or me.

With the lack of a plan, we urged her back inside her home, gathering in the kitchen. Not for fear we were imminent targets, but that we might attract unwanted attention from her neighbours. It was already surprising that our brief scuffle hadn't brought out the neighbourhood, but for now we'd gone unnoticed. I wondered if Sue had chosen to live there because people minded their own business. I asked if there was any danger of Suzanne Carter returning home and discovering us. Sue smiled at the notion.

'I'm Suzanne Carter.'

'Yours isn't the face on Miss Carter's social network profiles,' I said, although I already suspected where this was going.

'I'm hardly going to use my own picture, what with facial recognition software being all the rage.'

'So Carter's a legend?'

'Yes. It was a clean skin invented for me, so I could safely live here. Don't forget, Joe, Suzanne Bouchard drowned while scuba diving off the coast of Tenerife.'

Rink made a sound in his throat.

Sue smirked at him. 'You sound as if you actually missed me, Rink.'

'I did.' He rolled his neck. 'We had a falling out, Sue, but I didn't stop caring for you.'

'Sweet,' she said, sounding insincere. But then she shrugged. 'But it's academic now. Who was it that said, "Reports of my death have been greatly exaggerated?"'

'Elvis Presley?' I quipped. 'Rumour is he's flipping burgers in a Seattle diner.'

'It was Mark Twain,' Rink corrected me, and turned his attention back to Sue. 'Why was it necessary for you to go off grid? You didn't make the grade for selection, why would Arrowsake care if you were dead or alive?'

'Who says I didn't make the grade?'

Rink eyed her spuriously.

'What? You don't think I had it in me? That's not what you said when you were supposedly consoling me after I rang the bell.'

'You were the one cryin' on my shoulder. You tellin' me that was all an act?'

'Arrowsake recruited me, just not through the normal channels. And no, before you damn well ask, I wasn't recruited to be a honey trap.' She tapped the side of her head. 'I was recruited for this. When they wanted to fill their quota of hairy-assed grunts, they chose the likes of you guys.'

Rink and I exchanged a look, and after a moment of feigned ignominy we broke into grins. To be fair, she'd hit the nail on the head with her description of most of Arrowsake's paramilitary wing. I took it that she'd been secretly enlisted for one of the supporting logistical roles because not all Arrowsake operatives got their boots on the ground in foreign conflicts. Back then there were international, national and regional controllers, each with a support team at their disposal: a case in point being Walter Conrad, who in his official role as a CIA Sub-divisional Director of Black Ops, also helmed one of the US-based Arrowsake task forces. The likes of Rink and me were the ones to pull the trigger, but behind each bullet there was an army of helpers — most with no idea whom they were actually assisting — ensuring it reached its target.

'To escape them you felt it necessary to fake your own death?' Rink asked.

'I had to.' She gave us an earnest look apiece. 'Arrowsake is still pulling your strings, right? I bet neither of you are happy about that.'

'You're not wrong,' said Rink.

I massaged my hot ear. It was still a bit swollen, but the pain had subsided to a dull throb. I used it as an excuse to avoid answering her. Whatever Walter was, he was still a father figure to me, and in a fashion I even loved the bastard. My relationship with our old controller was the one point of acrimony between Rink and me. Didn't mean we couldn't respect each other's personal opinions.

Sue sat at the breakfast counter. She folded her hands in her lap as she bent at the waist to regard Rink. 'So don't let them rule you now.'

'They don't rule me,' he growled.

'Then leave Jason alone. In fact, leave me alone. Get on with your life, and leave us to ours.'

'I do that,' he countered, 'and I'm leavin' you to die. It ain't somethin' I'm prepared to do.'

'You said Arrowsake don't know about me. Is that the truth?'

'Yes.'

She opened her hands in silent question.

'You'll go to warn Mercer, and you'll get caught up in his crap. You'll die, Sue.'

'I disappeared once before, I can do it again.'

I'd stood idle for too long. 'Not if they learn you're alive. They'll move heaven and earth to find you, especially if they learn of your connection to Mercer.'

'If they come at us, I'll go to the press. I'll blow the whistle on all their dirty secrets. If we are out in the open, how can they touch us without incriminating themselves?'

'That,' I pointed out, 'is the exact attitude that'll get you killed. Going public won't make you untouchable. An organisation like theirs can influence the media any way they desire. They'll publicly discredit you, destroy your reputation, make you the villain, and once they've done that you'll either die in a freak accident or be made to look as if you've taken your own life.'

She placed her face in her hands, and groaned at the inevitable.

For years she had lived free of Arrowsake, but she must have known that this day would come. She would have considered her options, and threatening to go to the press with dirty secrets would've been one of them. Hell, Rink and me had considered a similar plan, but realised it wouldn't save us. Sure, while we were in the media spotlight we'd be safe from harm, but the world moves so quickly these days, with opinions shifting rapidly from one day to the next, that we'd either be forgotten or vilified in no time, and fair game for Arrowsake's killers. Although neither of us was afraid of a fight, and wouldn't make it easy for our enemies, it wasn't how we wanted to countenance our futures. We were soldiers, and accepted that each fight we had could be our last, but this modern incarnation of Arrowsake wouldn't shy away from targeting our friends and families in order to get at us. We'd concluded that there was truth in the old saying "keep your friends close, and your enemies closer", and had agreed a kind of truce. We wouldn't meddle in their affairs if they left us alone. Simply by warning Sue, let alone defending her, we were instigating a knock down drag 'em out fight.

8

Jason Mercer clutched at the edge of a counter to avoid falling. Vertigo surged over him, followed by nausea and he retched. He stayed supported by the counter for a few seconds, before sinking to the floor. Sweat dripped from his forehead.

'Fuck you all the way to Hell, Jared Rington,' he groaned.

His vision swam, and after a moment more he could sense his eyeballs jittering in their sockets. He screwed his eyelids tight, and ran his hands over his face. Another few seconds and he tested his vision and found that the world was jumping back and forth as his damaged brain attempted to regain control of his depth perception. He counted his breaths — in and out, in and out — and finally pushed to his feet. He slapped both palms flat on the counter top, not yet ready to trust his legs to support him.

Crippling neurological dysfunction had been an aspect of Mercer's life for so long now that it rarely sent him to his knees anymore, but there were occasions. He'd been shot twice, and each of those bullets should've been enough to kill him. He didn't know the odds he'd bucked, but his chance of survival must have been astronomically slim. One round had taken off a chunk of his ear, and rebounded off the curvature of his cranium, the second had landed cleaner and shattered the occipital bone at the rear of his skull. The trauma to his cerebellum had been significant, and yet he'd defied the reaper. In the first years following surgery he'd struggled with basic motor skills, couldn't walk without staggering like a lush on a weekend bender, and his voice had slurred so bad even he wasn't sure what he was trying to say. His road to recovery was long and not without bumps. He'd lost portions of his memory, and of his vocabulary, and had to relearn some simple motor skills like how to button his shirt or eat with cutlery. His eye-to-hand coordination was shot to pieces, but with practise over the years he'd regained most of his former skill sets, albeit these days he sometimes was slower to respond to certain stimuli than before. With concentration he could fire a pistol and hit a target, but don't ask him to draw and aim his weapon too quickly or he'd be likely to drop it. There were times where if he was observed closely that a trembling of his pupils would be noticed, the same with an uncontrollable tremor of his fingers.

Most days were good now. He could get by, and despite his scars, nobody would guess that he'd survived two bullets to the head. It was only if he was taken by surprise, or struck by alarm, that his symptoms intensified. Ordinarily they weren't bad enough to drop him to his knees, but the shock at spotting Joe Hunter had set off a neurological time bomb inside him. At first he didn't credit his eyes; he'd spotted Hunter seated in the foyer, and just as recognition struck the doors of the elevator had swished shut leaving him with a degree of disbelief in his senses, and also sick with anxiety. He had aged, gotten a bit grayer in the hair and had a few more lines around his eyes, but it was Hunter! Why was

Hunter there? Was his attendance in the building purely random, or specific to Mercer being there? Hunter hadn't shown a similar degree of recognition, just continued reading a glossy pamphlet but that meant nothing. If Hunter had followed him there, and had set up surveillance, he wouldn't have shown surprise. He'd convinced himself that Hunter hadn't recognised him: why should he? As far as Hunter knew, Mercer had died years ago. Hunter had been there when Rington gunned him down. Even if his features had been familiar, and Hunter had scrutinized them at more length, he'd have concluded he had to be mistaken. Yes, Mercer had managed to convince himself that Hunter's presence was down to pure chance and the fleeting look he'd gotten at him through the elevator doors — especially when he was partially blocked from view by a businessman — wasn't enough for Hunter to recognise him.

His conviction had lasted only until Sue called him with the next shock. She'd returned home to find Hunter and Rington staked out on her street. Hearing that Rink was with Hunter in Panama City was a terrible blow, but unsurprising. From his past experience of them, where one went the other did too. Recklessly she'd confronted them, firing a warning shot at them in the ridiculous notion it'd chase them off. He'd said that she should've shot them both dead, but she was having none of that crap, because, she argued, it would've made her no better than they were. He'd concurred; killing them outright wouldn't make their new position any more tenable. He'd warned Sue to flee, but she had to return to her house to fetch what she needed to help disappear again. He had returned to his own apartment for the same reason.

Unlike Sue, he'd prepared for this day. He didn't expect Hunter or Rink to be the ones to come after him, but somebody could. He had stocked a bag with all the necessary items he required to run, and more. His cache was hidden in a false compartment at the rear of his bedroom closet, along with a selection of weapons. He'd collected the bag and two pistols and ammunition, and carried them into the kitchen. It was there that the time bomb had detonated and sent him to his knees on the floor. Standing once more, he reached for where he'd set the bag on the counter and dragged it to him.

He took a last look around at the place he'd called home for the past few years, and felt homesick already. This was the last he'd see of it; now that he'd been flushed out there'd be no returning. He lugged the bag through into the living area, and paused. Is there anything here that could give a determined hunter a clue about where he intended running next? He knew there wasn't, but he should cover all bases. Maybe he should burn the apartment to the ground, and make sure.

He shook his head at the absurd notion. A fire would only attract attention, and it was the last thing he wanted right now. He pulled out his cell phone, wondering why Sue hadn't called yet. She was supposed to return home, grab what she needed and contact him the instant she was clear. He was tempted to call her, check she was OK, but what if she wasn't the one who answered?

Was Sue dead already? Worse still, was she alive and being forced to guide his hunters to him?

Bile spilled into his throat, and again his knees felt on the verge of collapse. He swallowed down the bitterness, and headed out of the front door, towards the adjacent carport. If Hunter and Rink had made Sue's Mercedes-Benz, they shouldn't rely on it to get them out of town now. Mercer had a Toyota Camry, one of the most popular cars in the US. It was black, one of the most popular colours. Out on the road the Toyota would be as innocuous as he could hope for, and far less noticeable than Sue's Merc SUV. If they'd taken Sue alive, Hunter and Rink might force the details of his car from her, but without digging much deeper they wouldn't learn the license number. He felt that the Toyota would do to get away, and he'd switch to another form of transportation at first opportunity. He aimed the key fob and the lights flashed and he heard the distinctive clunks of the locks disengaging. Only then did he smart at his reckless move. What if his hunters were already here and had rigged the Toyota to explode?

Paranoia was a killer!

It didn't matter how pervasive Arrowsake was, finding him and getting a team on the ground to install a car bomb in this short a time was an impossible task. Nevertheless, as he approached the car, it was tentatively. He eased open the driver's door, and when he was still alive a few seconds later, he allowed a held in breath to slip out. He chucked his bag across onto the passenger seat. Then turned to check around.

His duplex-style apartment was at the end of a row of six, in the residential neighbourhood of Wainwright Park on the west side of Panama City. It wasn't situated at the most defensive of locations, but it gave quick access to US Highway 98. He could be across Grand Lagoon via Hathaway Bridge in minutes, and on the road to Pensacola in no time. They'd discussed an escape plan before, agreeing that if they were split up, they should meet in Pensacola. He'd agreed with Sue that they'd wait for each other at University Town Plaza for two hours maximum; if either was a no show then they'd move to their next rendezvous point across the stateline in Mobile, Alabama. Mercer knew there was several car rental dealerships located in the mall at the plaza, and decided he'd swap his Toyota there for the ongoing drive. From there it was only a short journey to Mobile Downtown Airport, and ordinarily switching cars could be an unnecessary step in his getaway plan, but it'd help muddy the waters. After Mobile he'd no real idea where they'd flee next, that was probably down to which flights were due to leave with available seats.

There were a few people about. Lights had begun to come on in neighbouring homes. There were no suspicious glances aimed at Mercer, and from what he could tell no unfamiliar vehicles parked in the street. Anyone spying on him wouldn't be obvious, but with the short timescale since Sue had her run in with Hunter and Rink, it'd be unlikely they'd arrived yet. He got in the

Toyota and turned on the engine. He backed out of the carport onto the road, and aimed the car towards the highway. Two blocks later he brought the car to a stop, digging in his pocket for his cell phone. It was ringing.

Sue's number was on the screen.

He held his breath, thinking, thumb poised over the screen.

The phone rang a few more times.

He didn't answer.

He'd been desperate to hear from her, but now he was unsure.

He shoved the phone aside, on the seat alongside his grab bag and set off driving again.

The phone began ringing a second time, and in his state of paranoia he'd swear it sounded more persistent.

Without stopping this time, he reached for, and had to fish the phone out from where it had slid under his bag. He continued driving, glancing from the road to the screen and back again. He hit the accept button, but didn't speak.

'Jason, it's Sue. Can you hear me?' Sue's voice was distant, but that was due to Mercer holding out the phone at arm's length, as if he could distance himself from the inevitable.

'I can hear you,' he replied.

'Jason, it's super important that—'

'You aren't alone.'

'I'm with Joe and Rink.'

'Then we're done.'

'Wait, Jason. Hear me out before you—'

The Fourth Option

He ended the call.

Seconds later the phone began ringing.

Sue's number again.

He powered down the car's window and dropped the phone in the street as he hit the gas and hurtled for the highway.

9

I exchanged a knowing glance with Rink.

Sue had her back to us, her face tilted down to the screen of her phone. She studied it as if it was a surprise that Mercer had ended the call.

'Shall I try again?' she wondered aloud.

'Pointless, seein' as you've warned him to run,' Rink said.

'I didn't get a chance to explain. I should ring and—'

'He's probably ditched his cell by now,' I said. 'Sue…a little advice for you. If you're going to use a prearranged signal, you should choose a less obvious code word than "super". Even to my ear it sounded forced.'

She turned and glowered at me, opened her mouth. She was about to lie, but it was obvious that Sue and Mercer had agreed on a code to establish whether or not it was safe for them to speak. Denying it would make her look stupid. She shut her mouth and shrugged. 'For all you know he had the sense to hang up the second I mentioned I was with you guys.'

'So what's supposed to happen now? You try to give us the slip and meet him at a predetermined rendezvous?'

Sue ignored the question. 'What do you have in mind for me?'

I checked with Rink, as a plan wasn't something we'd devised yet. His eyebrows jumped, but that was the extent of his input. It was as much as a go-ahead as I needed, though. 'Our priority's getting you out of harm's way. The problem is where to take you. We aren't with Arrowsake, and haven't been for years, but that isn't to say Walter Conrad doesn't keep tabs on us. He knows where we live and work, and knows most of our closest contacts too.'

Sue exhaled in scorn. 'I bet you regret following us now?'

'We don't have a rewind button,' I said, 'so let's just concentrate on here and now.'

Rink's mind was still in a dark place. 'If I could turn back time, I'd put a third bullet in Mercer's skull, make sure the sonofabitch was dead. Then there'd be no need for any of this.'

'I was right in warning him to get away from you then,' said Sue.

Rink growled something deep in his throat. He clearly wasn't fully conversant with an agreement we'd made with Sue only moments ago, to let Mercer be, even though Rink had done so grudgingly. By speaking her code word, it was academic now, because Mercer was in the wind and out of our reach. It was probably for the best, because once Rink and Mercer laid eyes on each other again there'd have to be a reckoning. I didn't blame Sue for warning Mercer, she'd more loyalty to her friend than to us, and I respected that, but she'd stretched my trust in her going forward. It begged the obvious question: Why should we put our lives at risk for her?

The answer was plain.

It was what we did.

I'm a sucker for championing the underdog, and Rink's so strong a pal that he backs me up even against his personal misgivings. My nature had placed us in some dire situations in the past and I didn't expect things to change for the better soon.

'What's done is done,' I reminded my friend, then to Sue, I added, 'but next time somebody offers a helping hand, don't go pissing on it.'

She nodded, then glanced under her eyebrows at Rink. Arms crossed, chin out, he scowled a second longer. Then he swept a hand. 'What are you waiting for, Sue? Get your shit together and let's go.'

She'd already packed some essentials, but they weren't enough.

'Grab an extra set of clothes and underwear,' Rink suggested. He pointed a finger at her mane of red hair. 'And that red's too distinctive, it's gotta go.'

'Easily rectified,' Sue said, and began undoing some strategically placed bobby pins. Next she pulled off what neither of us fellas had realised was an expensive wig. Beneath it, her hair was short and if not raven black, a natural shade of dark brown, and not unlike how I remembered it. She dumped the wig on the kitchen counter, then pushed her fingers through her flattened hair to get it in some kind of order.

The wig, I thought, hadn't been a disguise for our benefit, and before today Arrowsake hadn't been her concern; made me wonder what Sue and Mercer had been up to prior to me spotting them in Mexico Beach. Yeah, and there was still her suppressed pistol to consider. Perhaps it wasn't the only weapon she had access to.

'Let's grab that clothing,' I said, and aimed a nod at the upper floor. 'I'll come with you.'

'I don't need fashion advice from a man,' she said.

'No, but from what I've witnessed you need some on how to stay alive. I'm coming with you so you don't do something stupid again.'

Rink waited in the kitchen, keeping an eye on the bags Sue had already stuffed. She led the way upstairs, and I stayed close enough to grab her if she tried to run, but wary of a backwards kick to my chest or jab of an elbow to my face. We got to the bedroom without a repeat performance of our earlier tussle.

She collected clothing from a wardrobe, then dug through drawers for underwear. I averted my gaze while she sifted through her smalls, deciding on which to take.

Done, she stood watching me, the clothes in a pile in her arms.

I met her eyes, but her chin dipped and she stared at the floor. She said, 'Y'know something Joe? Judged on my behaviour, it might not seem that I'm happy to see you guys. In my own way, I am, and I'm thankful to you both for helping me like this, but really there's no need. I can look after myself. I disappeared before, and can do it again. You and Rink needn't put yourself in danger because of me. Why not just leave, pretend you never saw me?'

'I can't. I've promised to help, and I keep my word.'

'What about Rink? He sounds more interested in ending things with Jason than helping me. If he thinks he can use me to get to Jason he can think again.'

'Rink isn't like that. He hates Mercer, but—' there was no denying it '—he still cares for you. He doesn't want you in the firing line, Sue.'

'He isn't making his feelings for me very obvious.'

'What do you expect? He's angry and confused. He thought you'd died, Sue, only for you to show up years later with one of the few people he genuinely hated. It might take him time to get his head straight, but it will happen, and he'll be the old Rink you once knew and loved again.'

It was a turn of phrase, but I caught the slight crinkling of her eyelids at my mention of the "L" word.

'Back then,' she said, 'things grew too complicated. I didn't know whom I could or couldn't trust. When I planned disappearing, it was too risky to take anyone into my confidence, especially Rink. He was still an active member of Arrowsake then, ferociously loyal to them, and I couldn't put him in a situation where he'd be expected to lie to them. It was best that I just—'

I'd stopped her with a raised hand. Perhaps she thought I was about to tell her that it was Rink she should explain herself to, not me. But that wasn't it. My ear was still smarting from earlier, but it didn't affect my hearing. A vehicle had come to a halt outside.

It was doubtful that Mercer had raced to Sue's rescue, but the arrival of the car couldn't be ignored.

'Incoming,' said Rink from below, having moved from the kitchen to the foot of the stairs.

The Fourth Option

I held up a finger to Sue for silence and checked we weren't casting shadows on the blinds as she had earlier. I circumnavigated the room to stand alongside the window. Rather than tease open the slats, I positioned so that I could spy out through the crack at its edge. A plain grey van idled at the curb, blocking the drive. The wash from a nearby streetlight painted the windshield and made it difficult to see inside, but I could still make out the indistinct form of one figure.

'Expecting anyone?'

'No,' said Sue.

'You're certain?'

'Joe,' she reminded me at a harsh whisper, 'I was in the act of running away when you guys got here. What, you think maybe I rang for take-out pizza or something first?'

I didn't rise to her sarcasm. 'We might have to act decisively,' I said, 'and don't want to harm an innocent.'

She bit her lip. 'I'm not expecting anyone.'

'Let's go,' I said, aiming a hand at the stairs.

Sue went first, carrying her stuff. Rink met her. He'd lugged her bags with him and set them down. He nodded at her to jam the fresh things inside. By then I was at ground level again, and I left them to scoot through into the front room. The lights were off here, but I still kept well back from the window. I could make out the front of the van, and discern slight movement behind the light washing the windshield. The driver was still inside, but I couldn't swear if there was anyone in the back, or even if they'd climbed out yet. I crabbed around further, staying in the deepest shadows to get a fuller view of the van. As I did so, the door opened and the driver stepped onto the sidewalk at the foot of Sue's driveway.

It was a man aged in his late thirties, tall and thin and severe looking. He was dressed in what could pass as a courier's uniform, but the jacket and cap lacked any identifying decal or logo. He was holding a smart phone in one hand. His other hand was empty. He craned to and fro, and I got the impression he was studying Rink's Ford, and the Mercedes-Benz. He glanced at his phone's screen and gave a tiny nod of reassurance. He held it up, and snapped a sequence of photographs, without using the flash function. He tapped details into the phone, probably sending out the photos to interested recipients.

He got back in the driving seat but left open the door. He tapped his phone again

He began a conversation, but his words were too muted to hear.

In the kitchen, Rink and Sue were preparing to move.

We were stuck for the moment because our car was effectively blocked the same way in which we'd blocked Sue's. We had to consider the obvious: this guy was involved in some sort of recon, and now he'd identified our rides he could be arranging an assault.

How could Arrowsake be onto us as soon as this?

Rink poked his head into the living room.

'Shit could be about to hit the fan,' I told him.

He drew Sue's pistol from his belt. 'How many?'

'Only one guy that I can see.'

'It's the one's you can't see we've to worry about.'

'I'm pretty sure he's alone, but you know that isn't going to last.'

'Time to move,' he agreed.

'Hold up.' Outside the man was out of the van once more. He studied the house, and for the briefest moment I thought he'd spotted me, as he stared directly into the darkness where I hid. But then his gaze roamed again and came to rest above, concentrating on the bedroom I'd been in moments ago. He turned and reached into the van, leaning over the driver's seat to grab something. He pulled out a flat parcel about the size of a shoebox, and moved up the drive. I could no longer see him, but as he'd ignored the front door completely, I could reasonably assume he was up to no good.

'He's working his way around the back,' I warned Rink.

He nodded, and immediately headed for the kitchen. I heard him exchange whispers with Sue, and pictured her ducking down behind her breakfast counter. I unlocked the front door and exited the house. As I moved around the house, I caught a glimpse of the man's shoulder disappearing around the back. I swiftly went after him.

I heard him knuckle the door.

I peeked around the corner, and for that moment he was unaware of my presence. He stepped back from the door, and I anticipated him kicking his way inside, but before that he pulled the lid off the parcel and delved inside. He dumped the empty box at his feet, and despite the dimness I recognised the shapes in his hands: a Micro Uzi and a magazine that he began fitting into the gun. This wasn't the recon guy; he was the hitter!

He pulled back the cocking lever, and I moved.

Don't let the name fool you. A Micro Uzi is still a machine pistol designed to rip an enemy combatant several new buttholes. Without a shoulder stock they're notoriously difficult to control on full auto, but this close it wouldn't matter. This guy would have to be the worst shot in history to miss me. Luckily for me, my surprise appearance made him pause for the split second I required to throw up my hands in surrender, and exclaim in fear. I had his full attention. The barrel of his gun wavered from me to the door and back again, and I saw the workings behind his eyes as he tried to comprehend my sudden appearance.

Before the guy could come to a decision about me, Rink shot repeatedly through the back door, the hail of bullets smashing the windowpane, and the man's chest and throat. Without a word, our would-be slayer fell and slumped on the porch where earlier I'd grappled Sue. I immediately dropped my frightened act, stepped in and kicked him over onto his back. My foot went down on his wrist, and I stripped the weapon from his grasp, and at once turned it on him. Covering from the shattered door, Rink met my gaze.

'We're clear,' I said.

There was no need for further discussion. He grunted an instruction at Sue. She came out, carrying her bags, and I turned from the corpse to lead her down the drive. As we passed the Merc, I pushed the open door to. Rink followed on our heels, alert to further danger. The suppressed pistol had made a series of clacks with each shot, but unless a neighbour was familiar with the sounds of gunfire it'd leave them unperturbed. The shattering of the windowpane might be a different story. A light came on and illuminated the yard behind the nearest house and I imagined the householder taking a look outside, wondering what the ruckus was about.

We were down the drive by then, alongside the Ford, and out of the nosy neighbour's line of sight, and there'd be no way of them seeing the dead man in Sue's backyard, without coming out and peering over her fence. We were reasonably assured of a few more seconds' grace, except there was nowhere for us to go while the van blocked us in.

Planning a quick spray of bullets at Sue and anyone accompanying her in her kitchen, the assassin had left open the van's door and the keys in the ignition for a fast getaway. I passed the Uzi to Rink, jogged to the van, jumped in and drove it clear, even as Rink backed off the drive. In seconds I was out of the van, and piling in the back of the Ford alongside Sue.

Rink pulled away, just as Sue's neighbours, an older couple, appeared on their drive. There were questions in their gazes and open mouths, but we weren't hanging around to answer to them. Thankfully neither of them followed to the sidewalk to get a better look at our car, and hopefully their suspicions hadn't been piqued too much and they'd go back to their evening meal or whatever we'd disturbed. If luck stayed on our side, the dead man wouldn't be discovered until we were well on the road out of Panama City.

10

'Who was that guy?' I asked.

Sue was seated alongside me in the back of the Ford, her bags piled between us like an insurmountable wall. Her skin was ghostly, almost translucent, and her eyes haunted. Events had robbed her of the earlier starchiness she'd exhibited and now she looked totally lost and reliant upon us to bring her back to reality.

'Sue,' I pressed, 'who was that guy back there?'

Her mouth worked but she had no words.

'One thing I'm reasonably certain of, he wasn't from Arrowsake,' I said.

Rink was driving, only taking his eyes off the road to check his mirrors. He grunted in agreement, then added, 'If that amateur's all Arrowsake can field these days, we've nothin' to worry about, brother. I almost feel bad about killing the frog-gigger.'

I'd taken an incredible risk in distracting the gunman the way I did. An experienced hitman would have shot me the instant I showed my face, then immediately turned his wrath on his intended target while I bled out on the ground. The guy from the van had allowed surprise to throw his mind into momentary turmoil, giving Rink the opportunity to shoot him instead. I was thankful it was Sue's would-be killer who'd died and not me, but there was still regret that we'd gone with the lethal option. Pick up a gun with murder in mind and you kind of deserve what you get; he'd chosen to live by the sword, but we didn't understand his motivation. It's a pity we hadn't wounded him, taking the fight out of him, but left him with enough strength to answer some questions.

'C'mon, Sue, you have to level with us,' I said.

She ran her hands over her face. 'I don't know,' she croaked, 'I've never seen him before.'

'You don't need to have seen him to know who he is, or who might have sent him.'

She screwed up her face, as if I was talking gibberish.

'You came at us with a silenced pistol. Don't try convincing us you only keep the gun for home defence because it's bullshit. This company you work for, what is it, some kind of front for something else?'

She didn't answer. She turned from me to stare out of the window. By now we were astride the Tyndall-DuPont Bridge, and her near view was of East Bay. The water was black, undulating slowly like oil under the moonless sky. 'I've no idea who he was,' she said again, barely above a whisper.

I wasn't fooled.

It was apparent that she was connected to the estate agency, posing as a realtor to carry out something more nefarious than showing around prospective homebuyers. Her house was listed on the company's property portfolio, and she'd stayed there under the bogus credentials of Suzanne Carter, and — I'd formed the opinion — the company must have been complicit in her duplicity. Either that or their due diligence was abysmal: I assumed that realtors must undergo some kind of security checks before any offer of employment, and to miss that Sue Bouchard and Suzanne Carter were two different individuals would be a shocking lapse in procedure. Then it struck me—

'Sue, that house back there, was it a safe house?'

'You're kidding, right?' She turned her gaze on me again, and some of her snarkiness had returned. 'Twice in one evening it has been attacked, is that your definition of *safe*?'

'You know exactly what Hunter means,' Rink growled. We were now off the bridge and adjacent to the sprawling air force base, rolling south towards Mexico Beach, and again beginning to notice signs of the recent hurricane. 'Maybe it's time to drop the act, and show us some gratitude for saving your ass back there.'

'Yeah, Rink, thanks for nothing. If you hadn't been holding me prisoner, I'd have been long gone and that guy would've shot up an empty house.'

Silence descended. All that was apparent was the low growl of the engine, the whistle of tires on asphalt. We allowed the silence to do our work for us. Finally Sue threw up her palms. 'What do you want to hear, guys?'

'For starters you can tell us who you're working for these days,' I said. 'I'd guess it's the CIA except Arrowsake would've known about you and Mercer before now.'

'I work for a private body.'

'Hitmen for hire?' Rink posed.

Sue snorted. 'I think I already made my feelings on assassins quite clear. No, we are better described as a private protective service.'

'I pity your clients,' Rink said, 'seeing as how *you* needed protectin' back there.'

'There you go again, making the assumption I needed your help. Hasn't it occurred to you that the only reason you took me so easily was I didn't intend hurting either of you?'

I rubbed my swollen ear, grinned lopsidedly. 'That was you trying not to hurt me?'

'I could've shot you both dead when I drove up on you,' she reminded us. 'I chose not to. These days I prefer to preserve life than take it.'

They were fair points.

'Mercer's in the same business?' Rink didn't sound convinced. It was a stretch to believe a man once deemed too dangerous to be allowed to live had enjoyed such a paradigm shift. 'Maybe puttin' those two bullets in his skull addled his brain and changed his personality for the better,' he suggested, but his words were delivered with a hefty dose of cynicism.

'You might be surprised to find you're not far off the mark,' said Sue. 'Except for one thing: he never was the rogue agent you were led to believe.'

There was the tiniest shake of Rink's head as he absorbed her words. Could she be telling the truth? The evidence that Jason Mercer had been killing for all sides, mainly for the highest payer, had convinced us and we'd willingly carried out the executive order to stop him. In lieu of what we'd later learned about Arrowsake, in particular in its new incarnation, it wouldn't surprise me to learn we'd been played.

'Convince us we were wrong,' I said, and caught a sharp glance from Rink. He restrained his disbelief though. It was highly likely he didn't want to hear he'd been fooled into shooting an innocent man, the knowledge could become a burden on his soul, but he still wanted the truth. His trust in Arrowsake had diminished to negative figures already, hearing how they'd lied to him again wouldn't shatter his psyche.

'Consider this for a moment,' she offered. 'There's a reason why I staged my death; I *had to* escape Arrowsake.'

'You discovered a secret they didn't want anyone to know,' I said, 'and would have had you killed to protect it.'

'You've got it,' she said.

Rink had incrementally taken his foot off the gas. The Ford was entering the outskirts of Mexico Beach, and with no other destination in mind Rink was heading back to the wreckage of my home. I told him the name of my hotel instead, and caught a nod of agreement from him. If Walter chose to look, he'd discover where I was currently staying, but I doubted he'd go that route yet. We may as well make use of the room I'd prepaid. Besides, I'd left my grab bag in the room, and if events continued the way they'd been going, I was going to need it.

We drove over the waterway known locally as The Canal. Hurricane Michael had all but destroyed this end of town, some dwellings were in as much disarray as mine, others missed roofs or sidings, while some of them were whole but pushed off their stilts or concrete foundations. Trees lay where they'd fallen, though the road itself had been cleared of most of the heavier detritus. The beach sand was piled in drifts on the roadsides, burying the sidewalks and gardens. Many residences were still without power or water. There was a hush over the place, as if the residents held their breath in anticipation of worse to come. Driving into my hometown that night was like entering a post apocalyptic nightmare.

Continuing down Highway 98 we passed backhoes and bulldozers, and all manner of heavy construction vehicles — emergency response crews had arrived in their droves, and most of the remaining hotels and motels now housed workers from near and far. I'd been fortunate to snag a spare room at one of the surviving hotels towards the southern end of town. It had suffered only minor damage by comparison, and had been pulled back into reasonable shape in the last few days, though it still felt like it was being operated on a wartime footing. There was a subterranean parking lot — at ground level actually, built to either side of the hotel's swimming pool, beneath an elevated courtyard sundeck — but it was currently out of use. The work crews and dispossessed townsfolk temporarily in residence had left their cars elsewhere. We needed our Ford out of sight, though, so Rink drove inside, and I guessed it was his intention to abandon the Ford there for the foreseeable future. At first opportunity I'd collect my Audi from home to use in any onward journey.

The Fourth Option

An elevator gave access directly from the parking garage to the residential levels, so we were able to avoid the reception area. My room card allowed us into the lift. We entered it, Rink having taken charge of one of Sue's bags, in which we'd concealed her pistol and the liberated Uzi. She'd slung her heavy tapestry bag over her shoulder, while I kept a close eye on her: it still wasn't too late for her to try to escape from us before the doors closed. Once we were on the way up, I relaxed a little. The doors opened onto a deserted hallway and we made it to my room without attracting attention. The room, with its compact adjoining bathroom, wasn't furnished to accommodate three, and with the door shut and curtains closed, felt on the verge of claustrophobic. We manoeuvred around, uncomfortable in each other's space until we'd found respective perches. Sue, having deliberately been jostled to the far end of the room, sat on one side of the bed and Rink the other. I took the only available tub chair and stretched my legs out as best I could. We were each lost in our personal thoughts for a minute or more. Finally Sue broke the silence.

'So this is the plan, guys? We just sit here until either the cops find us or Arrowsake does?'

'We need to catch our breath and think,' I pointed out, 'and this is as good as any place to do it.'

'I'm gonna take stock.' Rink delved in Sue's holdall bag and pulled out the guns. He checked each for ammunition. The Uzi had never been fired so the magazine was full; the pistol though was another story. He'd depleted its mag by half when shooting the gunman, plus there was the bullet Sue had wasted firing that half-arsed warning shot earlier.

I got up and dragged out my backpack from where I'd left it in the room's only wardrobe. Inside I'd paper cash, fake ID, and some spare clothing, plus my SIG Sauer P226 and spare ammunition. I tossed him a box of 9mm rounds, and he set to reloading Sue's pistol.

Sue eyed the room spuriously. It was stocked with only the rudiments for survival. There was a coffee maker, but none of the makings. 'Nothing to eat or drink?'

'I take my breaks at that cafe down the road. You know the one, Sue? I followed you and Mercer from there earlier.'

She danced her eyebrows in reply but didn't rise to the bait.

I said, 'Was your reason for being there related to why a gunman came to your home?'

She knitted her fingers together, and I could tell she was in internal conflict. Finally, she looked up at us and said, 'Maybe.'

'Only maybe?'

'One of our clients owns property in Mexico Beach. Jason and I were asked to accompany him here while he attended meetings with council officials and others involved in the reclamation of the town following Hurricane Michael. It was just boring stuff, about the recovery efforts, funding, insurance, and other stuff.'

'Your client needed protecting at a town meeting? I find that hard to believe.'

The Fourth Option

'We were asked to attend for appearances sake. Our client likes to portray a sense of gravitas, you see. He's an important man.'

'Sounds like he's an asshole full of his own self-importance,' Rink said without looking up from the guns he was working on.

Sue didn't disagree. 'Emotions were running high at the meeting, and there were several angry residents that took umbrage with our client, and at one point we'd to step in and separate a couple of them looking for a fist fight. A few angry threats and challenges were exchanged before we got them outside and out of our client's hair. Once the meeting was over, he went off to conduct some personal business, and it left us at a loose end. Before returning to work we decided to grab some lunch at the café you spotted us at.' She raised her palms. 'Maybe you weren't the only one to follow us back to Panama City, Joe. Maybe one of the guys we threw out of the meeting wanted payback and sent that gunman after us.'

She read the incredulity on my face.

'Like I said, I can only say *maybe*, it's the only theory I have.'

I caught Rink studying my response with an equal look of disbelief on his face. In unison, we said, 'Bullshit.'

There was absolutely no need for Sue to have attended any town meeting tooled up with a silenced pistol and disguised in a crimson wig. I didn't doubt that she'd accompanied a 'client' to a meeting, but I'd bet that the other attendees weren't town councilors, or if they were they were of the corrupt type. The thing was, I'd lived in Mexico Beach long enough that I'd've gotten to hear if there were any major criminal types or dodgy politicians around, and probably would have had a run in with them by now. Whenever disaster strikes there are always parasites ready, willing and able to profit off the misery of others; I imagined Sue's client, and those he'd gone to meet with were blood-sucking leeches. Had something bad happened, and somebody had gotten upset, and the attempted hit on Sue was supposed to be some kind of reckoning? There was a certain amount of logic in my theory. I didn't bother sharing it though.

I straightened my T-shirt that had become rucked up from sitting in the tub chair, and fed my SIG into my belt at the small of my back. 'I'll go fetch my car,' I said, 'and see if I can grab some food on the way back. If we're going to get through this together, you two need to speak, get things off your chests and clear the air between you.'

Rink and Sue glowered at each other.

But I left them to it, hoping that by the time I returned they would have made peace.

11

I could have left deep tracks in the amount of dirt that had accumulated on my car over the past couple of days while I'd worked: it was in need of a thorough cleaning. I made do with spraying the windshield and letting the wipers do their job, then drove away from the wreckage of my home, heading back towards the hotel. I fully intended killing some time by pulling in at the same diner as earlier, hoping that the owners would rustle up enough grub to help put us on the road, thus giving Rink and Sue an opportunity to clear the air. However, it was never to be. As I drove along the main road, again surrounded by heavy machinery and destroyed buildings, the presence of other vehicles ahead impinged on me. Mine wasn't the only car in Mexico Beach coated in dust and fallen debris — the majority were — but the two black SUVs I followed glistened under the arc-lights set up by construction crews, giving me the impression the cars belonged to out-of-towners. The cleanliness of these cars alone wasn't enough to get my Spider Senses tingling, but it made me look closer. The SUVs were identical models, and if I could see both, it wouldn't surprise me to learn that their license plates were similarly numbered: it was often the case where fleet cars were concerned, when vehicles were purchased in batches direct from the manufacturer. I guessed that they were rentals, collected very recently, most likely from a dealership at

Northwest Florida Beaches International Airport, northwest of Panama City.

I stayed back far enough not to attract attention, then found a spot at roadside to stop. I observed the SUVs crawl past my hotel and continue on for a hundred yards before both found a place to turn and came back. There was always the possibility that these were more rescue workers, newly arrived, searching for accommodation, and who'd noticed signs of life in the hotel. Perhaps they'd checked out the hotel as they passed, debated its suitability and decided to try to hire rooms there, but I doubted it.

The front SUV turned off the road into the hotel's grounds. At the main doors there was a turning circle, used by coaches and taxis dropping off or collecting fares. The first SUV halted there. Not unusual, but its twin carried on past the hotel towards me and stopped at curbside. Nobody got out yet.

I guessed that calls were being made between the occupants of both cars as a plan was formulated. Moments later, the rear doors opened on the curbside SUV and two figures got out. Both were males, and both immediately walked towards the entrance to the subterranean parking lot.

I reached for my phone, but, damn it, I'd earlier switched it off to avoid Walter Conrad tracking it, and so too had Rink with his. I'd no immediate way of calling my friend and warning him to expect company.

My pulse rate accelerated.

My SIG was a reassuring weight in the small of my back, but I didn't draw it yet.

The Fourth Option

I got out my Audi, hopeful that I wouldn't be noticed by those still in the nearest SUV. I avoided going towards the hotel, instead walking into the front yard of a damaged house, and I put the seriously off-kilter construction between us. I wasn't done with my phone. I switched it on and found the hotel's number in my telephone call log, rang it and asked to be patched through to Mr Hunter in my corresponding room. I could imagine both Rink and Sue eyeing the ringing phone with suspicion, and deciding to ignore the call that couldn't possibly be intended for them. However, Rink did pick up.

'Hello?' His tone was noncommittal.

'It's me,' I said, with no further need for clarity. 'You need to get Sue out of there right now.'

He dispensed with unnecessary chatter. 'How many?'

'Undetermined. As few as four and as many as ten. Two SUVs, one outside reception, one at the roadside. Two men are on foot already, entering the basement.'

'Cops?'

'Unlikely.'

'Where are you?'

'Coming to clear a path. Get Sue downstairs to the Ford, and I'll do the rest.'

'Copy that, brother.'

We hung up.

While we'd talked, I'd made it past the tilting house into its rear yard. A retaining fence around the yard had felt the full wrath of the hurricane. Splintered boards were scattered in a wide swathe, extending out into the darkness of a stretch of fallow ground beyond. I clambered over a few remaining cross spars and came to a chain-link fence surrounding a vacant lot directly adjacent to the hotel. I wondered if this ground was occasionally used for over-spill parking, but was currently the dumping grounds of large haulage containers destined to cart away the debris once more repairs on the hotel were completed. A portion of the fence had sagged, and I stepped over it. The containers offered cover as I made my way towards the hotel. I was reasonably confident nobody in the nearest SUV was aware of me, but I kept a close eye on them. The front passenger door opened and a third figure got out, this one a female. She remained standing at the edge of the road, peering towards the hotel, even as the SUV drove off towards where I'd abandoned my Audi: I guessed it was going to turn around to offer a quick getaway for when its passengers returned. I'd no idea what was going on with those in the other SUV, now out of my line of sight, near the reception doors. Perhaps they'd never leave the confines of their car, and only served to block that exit.

As I approached the hotel I was in danger of being illuminated by the lights spilling from the windows. I took care to move with caution and reached the fence, this time finding an open gate. A path of trodden sand separated the vacant lot from a low wall that I easily negotiated, but on the other side was a greater drop to the concrete floor of the parking garage. I tried to be as quiet as possible, but to me the soles of my feet slapping the ground sounded like gunshots. I crouched, holding my breath, in anticipation of a hail of bullets, but they didn't come. I moved, keeping a row of support stanchions between the elevator and me. It occurred that the two men that'd entered the parking garage would be unable to use the lift without a key card. Perhaps it wasn't their intention, rather that they were positioned to ambush anyone exiting at this level. I moved through the dimness, alert to the slightest hint of their presence.

Rink's Ford sat in the shadows where he'd left it. It appeared unmolested, but I assumed the couple had checked it out before moving on. Where were they?

My gaze tracked left. I'd never needed to use it during my stay, but I knew there was a fire escape door to the back right of the parking lot. It made sense that there was direct access to it via a stairwell towards the rear of the building. I spotted a set of doors, and moved cautiously towards them, finally feeding my hand under my shirt and drawing my pistol. For security purposes opening the doors under ordinary circumstances would be via a push bar on the other side, but I could see that the two doors weren't flush, and that they could indeed be opened from this side by way of a key card and handle. Without a card to disengage the magnetic locks the doors would have to be physically levered open with a pry bar, and this would set off an audible alarm, but apparently the couple hadn't entered the hotel using brute force. Security arrangements are only as effective as the people using them: at some point somebody had opened the doors from inside, and walked away before they'd fully closed. One of the doors had hung up on a drift of sand that'd invaded the parking garage during the storm. The two men had found their way into the stairwell unimpeded. I moved to follow, fully expecting that Rink would choose a back exit from the hotel over the elevators or main stairwell nearer the front.

I reached the doors, but before opening them further I stood and listened. The two men I'd followed could be standing on the other side, waiting at the foot of the stairs for anyone coming down. I heard nothing from beyond the door, but my attention was drawn elsewhere. There was the distant scuff of feet from the front of the garage, and I turned in time to spot a figure vaguely silhouetted at the drive-in entrance. It was the woman I'd watched decamp from the SUV, moving in to offer support to her colleagues now that they were inside. She was entering into deeper darkness, so the hotel's lights didn't limn me as they did her and she'd no hope of spotting me. I took another second or two to study her before slowly moving away from the doors and crouching in the lea of the retaining wall. I braced my gun butt alongside my chest, so I could track her with the barrel without making any give-away movements.

As she approached, she grew more alert. Her head darted as she checked out the nearest hiding places, and in response to some perceived threat she halted and listened. Down by her side she held an object I couldn't quite define, but suspected it was a weapon. In the next second she presented her profile to me and also raised what was in her hand, and I could now make out the shape of a pistol. Similarly to Sue's gun, it was fitted with a tubular suppressor. The presence of a silencer was significant, and only enforced my opinion that these people had arrived here specifically to do us harm: in general, cops didn't use sound suppressors, hitmen did.

She approached within thirty feet of me. She was alert, but her attention was on the elevator doors, so I was just another shadow within a clump of shadows in her peripheral vision. I could have easily shot her there and then, but I waited. There was probably zero chance that someone other than Sue was the target of this hit team, but still, shooting the woman without first confirming matters was next to cold-blooded murder. I'd happily shoot an enemy combatant, but I had to be sure.

From somewhere overhead there came the chatter of a machine pistol, and I knew for certain then: Rink had engaged the enemy. Shouts from startled guests rang out, but the men on the stairs kept their cool heads for now. The woman's attention jerked to the fire exit doors, the sounds of gunfire from above echoing down the stairwell. She shifted position, moving central to the elevator and stairs, her gun tracking from one location to the other.

I shot her without warning.

She dropped with a startled yell, one leg collapsing completely, the other skidding away on the concrete. Her back was presented to me, an inviting target.

Immediately I pounced towards her, and rather than shoot and finish her off, I planted the sole of my foot between her shoulders and stamped her to the floor. I jammed the muzzle of my SIG to the base of her skull.

'Lose the gun,' I hissed.

Her arm was extended, the gun pointing away from me. She flexed her fingers, and the gun was flicked a few inches from her grasp: still too close for comfort. I adjusted position so I could reach and snatch up the gun. I shoved it down the back of my trousers.

'Who are you and who are your targets?'

The woman moaned. 'You shot me.'

'Yes, you'd better believe it. I'll shoot you again if you don't speak.'

'Do it then. I'm going to die anyway,' she croaked. 'I'm going to bleed out.'

'Quit your bullshit,' I snapped.

There was blood dripping on the dirty concrete. I'd deliberately aimed to hit her in the thigh, avoiding the major arteries but apparently I'd nicked a vein or two. She wasn't going to bleed to death from her wound, but the pain would make walking difficult. Didn't matter, I'd no plans on letting her stand. I grabbed her by her collar and dragged her back into the shadows I'd pounced from. There was a pile of litter — junk and palm leaves, blown inside by the storm — and I threw her down on it. She rolled onto her back, drawing her injured leg up against her abdomen, while staring death up at me.

'If you won't speak,' I warned her, 'then I've no time to waste on you.'

I whacked her on the top of the head with my gun barrel. She was a tougher bitch than she'd initially made out — which I'd taken as an act to get me to lower my defences — and the pistol-whipping didn't knock her unconscious. It split her scalp though and blood poured from her hairline into her eyes. It didn't stop her from trying to lunge and grapple my legs. I kneed her square in the face, and this time the concussive effect of the blow knocked her flat.

Beating a woman never sat well with me, but fuck it! Her gender didn't come into it when she was intent on murder. She'd live, but if the ambush had gone in her favour I doubt she'd have shown me any mercy.

More gunfire chattered overhead.

I raced for the stairwell.

12

Only minutes had passed since Hunter's brief and urgent warning to get Sue out of harm's way. Rink hadn't tarried. Neither had Sue given him any argument when he ordered her to grab her essential stuff and leave the rest. Heeding his own advice, he snapped up Hunter's backpack, and slung it on his shoulders. He weighed the Uzi and Sue's pistol in his hands, and tossed her the latter. 'If you decide to shoot at me again, you'd better not miss,' he drawled.

She smirked at his warning. Before Hunter's phone call they'd grudgingly began conversing, and the awkward tension had left them, but now was not the time — for either of them — to forgive or forget. She checked the gun out of habit, even if there was no need as she'd watched Rink reload it. Then she slung her tapestry bag over her shoulder, and folded her hands over the gun, its butt nestled between her breasts and the suppressor and barrel concealed under her left forearm. If they came across another hotel guest they'd be unlikely to realise she was carrying a deadly weapon. Rink couldn't do much to conceal the Uzi, so didn't bother. He carried it openly, even folded out the stock for greater accuracy.

He opened the door and took a peek out into the hallway. It was deserted. 'OK, let's move,' he said, and immediately stepped out the room. He covered the approaches while Sue slipped out past him. Without instruction she went towards the back of the hotel, moving fast but warily. Rink followed, walking backwards, the Uzi raised. From Hunter's room to the main bank of guest elevators and stairwell was about fifty yards, and the distance grew with each step he retreated. He didn't trust the gun to hit anyone he pointed at over that distance, but a sustained blast of projectiles would keep their heads down.

They reached the back of the hotel unchallenged. The elevator they'd earlier used to gain access to the upper floor was the most direct and fastest route out of danger, but Rink had no intention of cornering them in a metal box where they could be mown down with impunity by anyone waiting at ground level. He trusted Hunter to level the odds in their favour, but still, he wasn't getting into a moving coffin. Sue apparently had the same idea: she went directly past the lift doors towards the fire exit at the back corner of the hotel. They'd still be in a precarious position descending the stairs, but it was better than the alternative.

From a distance there came the hum of machinery. One of the guest elevators was on its way up. Hunter had warned that they faced as few as four hitters but as many as ten. He'd reported the arrival of two SUVs, one was outside reception, and one had stayed at roadside. The two men on foot had allegedly entered the basement parking lot, so it was unlikely that either of them was in the guest lift. Some of those from the SUV outside reception must have entered the hotel to spring the hit. He sucked his bottom lip over his teeth as he braced for contact. Of course, he couldn't immediately shoot the second that a face was shown; the people riding the elevator could be innocent guests.

Sue had gained the door to the fire exit stairs. She didn't enter. She took care to glimpse through the small round window first. She gave Rink an earnest look. 'Clear,' she mouthed.

He didn't take his attention off the corridor for more than a second but it was enough for the dynamic to have changed. There was a ping to announce the arrival of the elevator at this level, but it was the stair door that opened just beyond it first and a guy stepped out warily. He was dressed in dark clothing, and had the peak of a baseball cap pulled low. He was toting a firearm. His attention was momentarily distracted by conflicting stimuli: the arrival of the lift, and also his attempt at reading the nearest room numbers to determine his direction. Rink backed towards Sue, even as he whispered, 'Go.'

She shoved open the door and entered the stairwell, but Rink was still seconds behind. The man at the other end of the corridor spotted him, and despite the intervening distance there was instant recognition. The guy's pistol came up, and it triggered Rink into action. His Uzi blazed.

Bullets tore holes in walls and the ceiling, and the gunman ducked back under cover of the doorjamb. Startled guests cried out in alarm. Rink understood the danger: any of the bullets he fired could cut through a wall and injure or kill an innocent, but he'd no other option. He fired another short burst of bullets, even as he backed into the stairwell. Sue's eyes questioned him.

The Fourth Option

'We can't stay here,' he said. 'Get down to the next landing. Wait for me there.'

She nodded and went down, her gun now extended before her in a two-handed grasp. The stairs switched back equidistant between floors. Rink waited until she was poised at the turn, checking below, before he again pulled open the door and leaned out a fraction into the hall. There were three gunmen now, spread out along the corridor, approaching tentatively. As soon as they spotted Rink, the nearest gunman opened fire, while the two behind sheltered as best they could in doorways.

The man's gunshots missed. His gun had a silencer, but in the echoing confines of the corridor, the reports were loud enough to set off another clamor as guests hid, or barricaded themselves inside their rooms. The snapshot Rink had taken of the three men's positions told him this burly gunman must have been one of those that'd emerged from the elevator. The guy in the baseball cap was to the rear, which told Rink he was probably the one in charge. If he could've done safely, he'd have called out to the man by name, but he was uncertain if it was the one the narrow-faced son-of-a-bitch used these days.

Instead, Rink called out, 'You fuckers are in a shootin' gallery, move another step and I'll blow you all to hell.'

His answer came by way of a volley of bullets. A window shattered at the very end of the corridor, and beside his shoulder bullets shredded the doorframe. Splinters flew and dust hung in the air.

Rink didn't show an inch of his head or torso. He stuck his hand around the corner and pulled the trigger on the Uzi, firing blind. Shouts greeted his action, but none of them sounded pained enough for his liking. Despite causing them to take cover, it would only be seconds before the gunmen came in pursuit. It would be apparent to anyone with any knowledge of gunplay that he'd spent the entire magazine in the three bursts of fire. They would expect him to reload. Under normal circumstances reloading the Uzi would take a matter of seconds, but Rink didn't have a spare magazine. He kept hold of it; even empty of rounds it weighed approximately four and half pounds of metal, and was a viable blunt instrument. He folded in the stock to make it less cumbersome, as he set off after Sue. He got to the switchback and spotted her below. She was peering over the bannister, trying to get a look to the two lower floors. Rink went down, training the Uzi back up the stairs: the gunmen had no idea he was out of ammo, and the gun a visible deterrent.

'I heard something,' Sue whispered, and nodded below them.

'The guys Hunter saw entering the parking lot.' Rink assumed so, but it could also be guests fleeing the sounds of conflict above. He was tempted to take the pistol off Sue, but if she were the intended target it stood to reason she needed its protection most. He said, 'I'll go first, you follow after five seconds.'

If she wished, she could push through the doors onto the second level and take her chances alone. It'd mean leaving Rink and Hunter to weather the storm on her behalf, use the distraction to escape while they got their asses gunned down. But he thought that old loyalties had been rekindled and trusted she'd follow instruction.

He descended on cat feet, alert to movement from below. Shortly he heard Sue's steps down the stairs and allowed a faint smile to tickle his lips. He reached the next landing. Only one floor to go and they'd be at ground level, and then, if his estimation of the building's dimensions was correct, a single flight after that to the subterranean parking lot.

Sue joined him on the landing. She stood near to him covering the stairs above; he could feel heat radiating off her in waves her back was so close to his. He checked the hallway to their left. At the far end there was movement, but it looked rushed and he assumed it was a guest or member of housekeeping staff making themself scarce. He contemplated using the hall as an escape route for no more than a second: Hunter had promised to clear a path to the Ford, and Rink wouldn't waste his friend's effort. If Hunter had already joined the fight, he was unsure. He hadn't heard any hint of a battle, but it could've been timed while he was opening fire with the Uzi and therefore missed.

From above sounded the scuff of a foot, and a tinkle of empty casings from the Uzi, kicked downstairs by a careless foot. Rink took a quick check upward, but could see nobody.

From below he heard a knock. Sue was onto the lower sound in an instant, aiming her weapon. A figure emerged and she fired, but the bullet struck a bannister and whined away as a ricochet. The figure returned fire then immediately ducked out of sight. So did Sue, breathing heavily at the near miss.

Gunmen above. Gunmen below. Perhaps the hallway to their left was their best hope of escape. But once again Rink discarded the idea. By now, the gunman he'd recognised above could've sent his two helpers across the hotel to come at them from the main stairs. He signalled to Sue to cover them.

'Hey up there,' he called. 'Why not come on down, and let me rip you a new asshole?'

Being out of ammo, it sounded as if he tempted fate, but he planned on the opposite. Acting ballsy might give the gunman upstairs more pause about trying to descend if he expected to face the full fury of the Uzi.

A voice answered. 'Hey, Jared Rington! Long time no see, old pal.'

'You forget somethin',' Rink snarled. 'I never was your pal. Never thought too fondly of you then and to be honest you ain't winning any points with me now.'

'Aww, man, that hurts.'

'Not as much as I'm gonna hurt you if you show your stupid face.'

'Rink, man, you have to hear me out. I'm not interested in fighting with you. I only want the woman. Let me have her and you have my word you won't be harmed.'

'Your word amounts to a pile of steaming dog crap.'

The gunman laughed, as if Rink was poking fun. He meant every damn word.

'Come on, Rink. Leave the woman. Walk away. No hard feelings.'

'Two things: only my friends get to call me Rink, and hard feelings are a fuckin' given. Some advice for ya, you're the one that needs to walk away, or be carried away in a body bag.'

The gunman laughed again, like they were two old buddies shooting the shit.

It had impinged on Rink that while he was in discourse with their leader, the other minions hadn't attempted to assail their position again. Rink was under no illusion; the gunman's words were equally a stalling tactic as Rink's. People were jostling for position. Perhaps others from the SUV's were on their way inside to help bolster the attack. An assault was imminent, because the stalemate couldn't last; hotel staff and guests would have called the cops by now. Rink signalled Sue, touched a fingertip to his lips. 'Get ready to move,' he whispered.

She nodded. Her eyes were diamond hard and her skin as pale as death as she moved incrementally for the stairs. She held the pistol in both hands, her tote bag jammed under one armpit.

Without warning, Rink stepped forward, lifting his right knee. He kicked open the door to the hallway with such force that the door rebounded off the wall. The double impacts resounded through the entire hotel, and got the desired response. A fresh clamour erupted as guests hunkered in their rooms exclaimed in horror at the renewal of combat. Above them, the gunman swore, and Rink was certain he began a rapid descent of the stairs — to him he'd think his prey was escaping along the corridor — and below, it brought out one of the other gunmen who must have thought the same. Sue fired, her gun spitting a rapid grouping of three rounds. The gunman below grunted, and collapsed against a wall. His gun clattered on the floor. He wasn't dead, only one of Sue's bullets had hit, and it was high on the outside of the shoulder, but Rink took a chance.

Rink was a scholar of martial wisdom. The famous undefeated swordsman Miyamoto Musashi once wrote "In battle, if you make your opponent flinch, you have already won". Well, this fucker had surely flinched. Rink bounded down three steps at a time and launched at the man. Startled by Rink's boldness, the gunman took a second longer to react than normal, and when he did it was with the wrong decision. He bent to retrieve his lost pistol. Rink slammed his skull with the Uzi, and bore the man to the ground. Dazed, verging on unconsciousness, the man was out of the fight, but only momentarily. Rink hit him another crushing blow with the Uzi.

Rink dropped the empty Uzi, snatched up the dropped pistol and stood.

Sue was by his side. They were on the final switchback, and open to fire from the remaining gunman below.

Except Hunter had kept his word.

__13__

The fire exit door opened about ten inches before it jammed on the floor. The storm, and possibly the sea, had pushed sand and plant litter deep within the parking garage, and some of it had accumulated there, causing drag. I took a sharp glance inside, noting I was clear to enter, then squeezed through the gap. The door caught on the liberated gun stuffed down the back of my trousers, but I made it through. I secured the pistol a bit deeper, but the addition of a suppressor made it uncomfortable against my backside. I'd live with the discomfort for the sake of the extra firepower, I decided, and went on. Rink's voice echoed down the stairwell telling somebody his word was equal to a pile of steaming dog crap. Corresponding laughter and then a reply was muffled by distance and echo, but caused me to frown. I'd swear I had heard that voice before.

Rink exchanged more words with the man, but I ignored them. I went forward, slow and measured, watching the stairs above. A single flight of concrete steps gave access to the first floor of the hotel. At the top, I guessed there'd be doors into the hotel, and also access to the fire escape Rink had used to descend. The volume of Rink's voice told me he wasn't far above me now, and also that any intervening doors had been opened — most assuredly by the two gunmen that'd entered before me.

I went up, cautiously, and as silent as possible. My SIG I kept trained above, ready to shoot.

Two successive bangs echoed through the hotel, and following them it sounded as if the gates of hell opened and set loose the souls of the damned. Events were kicking off in dramatic style, causing me to climb that much faster and reach the first level. Subdued gunfire, a curse and a thud, were followed almost instantly by sounds of a brief scuffle that culminated in a heavy clunk of metal on bone. I saw shadows play on the wall, and realised that somebody was emerging from an alcove to my right. It was a man — one of the two I'd earlier watched emerge from the SUV — but for that instant his attention was fixed on what was happening behind a second set of double-doors, the egress to the fire exit. I brought my gun around towards him, even as his attention snapped on me. We were so close that our guns almost struck barrels. Then we were closer again, and I grabbed at his gun hand, even as he snatched at mine. I had a token edge over him — I'd been expecting him to be there, whereas my presence was a surprise. Even as we moved to negate each other's firearm by pushing it aside, I stepped into his arc and headbutted him, my forehead flush across the bridge of his nose. He sagged, but didn't fall. His life was at risk and it gave him the fortitude to keep fighting. I headbutted him a second time, and bore him backwards as his knees began to fold. He slammed into the alcove he'd emerged from seconds ago. In the dimness the blood flowing from his nostrils looked as black as oil. He was stunned, though still alive. He tried to twist round the barrel of his pistol, to shoot me in the gut, and I forced his hand back, even as I inched around the barrel of mine. He kneed at my crotch, but missed. I headbutted him a third and final time, and felt his cheekbone collapse under my forehead. He croaked in agony, but he was galvanised into desperate action, and he began pulling the trigger of his pistol. Bullets missed my side by inches, forcing me to wrench further around to avoid being hit, but this only strengthened my position, and now my SIG was inches from him. I jammed the barrel under his armpit and fired.

A single bullet did the trick.

His knees gave out, as did his heart, and I had to step back rapidly to avoid being taken down with him on top of me. He fell face first, arse poking up in the air, stone dead. I didn't give his death a moment's remorse — not then, though it might trouble my dreams next time I slept — because you couldn't dwell on the actions you took if you hoped to survive an ongoing battle. I collected his dropped weapon; identical to the one I'd already taken from the woman in the parking lot. A gun in each hand, and one stuffed down my pants, I turned towards the fire exit doors in time to catch Rink's face peering back at me through the narrow glass panes.

Rink sent Sue to me first while he covered her. Her pale face, set against her dark hair, appeared almost luminous in the dimness. Her's probably wasn't the only face leeched of colour, I could feel the coldness in my own despite my brief but violent struggle. The loss of skin colour wasn't down to fear as such, more to do with the body's response to the endorphins flooding it in preparation for fight or flight. She glanced at the dead man, and gave a tiny shake of her head, but I doubted it was because I'd gone for the lethal option, more because she felt the man's death was somehow on her shoulders. Rink shouldered through the doors, and from my position I got a glimpse of a man he'd put down too, sprawled on the half-landing above.

Rink showed me three fingers, indicating there were three more hitters alive that he knew of. 'You ain't gonna believe who's up there,' he added. 'You remember that A-hole called Vince?'

I did believe, because I'd heard his voice.

In hindsight, it was unsurprising that Walter had sent Stephen Vincent after us. Since last we'd come across him in Manhattan a few years ago, the son of a bitch had climbed highly in this incarnation of Arrowsake. He was a lying, deceitful, murderous, dangerous bastard; the perfect example of an operative they could field these days. The last time we'd worked together under an uneasy alliance, in a dual effort to halt a greater evil, but we'd never been friends. In fact, before we realised we'd have to work together the bastard had tried to choke the life out of me with a guitar string garrote, and I'd promised him that somewhere down the line there'd have to be a reckoning. Seemed like that time might have arrived.

14

Rink gunned the Ford up the shallow ramp with enough speed that the tires lost contact with the ground for a second or two. Hitting earth, and finding traction, the car kicked up a rooster tail of dust as it powered towards the road. Even as the Ford emerged, our enemies were charging to cut off his escape route. The SUV at the front of the hotel reversed, engine whining, to reach the main road and block the Ford. The second SUV, only a dozen yards from where Rink would reach the road, had also prowled forward, as if the driver was preparing to hit the gas and ram him. Two men on foot, and the dazed woman I'd pistol-whipped earlier, ran after him, looking pathetic, as if they thought they could grab the Ford's fender and drag it to a halt. The woman limped with each step, her wounded leg on the verge of collapse. Rink hauled down on the steering, and the backend spun out so that the Ford hit the road parallel with the opposite curb. Immediately he stamped the fuel pedal and the Ford's tires screeched and sent up plumes of black smoke. The Ford rocketed away.

The SUV at roadside also lurched forward, the driver intent on pursuit. But then those on foot waved and hollered, and it slowed until the three of them could dive inside. Meanwhile, the SUV reversing out of the hotel grounds missed clipping the Ford by inches. The driver made a hurried correction, getting the SUV lined up to give chase. By the time the car was under control,

Rink was already fifty yards away and the distance lengthening every second.

Not all that'd entered the hotel to spring the trap had made it back to the vehicles — one man was dead from my bullet in his chest, and another's head was crushed by Rink. If the two men that'd chased Rink with the woman were the same two he'd earlier shot at upstairs, there was still another missing. Stephen Vincent hadn't shown his face yet. Possibly he had decided against following us into the parking lot, and had retreated to the other car, but I doubted he'd had time before it reversed wildly. He was probably still inside, but more likely creeping after us. Unlike the others, he might have realised the possibility that Rink was leading his team off on a wild goose chase.

As soon as we fled the stairwell, Rink had announced his intention to cause a distraction, and I hadn't objected. The key target was Sue, so she was the one that needed protecting. We jogged to the Ford together, where Rink only paused long enough to shrug out of my backpack and throw it to me. I jammed one of the liberated pistols inside it — the one I'd originally pushed down the back of my pants — but it still left me with two guns to hand. Sue still had hers but I'd no way of knowing how much ammunition she'd spent in the gun battle upstairs. Rink had the pistol he'd liberated from the man whose skull he'd crushed. We were good to go. 'Hey! Saint Joe. See ya down the road apiece,' he announced and clambered in the car.

Sue spotted the woman I'd crowned with my pistol. Those weren't the actions of any kind of saint she was aware of. I didn't make her any wiser, for fear of being overheard.

'C'mon,' I told her, 'before she fully comes round.'

Already the woman was surfacing from unconsciousness, twitching and groaning, but she was still out of it and hadn't a clue we were nearby.

'She's going to live?'

'For now.'

With her standing on my knee, I bunked Sue over the perimeter wall, and then scrambled up and over it onto the beaten path of sand. There we crouched, listening as Rink started the Ford and began a tire-squealing drive towards the exit ramp. The noise must have woken the woman, because next we heard her exclaim, and two men emerging from the fire exit replied. Their voices began to recede as they pursued the Ford. I raised my head over the parapet and watched the ensuing action, even spotting the reversing SUV through gaps in the farthest support stanchions. From our hunkered position on the path, we could see the ensuing action playing out at roadside. Rink's distraction was working, so I urged Sue to move. We went through the gate I'd used earlier and scrambled through the vacant lot, keeping the waste containers between the hotel and us as best we could. Climbing over the buckled fence wasn't as simple as it had been for me earlier, but we made it, although I left behind a patch of cloth when the wire snagged in my clothing and had to be ripped loose. I didn't worry about it being a flag for our pursuers because our escape route would become apparent to them.

I directed Sue around the back of the tilting house, and paused there for a second to assess. By chance I caught a flicker of movement between two of the containers, and I raised my SIG.

A succession of bright flashes had me ducking for my life. Two bullets whined overhead, a third struck the wall of the nearby house, punching a dime-sized hole in the wood. I returned fire, but my bullets were more a threat than a danger to our hunter, as he'd already gone to ground behind one of the containers. I backed up after Sue, searching for any sign of movement. I made it around the side of the house, alive and well, and more determined than ever that Arrowsake's minions weren't going to get their claws on Sue. We raced together under the dangerously tilting walls of the house and into the front yard. From there I could see the diminishing taillights of the SUVs in pursuit of Rink, but made a silent bet that one or more of the cars would be summoned back by our pursuer. The house blocked our views, but we could easily judge our respective positions. I expected the gunman to race directly across the vacant lot to get back to the road and stall us until reinforcements could arrive. We'd no time to spare.

'Get in.' I juggled my SIG so I could dig my car keys from my pocket. I unlocked the doors, cringing slightly at the corresponding bleep and flashing lights.

She headed for the front passenger door.

'In the back,' I corrected her, 'and keep your head down and your gun ready.'

The Fourth Option

Sue threw her tote bag inside, then scrambled onto the bench seat. I tossed my backpack on top of her as the most meagre of barriers I could offer against flying bullets. In the driving seat, I shoved the silenced pistol into the door pocket, and my SIG within reach on the central consol. My Audi growled to life, and I began a speedy reverse along the main street even as a wiry figure in a baseball cap lunged out into view. Even without the benefit of the distinctive pompadour he'd worn under the guise of Vince Everett — a nod to a movie character played by Elvis Presley — I recognised him. Part of me wished I'd sought retribution from Vince before now, but there was no turning back the clock. We'd been enemies at first, and then reluctant allies by necessity, but right then I was under no illusion: he raised his pistol and fired. Bullets embedded in the Audi's hood and ricocheted off the windshield.

I cursed him, but kept my foot on the throttle.

Vince pursued a few paces, shooting with each step, but knew as well as I did that he was only spending bullets. Frustrated, he threw his left hand in the air, kicking at the ground with a heel and completed a pirouette: typical of his Everett caricature. I popped a rapid turn, and sped off, racing towards the northwest end of town, aiming to get beyond 14th Street, before the beleaguered Mexico Beach Police Department responded to the reports of shots fired. This was trouble piled on top of a catastrophe I'd have preferred not to bring to the MBPD — I knew and was friendly with some of the officers — but it wasn't my choice. I certainly didn't plan on putting any cop acting in the line of duty in danger.

As it were, I sped past, leaving behind the PD office without seeing any sign of a police cruiser, but that wasn't to say we were in the clear. Officers out patrolling the devastated city would be hotfooting it to the hotel any second, and we could meet them en route. I slowed down to a more reasonable speed, checking my mirrors for signs of pursuit by Vince's team. Way behind on US Highway 98 I could see headlights, but there was a lack of gumball lights and sirens, and guessed the bad guys were coming.

Just after the canal, I found the entrance to City Docks. I knew from runs I'd taken around the back of the twisting waterway that there were several routes that would give me access back towards the coastal highway, though some of them were not entirely suitable for my car. Immediately having pulled off the highway I realised that the roads were in worse condition than usual, with storm wreckage spilling over them in places. However, the integrity of my car's suspension wasn't my concern at that time, so I pushed through or around the wreckage, only to find the little bridge to 44th Street gone completely. Even if the hurricane hadn't torn it away, we couldn't have reached the crossing as a mountain of debris confronted us; the remains of houses, boats flung from their moorings and uprooted trees were piled chaotically in our path. I'd boxed us into a dead end.

Sue sat up for a look.

The Fourth Option

'Keep your head down, will you.' I began reversing, hoping to find an escape route before the bad guys caught up. My hope was we were too far ahead for them to have seen my turn into the City Docks, but I couldn't be certain. Already they could have been prowling up on us.

I found a place to turn, though there was some pushing and shoving of the woodpiles to make room. The Audi began a slow crawl back the way we'd come, the car's lights doused so we weren't easily visible. We past the entrance to a track that led out towards Water Tank Road, in truth a cut through the trees that surrounded the entire town. Downed branches and fallen tree trunks blocked the track less than twenty feet in. It was impossible driving in that direction, but I thought if I could make it to Water Tank Road, the way might be clearer.

We headed back the same way we'd recently come. My original idea to circumvent pursuit, rejoin the highway behind our enemies and follow Rink southeast had been thwarted, so I'd no option than return. The City Docks is a grand title for what amounted to a boat ramp and a couple of launches. There was a wide space in the road, a crescent of hardpack, bordered after the storm by a larger boggy expanse of salt water pushed by the surging waves up the canal. The forest beyond looked as if some surly giant had been playing pick-up sticks, and tossed around the tree trunks he'd used as playthings. Here and there — even through the darkness — the hulls of boats picked up and hurled hundreds of feet into the woods stood out, luminous spots among the carnage.

Near the entrance to the dock there was movement. I halted the Audi. The dim shadow I'd noticed moving among other shadows coalesced into the front of a SUV. It too came with its lights extinguished — which kind of gave the game away, because any innocent road user would've had their high beams on to negotiate the wreckage. I presumed, being the hindmost and the one carrying most firepower, this was the latter SUV to chase Rink. I also assumed the SUV had halted momentarily so that Vince could jump on board. We could be facing five guns or more, and they were blocking our only escape route.

'Stay down, Sue,' I warned, and gunned the engine. I took the silenced pistol out of the door pocket and powered down my window. It was time for some John Wayne heroics.

Before Sue could question my rashness, the Audi shot forward, racing to meet the SUV as it also leaped forward. I hoped Vince was inside it, and on the receiving end of the bullets I rained at the SUV.

15

Jason Mercer felt another wobble coming on.

He stood with his eyes squeezed shut, spine erect, hands fisted at his sides as he counted his breaths.

'Sir,' said the young woman behind the service counter, 'is everything OK? You look…uh, should I fetch you a glass of water or something?'

Mercer exhaled, long and hard. He opened his eyes, and black spots danced in his vision. He steadied himself against the service counter with one hand. The other he held up to ward off the young clerk's concern. 'Sorry,' he said, 'I just felt a bit lightheaded for a moment.' He grinned in embarrassment. 'Too many late nights and early mornings for a fella my age.'

'Are you sure I can't fetch you something? A chair perhaps?'

He rubbed his face, feeling the rasp of whiskers under his palm. 'I'm fine…least I will be in a second or two.' He blew out again, with slight exaggeration, so it sounded as if he said, 'Hooey!'

The clerk watched him a moment longer, her big brown eyes full of concern — not concern for him, he decided, but at the prospect of maybe having to administer care to a fainting customer. He nodded, tight-lipped, to show her everything was all right, and she returned her attention to the forms she'd been processing.

'Sorry if I alarmed you just now,' Mercer said. 'It has been a long day, and I haven't eaten since breakfast. I promise I'll grab something before continuing my journey.'

'That sounds like a great idea, sir,' she said, and squeezed him a smile.

He relaxed by a tiny increment. For a second there he'd worried she'd withdraw his rental request if she thought him unfit to drive. He nodded again, grinning and he shuffled his feet. 'Yeah, I'll be good to go,' he said after his self-diagnostics check.

She smiled, but bent to go over the small print on the forms. With her gaze diverted, Mercer took another surreptitious glance at the TV bracketed on the wall behind her. It was tuned to a local news channel, the sound muted, but with the subtitle function on. The story had already moved on from the one that had caught his attention, and almost brought on another of his neurological meltdowns. But he'd seen enough. Police had responded to sounds of a disturbance at a home in the suburbs of Panama City and discovered a gunshot victim, and were now "concerned for the whereabouts" of one Suzanne Carter. The news footage had showed the buzz of activity at the scene, as well as a grey van abandoned outside Carter's home, and Sue's Mercedes-Benz on the drive. The snapshot image displayed on screen of Suzanne Carter was the one of a red-haired, burn-scarred woman loaned to build Sue's legend, which, as it happened was a small blessing: the cops would initially be seeking the wrong woman. Things might change once a nosy neighbour brought it to their attention that the Sue Carter they knew and the one reported as missing were different individuals. Sooner or later, the police would discover the truth in the anomaly, then the hunt really would be on.

The clerk was talking, going through the final instructions, but Mercer barely heard her. He simply nodded along with her, then scrawled his signature on the rental agreement with the proffered pen, and accepted his copies and his credit card from her, all robotically. His mind raced, and all he wanted was to leave. Done, and the keys in hand, he waved off another concerned question from her, and gave another promise he was fine, and he left the office, carrying his grab bag with him.

The clerk had already gone around the rental vehicle with him before completing the paperwork, ticking off a checklist and explaining the does and don'ts, so he knew which was his car. He bleeped the locks open and threw his bag into the passenger seat. Then he stepped back, turned and surveyed the approaches to the strip mall at the edge of University Town Plaza. He'd waited for the agreed two hours maximum in Pensacola, but it was time to move on. He should head for Mobile, Alabama, to their next agreed rendezvous point and a flight to freedom, but he paused. Maybe he should give Sue another fifteen minutes. No, he decided, Sue wasn't coming. It was apparent that they were faced with one of three scenarios: Sue had given Hunter and Rink the slip and was on the run and unable to make it to Pensacola in the agreed time; their enemies had recaptured Sue; Sue was dead. None of the three favoured him hanging around any longer. He should move immediately.

All well and good, but there was a moral dilemma attached to the first two scenarios, and one of vengeance to the latter.

He was still holding the car keys in his hand. He didn't get in. He retrieved his grab bag, dropped the keys on the driver's seat and closed the door. Using the rental vehicle was pointless now, when he no longer needed to add a false step in his trail. He walked back across the parking lot to where he'd initially abandoned his Toyota outside a JCPenney department store and aimed it for I-110, the fastest path to US-98 back to Panama City.

16

Unknown to us at the time, Jason Mercer set off from Pensacola with the intention of rescuing or avenging Sue at much the same time that I risked her safety in an insane game of chicken with her persecutors. We were outgunned, outnumbered, and the SUV outmuscled my Audi, so all of the odds were stacked against us. But I was of a similar mind-set as my pal Rink, in that if you took the fight to the enemy on your terms, you could win the battle. For us to survive I had to be audacious and fearless, and give them hell.

There was about one hundred yards between us when I hit the throttle, and the distance rapidly diminished. My left arm out the window, I fired repeatedly, more in the hope of causing a distraction than thinking I'd hit and kill Vince. My bullets struck the SUV's windshield and hood, and there was a noticeable reaction from the driver who jerked with each impact. The SUV didn't deviate from its equally mad plunge though. Also, somebody in the back of the SUV leaned out to return fire. Then I was the one flinching at the impacts as first my windshield cracked and then turned milky under the barrage. My instinct was to swerve, to try to get around the oncoming SUV, but I fought it: I sped the Audi like a dart at the bigger car.

As we plunged towards each other, I held my nerve, taking my cue not from John Wayne now but from James Dean in *Rebel Without a Cause*, and for all intents and purposes my opponent must have thought I was going to ram him in a head-on collision. He yanked down on the steering, the SUV pulling to my left with barely a few feet to spare. Ideally I should've then had space to sweep by, but the terrain was against me. The hardpack had been churned and stirred by the hurricane, and my tires found a soft spot. My Audi didn't respond the way I wanted, and continued arrow straight, and blasted the back end of the SUV. The sound was horrendous, and the impact not too pleasant either. The left wing of my car collapsed, and I felt the steering yanked out of my hands an instant before the airbag inflated and thrust me back in my seat, and filled my vision. Sue was instantly thrown forward against my seat and then back, and I heard her yell in consternation. The back end of the Audi spun out, and we were lucky it didn't roll.

I was momentarily stunned, but couldn't allow myself to be. I hit the airbag with my forearms, and it began to deflate, but now my vision was full of swirling powder. I craned around to see where Sue was. She was still on the back seat, but her bags had been thrown on the floor, and she was in the process of trying to regain her tote bag. She was alive and unhurt, and that was all that mattered to me. I searched for the SUV. It too had come to a halt, also spun out and its back corner had collapsed where we'd struck. The SUV had gone down into a wide ditch, and murky water was up to its door handles on the near side. I caught movement as those inside took stock. Any second now, they'd be clambering out and coming after us. I thought about shooting them as they piled out but I'd lost the silenced pistol. Where was my SIG?

It was in the footwell on the passenger side, thrown there during the initial crash. I popped out of my seatbelt and reached for it, scrabbling blindly as I tried to keep an eye on our enemies in my wing mirror – miraculously the mirror had survived the collision, whereas everything forward of it was a crumpled mess. The driver's door was also twisted in its frame, and I doubted it would offer a fast escape. I clambered across to the passenger seat and popped open the door, grabbed my SIG and got out. I levelled my SIG over the roof of my car, ready to cap anyone that showed their face, covering while Sue also slid out on the same side. She went to her belly in the dirt, but came to her hands and knees, clawing her tote bag to her chest. There was no sign of her weapon. She rectified that by reaching back inside and clawing it off the floor. She looked up at me, the whites of her eyes bright in the gleam of the interior light, and then it went out. Steam belched from the Audi's buckled hood. An explosion was not imminent, but we couldn't hang around.

From beyond the SUV I'd heard sloshing, and understood that somebody had already escaped its confines and was in the boggy pond on the far side of the ditch. Other figures kept low as they too slipped out the prison of the car. To keep their heads down, I sent a shot through the shattered back window. At once I jabbed a finger for Sue to follow and she checked out the direction of travel. On our side of the hardpack there was another salt bog, water left there after the sea receded. Beyond, the woods looked navigable but there were enough fallen trees to shield behind. Keeping the Audi between her and the SUV she began a run for the swamp. Before following, I retrieved my backpack and shrugged into it, then began a slow retreat, watching for targets.

'Hunter!' Vince called from the darkness beyond the swamped SUV. I couldn't see him or even pinpoint the origin of his voice. 'You really want to play this game out? C'mon, man, this place is gonna be swarming with cops in no time, so let's quit the bullshit, accept the inevitable, and hand the woman over before we all end up in prison.'

'The only inevitability is you getting a bullet in the face if you follow us,' I replied.

'You'd kill me? I thought we were good, man.'

'Vince, we were never *good*.' I scanned left and right, alert to the probability he was trying to distract me so his pals could outflank me. I continued backwards. Behind me Sue was already up to her hips in swamp water.

'I told Rink already; this isn't about you guys. We only want, Suzanne Bouchard. C'mon, Hunter, we are on the same team. Give me a break, will ya?'

'Isn't going to happen.'

'Hunter, think about it, man. You were told to stand down and leave things to us.'

'Walter doesn't tell me what to do, Vince. Besides, that *request* was regarding another subject entirely. Go back to Walter and tell him that Sue's under my protection and off limits.' I'd reached the bog and went backwards into it, feeling the chill of murky water invading my clothes. The footing was treacherous, thick beneath the surface with broken branches and wreckage from the nearest buildings. Choosing the swamp as an escape route might not sound like my finest idea, but any second I expected the second SUV to come roaring along from the highway so we couldn't go that way.

'You think that Walter sent us here?'

'Who else?'

Vince didn't answer, not in words. He fired and his bullets kicked up water a few feet from me. I returned fire, aiming for his muzzle flash, but they were wasted shots as he'd already adjusted his position. It dawned that the son of a bitch was trying to determine my exact location and had drawn me into returning fire. I spun away, plunging for the cover of the nearby forest. From two different sides of the SUV, silenced pistols spat rounds at me. One of them hit my backpack, but thankfully not my spine. I popped off an answering round, but continued wading through the muck. Ahead of me, Sue had taken cover behind a fallen tree trunk. She covered me, firing back at those that'd tried to bring me down. Another bullet whizzed past my head, liquefying the air. I vaulted the fallen tree, and went to my knees. Something jabbed the palm of my left hand, something sharper pierced my left side. I slapped away the huge splinter of wood that had stuck into my flesh. Even soaked as I was, I felt warm blood pour down my hip, but knew the wound wasn't serious.

'Where now, Joe?' Sue's words sounded accusatory, for putting us both in such a tenuous position, and to be fair, she had a point.

'We go through the woods,' I told her. 'There's a service trail back there that will take us around the town. If we make it out alive, we'll reconnect with Rink and get the hell out of Dodge.'

'Do you think Rink has made it?'

'I've all faith in the big guy.'

She didn't answer; maybe she realised I was trying to change her opinion of him following his actions concerning Jason Mercer. She only offered a nonplussed expression.

I gestured out into the darkness where our hunters were. 'Those guys out there, they've got their orders and are trying to obey them to the best of their abilities. We've become their enemies through circumstances beyond all our control. They might not like it. We might not like it. But it is what it is. It was no different for Rink.'

'Neither was it different for Jason,' she reminded me. 'What he was accused of in Sierra Leone, he was ordered to do. And when it was done, Arrowsake didn't want him around anymore. They still don't, and because they suspect I know their secret they don't want me around either.'

I nodded sharply at her logic. We could debate this all night, go round and round in circles and get nowhere. More importantly was getting the hell away before Vince's team got organised and outmanoeuvred us. Whether or not they'd woken that morning with murder in mind didn't matter; they'd kill us if they caught us. And I'd do my best to stop them.

'How are you for ammo?' I asked.

She dropped the clip on her gun, inspected it and then shoved it back in. 'I'm down to my last two rounds.'

I twisted around so my backpack was presented. 'Dig in there. There's another pistol that should be fully loaded.'

She did as instructed and pulled out the gun I'd taken from the female assassin. Her own pistol she tucked into her tote bag.

'Stay low and stay hidden,' I told her, pointing off into the woods, 'take a straight line and I'll meet you a couple of hundred yards in.'

'What are you going to do?'

'Dissuade anyone from trying to follow you.'

She eyed me again, but not with the expressionless features as moments ago. She sucked in her bottom lip, nodded at my selflessness and then moved away. As she progressed through the maze-like branches and fallen trees, I shifted too, so that I was in a better position to watch both sides of the SUV. At least two of my enemies were concealed behind it, and largely pinned down from showing their faces, but Vince and possibly two others had moved away, probably seeking to find a way to outflank me. At present, the strip of hardpack was between us, and nobody was eager to cross the open space. From way off to my left there came the sounds of crashing timber. One of Sue's hunters had made it further than I realised, and was currently trying to find a way to get behind us by scaling one of the demolished houses down by the collapsed bridge. They'd probably slunk off while Vince kept me busy.

Sue was invisible to me by then, but I could hear her crackling progress through the woods. Keeping my head down, I went after her. Twenty feet further into the woods I halted, and peered back the way I'd come. I'd lost some of the panoramic nature of the view I'd enjoyed before, but beyond the trees it was lighter, so I'd more chance of spotting movement. Beyond the hardpack, and the wrecked cars, I could make out the bulky shapes of some surviving buildings, and further back the glow of arc lights on the highway. I also noted the flickering play of red and blue emergency lights. The cops were on US-98, seeking the architects of this fresh calamity to strike their town. For now I was happy to note that the cops were unaware we'd taken our fight down the City Dock road; all the nearby buildings had been evacuated, so it was unlikely our crash and brief gunfight had been overheard.

Without an enemy target in sight, I followed Sue deeper into the woods. The hurricane had done a number on it the further I progressed, and I had to take more care. There was a thatch of fallen trees overhead, some only held precariously on the splintered branches of other fallen trees. A heavy sneeze could bring any of them toppling down to spear me with their shattered limbs. I came to one spot that resembled a log jamb. Sue had been forced off track by the mountain of fallen trunks, but it was OK, as my vision had adapted to the night and I could now pinpoint her moving to my left. I went after her, and once she was around the pile, saw her try to regain her original direction of travel: she was following my instructions to the letter. Once I'd negotiated the pile I again halted and listened. Distant sirens wailed, and something crashed down — possibly a damaged building that'd finally given in to gravity — but it was far enough away to be unconnected to our hunters. There was no hint we were being tracked, and the best-case scenario was that Vince had abandoned the hunt for now, in favour of escaping the tightening police cordon.

I moved on for a dozen steps. Sue was a little way ahead. She paused to check where I'd gotten. Backlit by the city lights, I was probably just another dark blob against the thousands of others we pressed through. I'd the benefit of seeing her figure limned by the hull of an upturned cabin cruiser wedged between the fallen trees beyond her. The boat's position spoke more of the ferocity of the recent hurricane even than the complete destruction of my beachfront home. The boat must've been snatched from its moorings and hurled end over end to finally come to rest on a nest of branches hundreds of yards into the woods. Hopefully its skipper had evacuated long before the hurricane made landfall, and he wasn't still inside the boat, a jumble of rags and broken bones.

A silenced pistol coughed. The bullet struck a branch alongside my head, showering me with splinters and dust. Too late I ducked — my right eye was full of grit — and turned and fired blindly at the source of the noise. My SIG barked by comparison, and a visible flame stood inches from the barrel with each squeeze of the trigger. Another gun returned fire, this one from the opposite side. Again I ducked — instinct — but fought the impulse to go to ground. I adjusted my aim and fired at the figure crouching alongside the log jamb. The figure took cover. Immediately I searched for the first shooter, but couldn't get a bead on him. I was exposed where I stood. A bullet smacked another tree inches from my left shoulder, and I was showered in stinging splinters a second time. With my compromised eye half shut and streaming with tears, I turned and ran, urging Sue to greater speed. We headed for the best available shelter nearby, the upturned boat. Bullets chased me all the way, and again my backpack saved my life when it absorbed a round destined for my spine.

17

It was apparent that Vince's team had abandoned pursuit of Rink long before he reached Port St. Joe, the next coastal city down U.S. Highway 98, but he continued on until then. Port St. Joe was the permanent home to less than four thousand residents, a small city set alongside the white sands of Saint Joseph Bay, at the intersection of the highway with State Road 71. Earlier, after throwing Hunter his backpack, he'd called his buddy "Saint Joe" and said he'd see them down the road apiece; it was an instruction where they should meet once they'd given their pursuers the slip that Hunter would understand without any clarification. On several occasions that Rink had visited with Hunter in Mexico Beach, he'd joined his buddy on fitness sessions that had seen them run the sands to Port St. Joe and back. Usually the historical Cape San Blas Lighthouse or adjacent marina marked the halfway point in their twenty-mile runs. Hunter would know where to find him.

He took the turn towards Marina Drive, and found a space on a visitor parking lot. The hurricane that had devastated Mexico Beach had also touched here, but with less fury. Nevertheless, it wasn't a destination for the usual sightseers and vacationers just then. The lot was otherwise empty but for some mounds of detritus piled up and awaiting collection. He parked so that one of the piles hid his Ford from the entrance. He kept the engine running.

The pistol he'd taken from the gunman on the stairwell was beside him on the passenger seat, in easy reach, but not the tool he required just then. Earlier in the day both he and Hunter had switched off their phones, and Rink had gone a step further in separating the battery from the handset. He dipped in his pocket and took out the components and reassembled his cell and switched it on. He didn't care that Arrowsake might locate him through it, considering he wished to speak with Walter Hayes Conrad.

He rang a number from memory, and waited while he was shunted through the usual encryption and diversionary servers and then listened to his phone ring. There was no immediate pick-up, but Rink waited.

Finally, 'Yes?'

'I'm probably the last person you expected to hear from, you sumbitch.'

'Ah, Rink. You're right; I wasn't expecting you to call.'

'You were maybe expecting Joe? Joe's a bit tied up right now, kicking the asses of your goddamn attack dogs.'

'Hold on a minute, son. What are you talking about?'

'Don't call me son and quit your goddamn bullshit. The team you sent after us—'

'Team? Rink, what are you talking about?'

'You know fine well. The team led by your boy, Stephen-fucking-Vincent, or Vince-fucking-Everett, or whatever the hell he's goin' by these days.'

'Vince is out there in Florida?'

The Fourth Option

'Quit playing around, Walt.'

'Rink, I know you don't trust me, but—'

'You're right. I don't trust you. So keep your bullshit excuses. You sicked Vince on us, and that's unforgivable.'

'I swear to you, Rink. I'd no part in sending *anyone* after you. The only one I'm interested in finding is Jason Mercer. Remember? It was you and Joe who told me he'd resurfaced, and I asked you to step down. I wanted you guys out of the way, so you didn't get caught up in Arrowsake's business.'

'Bullshit! There's only you who knew where to find us.'

'Rink, I hear you. I understand your suspicion, but believe me when I say—'

'No. You should believe *me* when I say, if any harm comes to either Hunter or Sue, then I'm coming for you. I don't care how many killers you put in my way they won't stop me. I'll find you and cut off your goddamn head! Do you get me?'

'I don't take kindly to threats, Rink, but under the circumstances, I can expect nothing less. You're mad at me—'

'Damn right!'

'But your anger is misguided.'

'Is it? You didn't as much as pause just now, when I mentioned Sue. That tells me you knew she was with us, and you sent Vince's crew to capture or kill her.'

'Rink, I'm sorry, but I've no clue who this "Sue" is.'

'Yeah, right.' Rink paused. In fairness, he'd warned Hunter against mentioning Sue to Walter, and Hunter had been good to his word. 'Then if not you, who else would know where to find us?'

'I'm not denying I reported to my superiors, and advised that they mobilised a team — I was on it the second Joe got off the phone earlier — but they were sent to confirm that Mercer had survived. In the process I had to disclose you and Joe as my sources, but I did that with the express caveat that Arrowsake left you alone. I told my bosses I'd ordered you to stand down, and that I trusted you to do so. There's no reason why they should've sent Vince after you guys unless…this Sue you just mentioned? Who is she Rink, and why's she as important to them as Mercer is?'

Rink sucked in his bottom lip, and bit down. He had stupidly let his tongue get away from him by electing information that Walter had previously been unaware of. But it had been a fair assumption that Walter was the person behind the team that'd turned up at the hotel. Vince had proclaimed they were only there for Sue, so it stood to reason that Rink would think he'd gotten his information from Walter. However, he now understood where he and Hunter had fucked up. Walter — for all that Rink still believed him to be an untrustworthy conniving weasel — had inadvertently given the game away when demanding clemency for him and Hunter.

'Son of a bitch,' he growled in self-admonishment. He worked through a hypothesis as it came to him. 'When you told them about Hunter spotting Mercer, they must've interrogated Hunter's cell phone data to identify where exactly he'd been, and where they could therefore locate Mercer. They saw that he'd spoken with Velasquez back at the office, and that led them to check out Val's subsequent research into Suzanne Carter. They'd have figured it out that Sue was somehow connected with Mercer, and that she was their conduit to him. That led them to Sue's house, and once they realised they'd missed grabbin' her, they deduced she was probably with us. They'll have been aware that a hurricane had ripped Mexico Beach apart, but that Hunter must still be stayin' local. Hunter was registered under his genuine details at the goddamn hotel, so it'd have taken them minutes to find out where he was livin'.'

'Sounds plausible,' said Walter. 'Enough that you believe I didn't have anything to do with sending Vince after you?'

'You ain't off the hook yet.'

'Who is Sue Carter? The name means nothing to me.'

'It wouldn't,' said Rink, but didn't expound this time.

Walter didn't push for more. He didn't need to: Rink supposed he could learn all he needed about her from Arrowsake.

'You need to pull Vince's team off her right now,' Rink said.

'I would if I'd anything to do with the operation. It was taken out of my hands, Rink.' Walter sucked air through his teeth. 'My influence with Arrowsake isn't what it used to be…'

'Don't give me that! You've been calling the shots for years.'

'You're wrong. This Arrowsake is a different beast than the one you belonged to. It's different even to the version you'd the unfortunate experience of in Manhattan. There was the recent incident down in Miami where I was able to pull a few strings to help, but we've had little to do with each other after that job you helped Hunter with in Mexico, so you won't be aware that I've taken a step back. In fact, I've been pushed back several steps too. If I had my way I'd gladly sever all ties, but you know that isn't possible. You got him back for me, Rink, and I want to enjoy my great grandson for as long as I can. But that won't happen if I fully turn my back on Arrowsake. Ha! Even that would be impossible; I'd spend my last few years with one eye over my shoulder. I know too much for them to let me go free — I'm too much of a security risk to them — and these days I'm kept out of the inner circle so I don't learn more.'

'You must still have influence, even if it's as an advisor. You should tell them they've nothing to gain from making war on us, and lots to lose. Maybe you've lost your footing in the hierarchy, but surely your experience still means something to them? What about with Vince? He's still loyal to you, right?'

Walter laughed scornfully. 'You've got to be kidding me! Vince has no loyalty to me whatsoever. Why'd you think it was you and Joe I came to when I needed help getting Benjamin back? Vince doesn't give a goddamn hoot for me, or for anyone else. In fact, if ever I escape

Arrowsake, I said I'd have to keep one eye over my shoulder; it's Vince and his damn garrote I'm most fearful of.'

'Maybe Hunter will do you a favour and put the frog-gigger down,' Rink said. 'But I'll say again, if things go the other way, there's gonna be hell to pay.'

'Not by me though?'

'Didn't say I believed you yet.'

Walter grunted in mirth. It was apparent from Rink's change of tone that he'd accepted Walter's word on the matter – a paradigm shift for Rink, admittedly.

'Look, son, I'll make contact, see what I can do about having Vince stood down, but as I pointed out, I have little influence these days. I will, however, do my best.'

This time, Rink allowed Walter's misguided term of endearment to slide. It didn't pay to alienate Walter further when he was probably the only ally in an otherwise hostile camp.

'Thank you,' he said, with sincerity.

Rink ended the call. He was undecided: should he disassemble the cell phone again or not? He left it intact. He hadn't agreed a timescale with Hunter, but if he'd evaded pursuit, he should've made it there to Port St. Joe by now. Several scenarios went through his mind: Hunter was still on the road but was unable to find a clear route to their rendezvous site; Hunter was pinned down and unable to escape; Hunter was in police custody; Hunter was dead. Whichever way he looked at the possibilities, none of them was good, and getting no better while he idled there at the deserted marina. Walter had meant it when he'd offered to do his best to call off the hounds, and Rink believed him more than he'd have admitted before; sadly, he also believed that Walter's influence over Arrowsake was waning, and probably next to zero. He glanced over at the pistol on the passenger seat, came to a decision, and aimed the Ford at the highway back to Mexico Beach.

18

The upturned hull of the boat offered shelter, but if we stayed hidden by it, it could become our tomb. It had absorbed a couple of potshots taken at us, but wouldn't protect us from a sustained assault.

'We can't stay here,' I said, blinking crud out of my eye.

'They're moving in around us,' Sue said, adding validation to my words.

Though I couldn't pinpoint their exact positions, I could hear movement, and understood how perilously close we were to being flanked, or worse still encircled. While the opportunity presented, I shucked out of my backpack and delved inside for extra ammunition. While Sue covered me, I quickly reloaded. My SIG currently had a ten rounds magazine; I'd enough bullets to kill all of our pursuers if they did the honorable thing and came at us one at a time. As if that would ever happen.

I squirmed into my backpack. Sue was hunkered down, her tapestry tote bag between her knees as she scanned the woodland for movement.

'We're going to have to move fast,' I warned her, 'maybe you should dump the bag; whatever you need, we can replace later…if we make it.'

Sue didn't acknowledge my words. Instead she grasped the bag with her left hand, protectively, as if I was about to snatch it.

'It's too heavy and cumbersome,' I said. 'It will slow you down.'

'It hasn't slowed me down yet.'

'Your choice.'

She drew it tighter between her knees.

'Okay,' I said, changing the subject. 'Any minute now, the shit's going to hit the fan. The cops can't be far off, and that means the window of opportunity for these fuckers is closing. They'll assault us or they'll be forced to leave. We've hurt them, and we've embarrassed them, so it's my guess they'll go for broke rather than run with their tails between their legs.'

'If we hold them off long enough for the cops to arrive—'

'No. I'm not prepared to risk the life of a cop, just so we can get away. We have to keep moving, draw them out into the woods until they realise we've reduced their opportunity of escape. They'll be forced to abandon the chase then, and will concentrate on evading law enforcement rather than get into a shoot out.'

'If we leave cover, we'll probably be gunned down.'

We required a diversion; one that'd work better than the ad hoc plan Rink had come up with earlier.

'Do you smoke?' I asked.

When Sue replied with a look of confusion, I held up my fist and rolled my thumb over my index finger. 'Got a lighter?'

'No.'

I looked around.

When the boat had been thrown here by the high winds it had spilled most of its guts along its tumbling path through the trees. It was unlikely I'd find a flare or anything else I could use to ignite a fire. My initial idea was to set the boat ablaze, making a beacon to draw the police to the area that much faster, forcing our enemies to abandon the fight. Ironically, without a lighter, my plan had gone up in smoke seconds after I considered it.

'Do you see that, Joe?'

Sue indicated an object wedged under a fallen branch approximately ten feet away. I'd no way of knowing if it had fallen off the tumbling boat or had been blown here from another source, from one of the nearby demolished houses, perhaps. It was a propane canister, the type used in camping stoves.

'You want to shoot it?' I asked. 'If you expect it to explode, don't. You still need a flame to ignite the escaping gas.'

'Yeah, but it'll still make a big-assed noise, right?'

She was correct. The sound of an exploding propane canister wouldn't carry to the ears of the cops on the highway, but it might force an exaggerated response from our attackers.

'Cover me.'

Before she could reply I ducked out from under the boat and crawled for the pile of debris. Thankfully I went unobserved and I drew out the propane canister, and found to my satisfaction that it was heavy with gas. As I turned to retreat to the boat, Sue began shooting. The boat's hull acted like a resonance chamber, so her silenced shots sounded like a series of echoing claps. From the far side, somebody returned fire. I wormed my way back on my belly, the canister clutched in one hand, my SIG in the other. As soon as I was under cover I put down the canister and clutched Sue's shoulder.

'Go out the way I just did. There's none of them back there yet. Beeline into the trees so I know where to find you after.'

She gathered up her tote bag, and did as instructed. I watched as she crawled the first ten yards, before she rose up to a crouch, hugged her bag under one armpit and darted among the fallen trees. I wondered if I should forego a distraction in favour of stealth, but couldn't guarantee I wouldn't be spotted, despite Sue getting clear unobserved. I leaned to see from under the boat, and heard the crackling of branches breaking underfoot. Somebody was out there, less than fifty feet away and moving in under cover. I fired at the source of the noises and heard a curse in response. The gunman went to cover, but from near the front of the boat someone took up the fight. Bullets drilled the capsized prow. Good, I'd caught their attention. I squirmed back to where Sue had just left. I checked my anticipated route through the trees, then lined up the propane canister. I backed out on hands and knees, keeping my eye on my target. As I retreated, I hoped nobody had slipped around behind me, or my arse would make too resistible a target to miss.

Twenty feet out I stopped, rose to one knee and aimed at the canister.

For a nanosecond I paused, worried that Hollywood was correct; that a gas canister shot with a bullet would explode, and I'd be scorched. I caressed the trigger and my SIG kicked in my hand. The propane exploded, but not with flame. There was a tremendous *pop* and a wail of escaping gas! The upturned hull of the boat amplified the racket, and hanging precariously on some branches before, it shifted, gained momentum and canted on one side with an even larger crash. Immediately the escaping propane clouded the scene, almost glowing with luminosity against the darkness. The result was greater than I'd imagined. To anyone watching, they'd be forgiven for thinking we'd blown ourselves up.

I heard the gunmen's startled responses. Heard the clatter as they moved through the brush and debris. They were converging on the boat, though with some trepidation, perhaps expecting a second explosion. I moved away as stealthily as possible. Once I was a hundred or so yards deeper into the forest I checked behind, and was satisfied we'd momentarily given Vince's crew the slip. Also, I heard a siren grow louder and thought the cops were on their way. Hopefully Vince and his team would run, and not risk a pointless showdown.

19

We made good progress once we were on the service road, though I saw neither hide nor hair of the water tank it was named for. The going was mainly good, except every now and again we'd to climb over or circumnavigate trees strewn across our path. Alert to the possibility that Vince's team might chase us in their surviving SUV, I kept one eye on our back trail, another ahead incase they somehow anticipated our plan to circle back towards town once we were clear of the area. The road went around the back of Mexico Beach. We hurried through several dogleg turns and the further we progressed the less maintained it was. We reached a point where the hardpack gave way to ancient tire tracks in the sandy earth, and the trees loomed closer on each side. Here the hurricane had brought down branches but most of the trunks had withstood its ferocity. We made better time, and found ourselves approaching the city lights once more, probably a full two miles downtown from the City Dock.

We emerged from the forest trail onto the aptly named Joe Drive. I'd jogged most of the forest trails around town, and was familiar with Water Tank Road, and the one that we came out onto. It intersected with 15th Street, from where, with a strong arm, I could throw a stone and hit the police department building on 14th. It wasn't an ideal location to show our faces, but it was what it was. Hopefully every cop in town had converged on City Docks by now and we'd have a free run back to the main highway. We couldn't take the most direct route, not when the hotel where I'd stayed — and the scene of the recent gun battle — was only a few blocks southeast of the police station. At 15th Street, I directed Sue to go to the left, and follow the circuitous road until we were clear of the crime scene. Mercifully, most of the neighbourhood had survived the storm, and there were still residents at home. Unfortunately that meant there was the potential for witnesses. We were muddy, soaked to our waists, and could draw attention. We'd both hidden our pistols, mine down my belt at the small of my back, Sue's in her tote bag, but were ready to draw them in an instant.

We took several left and then right intersections, side-stepping our way back to the coast rather than take a direct path, and finally approached US Highway 98 near the demarcation point with Gulf County. I'd shopped at a Seafood Grill at the intersection on numerous occasions over the years, where they served an excellent shrimp po'boy sandwich, but one of my favourite take out spots had disappeared, all but for a pile of rubble and a low cinderblock wall that'd survived. The lot at the rear was currently devoid of the trailers and RV's usually to be found when I'd parked there on previous occasions, though there was a jumble of wreckage. I checked for observers, and when I saw none, urged Sue to enter the back lot and we hid from view, crouching in the lea of the cinderblock wall. Above us, the power lines had survived, but the poles themselves leaned drunkenly and some of the wires sagged perilously close overhead. I wondered if they'd affect my cell phone as I took it out and switched it on. They didn't.

Rink answered after the first ring, and I was relieved he'd had the presence of mind to switch his phone back on. I say he answered, though not in words. I could tell he was waiting for me to speak, to confirm I was the caller.

'Rink, it's me.'

'Good to hear you're alive, Hunter. Sit-rep?'

'We're in a bit of a pinch,' I told him. 'We lost the car and are on foot and exposed.'

'Where?'

I described our hiding place, and reminded him of the times we'd grabbed po'boys from the grill and sat on the beach watching the pelicans as we ate. 'I know it. Fact is, I'm only a few minutes away. Shouldn't have a problem gettin' to you, unless the cops have shut the highway between us.'

'I don't think they've the manpower.' Right then the beleaguered cops had two crime scenes to contend with, one of them at the far north end of town. 'I doubt you'll run into trouble.'

'Vince's team have been chased off?'

'Couldn't say.' I didn't have time to go into the events at the dock or in the woods afterwards culminating in exploding my improvised smoke bomb. 'I did what I could to alert the cops, and hope I forced Vince and the others to run. One of their SUV's are out of commission, but it leaves the other. They'll probably rendezvous with it once they're clear of the cops.'

'Yeah,' Rink said, 'it chased me a mile or two but gave up and headed back your way.'

'Your diversion worked at first, but Vince spotted us and called the troops back.'

'I guess I wasn't important enough to chase.'

'They're only interested in getting their hands on Sue.'

'Yeah,' Rink answered. 'Strange thing is, I talked with Walter. He can be deceitful at the best of times, but I got the sense he'd no idea that Sue was involved.'

'So it wasn't him that sent Vince after us?'

'Swears he wasn't involved.'

An icy sensation inside my chest began to melt: I'd carried it since spotting the SUV's prowling towards the hotel, and surmised that Walter had betrayed us.

'Seems there's been some kinda power shift in Arrowsake, and the old fart has been shoved out to pasture. He said he'll do what he can for us but didn't sound too hopeful. In fact, the way he put it, he's worried he could be next on Vince's list.'

'Not if I have anything to do with it. I'll—'

Sue stirred. She craned, trying to pierce the darkness beyond a nearby pile of debris.

'Hold on, Rink.' I turned my attention to Sue. 'What is it?'

'I thought I saw movement.' She aimed a finger, indicating a patch of ground near a collapsed shed. I watched, but saw nothing. Sue drew her tote bag closer, and draped her hand inside: probably feeling for her pistol.

'How far away are you now, Rink?'

'I'm just passing the memorial park.'

He was talking about Gulf County Veterans Memorial Park, and depending on his speed, should arrive at our hiding place within the next minute.

'Joe!' Sue stabbed towards the darkness this time.

A figure morphed out of the surrounding darkness, and I was under no illusion: this was not an innocent local out for a midnight stroll among the wreckage. It was a man wearing a baseball cap and dark jacket, and he darted from one pile of wreckage to another.

'They're here,' I said, for both Sue and Rink's ears.

We were exposed to gunfire.

Immediately I shoved away my phone, and grabbed for my SIG, and urged unnecessary action from Sue who'd clutched her bag to her chest and was already lunging to get around the cinderblock wall. But already it was too late. Distracted by my call to Rink, I'd allowed Vince to creep up on us.

Except, Vince wasn't the man sneaking up on us from the darkness. He'd crept in from the opposite side, and used his lackey's distraction to his benefit. As we scrambled to defend ourselves, he stood up from behind the cinderblock wall and snapped his garrote down over Sue's head and yanked it tight.

20

I had firsthand experience of Vince's guitar string garrote. I'd come close to death when I'd fallen foul of it, and only because Vince relaxed the pressure had I survived. A little tighter pull on it and the guitar string would've cut through my flesh right down to the vertebra. He'd only exerted enough pressure to throttle me unconscious, and there had been nothing I could do to stop him: almost instantly my mind had turned black and my oxygen-starved brain had refused my urge to fight back.

The bastard literally hauled Sue off her feet with one quick wrench, and dragged her bodily over the low wall before she could even drop her bag to claw at the noose. He pulled her in tightly to him, so that I could only see one side of his face peering over her shoulder. Sue's tongue protruded, and her eyes bulged. Her feet scrabbled wildly for purchase.

I didn't hang around; I immediately aimed my pistol, but couldn't shoot. I had another armed man to my right, and besides, there was no clear shot at Vince. I adjusted my SIG towards the gunman, but for the moment understood that Vince had beaten me.

'Don't try to be a hero, Hunter,' he said as he took a couple of steps backwards, dragging Sue with him. 'It will only take a little pull on this thing and Sue's head will come off.'

'Harm her, I'll shoot you in the fucking face,' I snarled.

Sue was still conscious, but I doubted there'd be any cognizance in her thoughts. She hadn't the strength to fight, and all her efforts just then were on trying to find her footing. Her heels barked at Vince's shins, but he took the discomfort in favour of using her as a human shield. He even relaxed the pressure on the garrote so she could suck in a breath. Her body shuddered. Instantly he tightened the coil again.

'You won't shoot anyone,' Vince corrected me, 'because you're going to throw down your weapon.'

'No chance.'

'Then I don't see a good way out of this for any of us, except maybe for Cayton over there.'

Cayton, the man who'd acted as bait so that Vince could spring his trap, emerged from hiding and approached a few steps. He had his silenced pistol aimed at me. His mouth was turned up at one corner in a sneer. His expression challenged me to try to kill him first.

The way Vince saw things, if he killed Sue, I would kill him, but then I'd die under Cayton's gun. Cayton, it appeared, was under the same impression.

Another scenario: if I threw down my gun, I'd get shot dead by Cayton, and Sue would still be their prisoner.

'Might not end too well for you either, mate,' I warned Cayton.

His sneer flickered, because there was always the possibility I'd shoot him, being the most direct threat, and he'd just put himself in my sights.

'Whatever you're being paid, is it worth your life?' I asked the gunman.

His tongue darted across his lips as he considered my words. For a second it looked as if Cayton had reconsidered the predicament he'd gotten embroiled in, and his gaze went from me to Vince for direction.

'Watch *him*, goddamnit,' Vince snapped at him, and he tightened the garrote so that Sue's legs thrashed. Her tote bag had been dragged over the wall with her, but she'd since dropped it between her feet. Her hands were behind her, squashed to her butt by the way Vince arched her over his thigh. 'Hunter! Lower your weapon or I swear to God I'll—'

'I'm not throwing down my gun. Let her go, Vince, or we're all probably going to die today. It's a price I'm willing to pay…are you ready?' I stared at Cayton, returning his earlier challenge. My gun barrel didn't waver. In the meantime, Vince continued moving backwards, taking Sue with him.

I heard the sound of an approaching vehicle. A minute felt like an eternity when lives were under threat, but at last Rink had made it here.

Unfortunately his wasn't the only vehicle to squeal to a halt.

The surviving SUV had arrived, and some of the others I'd fought in the woods were inside. They must've evaded the cops and rendezvoused with the driver, even as Vince and Cayton had tracked us along Water Tank Road, before splitting up to trap us after we'd gone to ground behind the wall.

I dared not take my eyes off Cayton, but I heard Rink's car door open, and assumed he'd taken cover behind it. I also heard a door on the SUV clunk open. Vince continued backing towards it, his hostage now angled to protect him from Rink's gun too.

Cayton had grown seriously nervous: if Vince made it to the SUV with Sue, it'd leave him exposed and at the mercy of two guns. I saw uncertainty flicker across his features, and knew for certain he was going to shoot.

I shot him first, and my bullets took him in the chest. He got off a return shot, but it drilled the wall next to me, as I was already spinning to acquire my original target.

Somebody shot from the car, muzzle flashes lighting up the interior. Rink returned fired, but with care not to hit Sue, so ineffectively.

Latterly Sue fired.

Unbeknown to us all, she'd had more presence of mind than anyone would've given her credit, and had slipped her pistol from the tote bag before it had fallen to the ground. Her silenced pistol coughed twice, and Vince danced behind her with a startled yowl. Sadly she'd missed shooting off his feet. She swung the gun up and over her shoulder and stuck the suppressor against his throat, and her eyes pinched in anticipation of the blowback as she again squeezed the trigger.

Vince was the luckiest son of a bitch alive. In her desperation, she'd grabbed the first gun she'd placed in her bag, and this one had only held two rounds. He yelled again, but in anger this time, and he employed the leverage of the garrote to twist her around and toss her into the waiting hands of his pals in the back of the SUV. He didn't hang around either. As both Rink and I fired, he threw himself inside, on top of them. The car was already revving away, the back door open, with Vince's legs kicking the air, as both of us rushed to slow them.

I tried to shoot out a tire, but my bullet rebounded from the spinning rubber. Rink aimed for the engine, but it was angled away from him and his bullet ricocheted off the side. If Sue hadn't been onboard we'd have peppered the SUV with rounds until it was as holed as a sieve, instead we lowered our pistols. The SUV took a wide squealing swerve around the intersection, almost mounting the grass shoulder on the beach side, and then it tore off at speed, heading down the highway with its engine roaring.

I met Rink's eyes. He had his teeth clenched, his features had darkened in rage and the old scar stood out on his chin like a thunderbolt. I probably looked equally pissed off.

From further up the highway sirens howled, and blue, red and white lights flashed. The cops were coming.

'This ain't over, brother,' Rink said.

'Not by a long shot,' I said.

'Let's go.'

I took a step after him, then glanced over at Sue's tote bag.

'Gimme a second,' I said.

She'd clung to that bag throughout, until she couldn't any longer.

I snatched it up, and then we ran for the Ford.

21

I'd returned to Mexico Beach with innocent intent and a sense of civic duty to assist with the clean up and reclamation of the town I'd called home for years. I'd toiled among the wreckage of my beach house, salvaging a few personal items, and the last thing I'd ever expected was to get caught up in a fight. With no reason not to, I'd booked my hotel room under my genuine details, and also I was the registered owner of the Audi I'd abandoned at City Dock. Even if we managed to give the police the slip now, I'd be identified and a wanted man. Back in the good old days, Walter would have exerted his influence to divert law enforcement attention off me, but I couldn't rely on his help this time. If his superiors were the ones that'd sent a hit team to my hotel, then they sure as hell wouldn't allow Walter to protect me as he had before.

The cops were not my enemies, but they didn't know that. I wasn't happy about potentially hurting a cop, but neither could I let them arrest me. In time I could probably prove my innocence, and convince a jury I was acting in self-defence throughout, but that could take weeks or perhaps months. I didn't have time to languish in a cell if Sue's life was going to be saved. There was only one reason that she was alive for now, and it was because Arrowsake believed she could lead them to Mercer. They might keep her as a lure, or they might torture the information they required from her, then kill her the instant she was no longer useful.

Rink hurtled the Ford down the highway, and I was happy to note the police lights were dwindling. Sadly Vince and the others in the SUV were too far ahead of us, and travelling without lights, so we'd no idea where they were. One thing we were both conscious of was the possibility of cops from Port St. Joe responding to calls for assistance from their neighbouring PD, and shutting the highway ahead. Rink took a left turn onto a forest trail running adjacent to a boggy waterway called Chickenhouse Branch. None of my previous explorations had brought me here, so I'd no more idea where the road would take us than Rink. As long as it was away from law enforcement pursuit, it suited me. Once out of sight of the highway, he slowed down and took more care navigating the trail. The tires crunched over downed branches but the road wasn't blocked. At a T-junction, he went right, perhaps guessing that the next trail might lead us towards the eastern end of Port St. Joe where we could pick up FL-71, while avoiding any police cordon. I wasn't confident there was any route hereabouts that bridged the Gulf County Canal, which to my reconning could be less than a couple of miles ahead, blocked our direction and was only spanned at the highway.

Rink decided on taking a narrow trail that sent us deeper into the woods and up along the crest of a low chalky bluff that shone almost luminescent under the starlight. Safely off the road he reversed the Ford off-trail so that the tree canopy hid it from above. Depending on the extent of the police pursuit, they could send up a chopper with thermal imaging cameras: the heat from the Ford's engine would stand out like a bonfire, but hopefully the dense tree cover would protect us for now.

Rink kept the engine running but all the lights off. We exchanged looks.

'You injured, brother?' he asked.

'I'm fine.'

'You smell like a swamp.'

'I hadn't noticed.' I'd walked off some of the water in my clothes, but was still wet from my waist down. My feet squelched in my boots. Now that he'd mentioned it, I got a waft of warm air rising off me and it was pretty rank.

When we'd run to the car I'd tossed Sue's tote bag, and also my backpack, onto the back seat. I'd a set of boxers, spare jeans and a shirt in my bag, but there was nothing I could do about my wet footwear. I got out and opened the back door, reached inside and dragged my backpack to me. I paused, my gaze alighting on Sue's tote bag: she'd been determined not to let that thing out of her sight. Letting my change of clothes be for now, I reached and grabbed the tote. It was heavy. I was conscious of Rink watching me over his shoulder. 'Lookin' for some fresh pantyhose?' he quipped.

'I just want to see what's so bloody important inside this bag.'

Rink reached up and flicked on the dome light. We were deep in the woods, and no cop would see the faint glow; if they were already close enough to see it, we would be in trouble anyway.

The bag had large handles, and a zip along the top, partly open. I fully unzipped it and folded back the edges to see inside. On top was the silenced pistol she'd missed grabbing when in Vince's clutches: it was a shame her groping fingers had found the wrong gun, or she would have blown his damned head off and then we'd have foiled her abduction. I picked the gun up and placed it on the seat.

I returned to delving through the bag. There were more of Sue's personal belongings, including her purse and another bag containing cosmetics, hairbrush and the usual accoutrements. There was a smart phone, and another cheaper model cell that'd gone out with Noah's Ark. The first was switched off, the second disassembled, with its battery and SIM card wrapped in cellophane. I showed Rink the latter and he nodded sagely. For the moment I set it aside.

I pulled out other inconspicuous items, and laid them on the seat. I came upon a sturdy tin box. It was the type often used to hold petty cash in an office. It was locked, but no problem to open. I put it down on the ground, raised a heel then stamped down on it. The lid buckled and the lock popped open. Inside I found what I'd largely expected: loose cash, amounting to about a thousand dollars, and several credit cards in the name of Suzanne Carter. There were also a few things I hadn't expected: small plastic wraps containing white powder…more accurately, narcotics. Sue hadn't struck me as a user, so I decided the drugs were probably there as incentives to buy help that required secrecy. I shoved everything away in the box and shut the twisted lid as best I could. Then I bent to what I was really searching for. In the bottom of the bag there was a large bundle wrapped in opaque plastic. It looked as if Sue had torn down a shower curtain, packed items inside it, then secured it all with duct tape. I hauled it out. Rink's attention was piqued enough that he got out of the car and joined me. I dumped the heavy package on the roof of the car.

'Got a knife?' I asked.

Often Rink carried a military issue KABAR, but that was on active missions, and he'd neglected to arm himself before his unexpected drive up from Tampa.

'Here, let me,' he said, as I reached for the bundle. 'You can get yourself changed into some dry clothin'.'

I stood aside for him, and he set to work ripping off lengths of duct tape. I was too impatient to see what he disclosed to bother with stripping out of my soaked trousers. He unwrapped the plastic sheet slowly, like a kid savouring the surprise on Christmas morning. He stepped back, mouth downturned, similar to some of those kids where the surprise didn't match their expectation. 'What the hell is this?'

There were six buff-coloured folders altogether, thickly packed with printed documents. I reached past him and flicked open the topmost one. I slipped out the first few printed sheets.

'Talk about takin' your work home with you,' said Rink.

The documents were pretty much what would be expected of a realtor. They contained the specs of houses and other properties, including photographs to show the homes off to their best ability. There were details on room numbers and dimensions, facilities, and even fuel and energy consumption ratings.

Rink exhaled through his nostrils. 'You should have a flick through those, see if there's anywhere takes your fancy seein'' as you're effectively homeless now.'

'Why would Sue waste her time protecting this stuff?' I dug deeper, but couldn't see anything unusual.

'She told us the realtors she works for is a front for a protective service,' Rink began, and I took his hint.

'You think these documents hide a network of safe houses, just like the one where Sue lived?'

'Yup. Don't know how that will help us find Sue though, and right now we haven't really got the time to check. Let's just bundle that stuff up and I'll put it safely in the trunk.'

I nodded without answering, deep in thought. Sue had given us a cock and bull story about attending a civic meeting with a client, and it had turned ugly. She'd intimated that the gunman that had come to her house was probably looking for payback for somebody she and Mercer had strong-armed out of the meeting: it had sounded like a bullshit story to me then, and even more so now. I'd bet that if I interrogated those files, I'd find a house matching an address in Mexico Beach. Disguised in her vibrant red wig, had Sue come to town earlier to check on the house, or more correctly the person relocated under false details to it? By no stretch of the imagination did I believe that all the documents pertained to safe houses, only that they were hidden among all the rest: when Sue had rushed home to clear out the documents before fleeing, she hadn't had time to sift among them. She'd grabbed everything she had, dumped them in the plastic and prepared to leave, and that was when we'd shown up, followed shortly by the guy with the Uzi. I'd disregarded that first gunman from being sent by Arrowsake, now I wasn't as sure. Back in our day, Arrowsake fielded only the cream of military operatives; it seemed these days, they were using any asshole that could point a gun. Case in point: Vince's team. Cayton had lacked killer instinct; he'd allowed indecision to gain control of him and had died for his mistake. Also, those others with Vince, they had the numbers, the firepower, but not the strategic training I'd have expected of them, otherwise none of us would've made it out of that hotel alive, and Sue and I would've been killed or captured back at City Docks.

The trunk lid clunked softly, and Rink leaned on it to fully close it. He'd loosely rewrapped the documents and put them in the trunk while I'd mulled things over. He was correct in that the documents wouldn't help us find or rescue Sue, but there was another item that might. 'Gimme those cell phones, Hunter.'

I handed over both, and while he interrogated the smart phone, I quickly shucked out of my wet clothing, wiped myself down with my discarded shirt, and dressed in the dry stuff from my backpack. The wet clothes I wadded up and stuffed under a fallen log, then kicked some leaf litter over them to hide them completely. I inserted my SIG in the back of my fresh jeans. By then Rink had scrolled through Sue's most recent activity on her smart phone.

'There's a number here that could be Mercer's. She called it after first spotting us, probably to warn him to run. I'm going to ring it but doubt it'll get us anywhere.'

'He has probably dumped that phone by now,' I said, 'the same as Sue probably intended to do with her's before the shit hit the fan.'

He nodded, but hit the call button anyway. Listened. I heard the tinny strains of an automated message advising that the call couldn't be connected. Just as expected, but Rink had to try. He switched off the smart phone and lobbed it on the back seat.

'If he'd answered,' I asked, 'what would you have said?'

He shrugged, not fully sure.

'We have to agree on something, Rink,' I said.

'Yeah.' He gave a rueful shake of his head. 'Sue comes first.'

'Do you think he'll let bygones be bygones for her sake?'

'If he won't, it will only prove I was right to shoot the scumball.'

'How do you feel about that now? According to Sue, Arrowsake sold you a lie, and had him executed to protect their wrongdoing…but then, Sue has lied to us about other things.'

He exhaled noisily. 'The reason she gave for them being in Mexico Beach when you spotted Mercer was obviously bullshit; she was thinking on the hoof and graspin' for a plausible lie, and it sounded paper thin. It was different with what she said about Mercer though. Knowin' what we do now about Arrowsake, it makes perfect sense. He was their patsy, and like a good little soldier I obeyed my orders to execute him. Does knowin' that change my opinion of him? Sure it does. Can't say he'll feel the same way about me.'

'We won't know until we make contact.' I held out my hand. 'Maybe I should be the one to make first contact.'

Rink studied the old cell phone and its sundry parts. He came to a decision, and handed them over.

I fitted the SIM and inserted the battery and replaced the cover. After switching it on I'd to wait for it to power up. The tiny display screen was in grey-scale.

'Jesus,' I said, 'I'd an Etchasketch when I was a kid that was more sophisticated than this thing.'

'Yep, it's barely a step up from two tin cans joined by string.'

The inexpensive model phone was what was often termed a burner: something to be thrown away or destroyed after use, usually untraceable to the users. I'd last used phones like it back in the late 1990s, and took a few seconds to get my head around the buttons. I found the menu and brought up the contacts list. As I'd expected there was only one number programmed in its memory. My thumb hovered over the call button.

'You sure we should go ahead with this?'

Rink sucked in his bottom lip and chewed down on it. Finally he nodded. 'If we're gonna save Sue, we need to use every tool in our box.'

I pressed the button.

22

It was a number of hours since the brief, but lethal gunfight in the backyard of Sue's house in Panama City. Law enforcement, and the media, had arrived en masse and the activity had barely diminished since. Sue's house was cordoned off behind police tape and a couple of stern-faced officers kept nosy onlookers back with curt commands. At the front of the house a van was being loaded on a trailer to be transferred to a secure compound where further forensic investigation would be completed. Sue's Mercedes-Benz sat on the drive at the side of the house, and would probably be next to be hauled away for examination. There were uniformed officers and also plain-clothed detectives in and outside the house, and several crime scene investigators were controlling the area where a man had been shot dead: the corpse had most likely have been recovered by the coroner's department by now. People had gathered in small groups on the sidewalks, local residents all gossiping about what had happened on their street, raising conjecture and probably concluding bullshit theories. Jason Mercer had inserted himself behind one small bunch, close enough to be mistaken as one of them, so that he didn't stand out as a stranger to any of the investigators. Still, it was risky being there.

He'd gained from attending the scene though, enough to temper his concern that Sue had been murdered. He'd overheard snatches of conversation, and the consensus was that the man that ended up dead had arrived in the van, whereas Sue had left with two different men in a dark coloured car. The descriptions he'd heard regarding Sue's abductors were that one was Caucasian, of average size and build, whereas the other was taller and muscled like a pro athlete. Two witnesses were in conflict as to the latter man's ethnicity, one claiming he was white while the other said Asian – they were both correct in part as Rink's mother was Japanese, his father Scottish-Canadian. Even without Sue's warning call Mercer would've been under no illusion about who'd taken Sue.

He was also reasonably assured that the dead man was an Arrowsake goon, although the manner of his death perplexed him. If Hunter and Rink were still puppets of their old masters, why the hell had they killed Sue's would-be assassin? Yeah, he was jumping to conclusions, but he was confident there was only one reason why that man had gone to the house, and it wasn't to spread the Gospel of Jesus Christ. He had all the hallmarks of a hired gun, albeit, until now his weapon hadn't been recovered, although the box he'd transported it in had — if Sue's next door neighbours were to be believed. Mercer had concluded that Hunter and Rink were already on the scene when the killer had turned up, and they'd killed the man and taken Sue with them. Why? Perhaps they wanted the kudos for the capture, maybe there was a reward to be claimed they didn't wish to share, but neither scenario rang true.

Mercer caught a couple of fleeting glances aimed in his direction. A big man, florid-faced, and splayfooted was paying too much attention to him. The guy was probably wondering who he was, and why he'd almost ingratiated himself into his group of gossiping friends. He saw the man bump the elbow of another man next to him, and they exchanged whispers. The second man looked fully at Mercer.

Mercer realised why.

He was lathered in cold sweat, and visibly shaking.

'Hey, buddy.' The red-faced man took a step closer, holding out a hand. 'You okay there? D'you need a doctor or something?'

Mercer shook his head, trying to divert attention away with a lie. 'Low blood sugar,' he said. 'Just need to eat some candy and I'll be fine.'

'You want me to—'

He turned away before the man could offer to fetch him something. He was conscious of being observed as he walked away. He kept going, avoiding the urge to glance back, and believed that the man's attention would shift within ten seconds. Mercer returned to his Toyota, which he'd left parked along the street, well distant of the bubble of activity around Sue's house. He leaned on the car, light-headed and trembling, and snuck a glance back to where the group of neighbours stood. Nobody was interested in him any more. He sat in the driver's seat for some minutes, gathering his strength, counting his breaths and settling his juddering vision so it would be safe to drive.

When he got that way, he sometimes suffered pins and needles in his extremities. He opened and closed his fists, wiggled his fingers, but didn't detect the numbness that occasionally afflicted him. He realised something important: this wasn't due to one of his neurological responses as before, but through a rush of endorphins. He was a battleground for a mixture of conflicting emotions.

By now he could have been safely aboard a flight out of Mobile, Alabama. He'd gone against their own strict escape plan to return here to try to rescue Sue from her abductors. He hadn't stopped to consider what returning to Panama City actually meant, only that he must if he was going to find out where she was being held. As a soldier he'd faced death on numerous occasions, and as Arrowsake's patsy had literally skated at the edge of the abyss after Jared Rington shot him, and he'd no great desire to confront it again, but returning here was akin to placing himself in the firing line. During the months he'd spent recuperating from his wounds, he'd suffered almost daily, his nightmares brimming with screaming terror, his waking hours filled with the soul crushing promise of the hell to which he'd go when death finally took him. As the years passed, his nightmares had grown less frequent and he'd been able to shuck off his illogical fear of burning for all eternity. It had suddenly struck him that by trying to save Sue, he could speed his own demise. Was his probable sacrifice worth it to save her life?

Yes. He owed Sue. If not exactly for his life, she'd helped him return to something equating normality. After being gunned down by Rington, Mercer had been left to rot amid the ruins of a scorched town in Sierra Leone. Local villagers discovered him, clinging to life. In a show of humanity they had carried him to a nearby *Médecins Sans Frontières* field hospital. The volunteer doctors were more used to assisting amputees — Sierra Leone was in the midst of a terrible civil war at the time, where groups of men travelled between villages chopping off the arms of residents, raping women, murdering entire families and razing villages to the ground — but were no strangers to gunshot wounds either. His life had been saved, and to which he'd be eternally equally grateful, his anonymity was also protected. He travelled throughout northern Africa and into Europe, and finally was repatriated stateside, where to his surprise he found Sue Bouchard — more correctly, she found him. Sue was also in hiding from Arrowsake, having faked her drowning he'd learned, after discovering Mercer's 'execution' had been ordered to conceal their dirty secret, and therefore fearing for her own life. It turned out that she was in the process of setting up a network to assist those in similar positions to her, and to Mercer. She'd recruited him, and brought him into the fold, giving him a new life and purpose. Without her support, he firmly believed that he'd have succumbed by now, maybe by putting the barrel of his pistol between his teeth and ending what Jared Rington started.

He loved Sue. She was attractive, smart and intelligent, but more so she was beautiful in her heart and soul. However, he convinced himself, his feelings for her were purely platonic. Another blow due to the damage to his neurology was that he'd lost any sexual desire, but that wasn't it. He regarded Sue more as the little sister he'd never had, and what kind of brother would put his life before hers?

It was obvious why a killer had been sent after her, but not why Hunter and Rink had then snatched Sue. Clearly they wished to keep her alive for now, and the only reason he could think of was to use as leverage against him. Where would they take her? Earlier when Sue had rung to warn him his old nemesis was in town, she'd surmised that they must have been spotted while out earlier that day, and she'd assumed it was during their trip down to the storm ravaged town of Mexico Beach. Was it likely they'd returned there after whisking Sue away?

He must check it out.

The police were seeking the wrong person for now. They were still of the mistaken assumption they were looking for Suzanne Carter, but once her neighbours returned home and saw the face depicted on the news bulletins, they'd put the story straight. Her neighbours knew Sue as Suzanne Carter, but not as the scarred woman from whom Sue had taken her bogus identity. Once they dug deeper the police would learn that Suzanne Carter had died years ago, that *his* Sue was another woman entirely, and the mystery of the shooting and her abduction would deepen, and attract further interest. He could of course go to them and throw his and Sue's fates at the feet of the police, but he feared that the cops couldn't protect them from Arrowsake. Sue's only hope of survival was for him to take the fight to the son's of bitches and hope his aim was steady enough.

The Fourth Option

He started the Toyota and made a turn in the street, heading away from the crime scene. He hadn't made it more than a couple of blocks before the burner phone in his shirt pocket began ringing.

23

My greeting was met by silence.

It was understandable. Probably the last person Jason Mercer wanted to hear from was the best friend of the man who had almost killed him. No, scratch that; he'd prefer speaking to me than directly with Rink.

'Don't hang up, Mercer,' I reasoned with him. 'Hear us out, for Sue's sake.'

'If you've hurt her I'll—'

'It isn't us hurting her you have to worry about. The opposite, in fact.'

'What do you mean? You have her. Don't try lying to me. I know you were here and took her. You want me, you can have me, but you let her go. Do you hear me? Let. Her. Go.'

'Trust me, Mercer, you've gotten hold of the wrong end of the stick.'

He laughed, a sarcastic bark. 'Well, haven't we just been there before? Oh, wait! It wasn't me that got things wrong that time, was it? It was Rink who handed me the shitty end.'

'Rink's here beside me.'

'Like I give a fuck about *him*?'

'Just laying our cards on the table, Mercer, so there's no misunderstanding. Rink's here beside me, and I speak for us both. We don't mean Sue harm, and we don't mean you harm.'

He clucked his tongue. 'So let her go, let *us* disappear.'

The Fourth Option

'If it was in our power, we'd do that.'

'You're still working for those bastards.'

'No. You're wrong. We are working against them.'

'Bullshit.'

'You said a minute ago that we were there and took her. You're talking about Suzanne Carter's house in Panama City. If you're there, then you already know that we stopped the man they sent to kill her.'

He snapped out another sarcastic bark. 'Only because he was in your way and you wanted the prize all to yourselves.'

'You know that's rubbish.'

'Then why take her?'

'We took her for her own protection.'

'So let me speak with her; let Sue convince me you aren't the murderous bastards I think you are.'

'We can't.'

'Ha! There you fucking go then!'

'We can't because we no longer have her.'

'You killed—' His voice was a squawk of rising anger.

'No,' I cut in to forestall him. 'We didn't. Sue was taken from us.'

'You handed her over?'

'I told you she was *taken*. We fought to stop them, but things went south and Sue was grabbed.'

'You handed her over to your goddamn bosses, you mean. Now what? You're trying to trick me into surrendering too? Well fuck you, Hunter, and fuck Jared Rington!'

For a second I thought he was about to blow. He was on the verge of hanging up, and perhaps throwing the burner phone away. The single conduit we had to him would be lost. He didn't though. I could hear him breathing, ragged, loud exhalations. There was a mutter after each breath, a word…no a number. He was counting, and it made me wonder if he was using some kind of mantra to keep his emotions under control. I gave him time.

'OK,' I said, 'now you've got that off your chest, are you going to listen to me? Sue's life depends on our mutual cooperation.'

'Don't take me for a fool, Hunter.'

'I'm not. I'm hoping you care enough about Sue to let what happened in the past slide.'

'That's easy for you to say. You weren't the one with the two bullets in your skull.'

Beside me Rink growled something about Mercer being a whining punk. His curse didn't carry to Mercer's ear though. 'You were being manipulated back then, we know that now. The same went for Rink – Arrowsake used him too, lied to him, and had him carry out their dirty work. You've got to see that, Mercer.'

'So what? I'm supposed to forgive him? You want us to hug it out, have a few beers and sing Auld Lang Syne?'

'No,' I answered, 'I want you to put the past behind you if you want Sue to have a future.' Even to me, I sounded trite. But I also meant what I said.

'I still have trust issues.'

'You needn't have.'

The Fourth Option

'Who says you're not lying to me, and you're only trying to draw me out so you can finish the job for Arrowsake?'

'Arrowsake are our enemies now.' As briefly, but emphatically as I could, I related what had happened, culminating with Sue's abduction by Vince.

He absorbed my story, and it was apparent that my words rang true to him, but he was understandably cautious.

'I don't recall anyone called Stephen Vincent,' he said, 'or what else was it you called him: Vince Everett?'

'Let's just call him Vince to avoid confusion. You won't recall him; he wasn't around in our day. He's one of a new breed…a different breed. They sing from a different hymn sheet than ours.'

'I'm not sure we were ever in harmony. Can't see as how we can work together now.'

Rink had heard enough. He muscled in beside me, so he was clearly understood. 'Listen up, Mercer. Quit the goddamn bullshit. You don't trust us, well the feeling's mutual. But I'm prepared to put aside my distrust of you for the sake of savin' Sue. You're in or you're out. We are goin' to try to get her back with or without you. If you care for her, you'll join us. Your choice, pal.'

Again Mercer grew silent, but there was no hint of his mantra this time. Finally he came back on the line. 'We need to meet. Somewhere neutral, somewhere—'

'Somewhere public,' I ended for him. 'Not sure as how that can work, Mercer, seeing as I expect my face to be plastered all over the news networks before daybreak.'

'You'll have to make it work, Hunter. It has to be someplace public,' he emphasized. 'There's no way I'm putting myself in your sights without plenty of witnesses.'

'Call it, then,' I said.

'How well do you know Panama City?'

'Barely.'

'Barely will have to do. Come here. Keep that cell handy: I'll be in touch.'

'The longer you make us wait, the longer Sue's in Arrowsake's hands.'

'I get you. But there's no way I'm showing my face til I'm certain Rink isn't gonna try and blow it off again.'

'You're going to make us wait til morning?'

'That's the way it has to be.' Mercer ended the call.

24

The following morning Mercer directed us to a sprawling shopping mall on Martin Luther King Jr Boulevard. He'd chosen it because it offered several escape routes, and plenty of potential witnesses should we try visiting violence on him. There were security patrols, and CCTV cameras in abundance, so it was risky enough entering the building without us causing any kind of drama. Rink parked the company Ford — now in possession of a different set of license plates we'd lifted off a similar model Ford down in Port St Joe — in the spacious lot adjacent to a Sears's department store, and we entered the mall and made our way to the central hub. Rink was a distinctive guy, whichever way you looked at him, but he also had a knack for stillness, for adopting a Zen-like tranquillity, so he could go unnoticed when he wished. For my part, I'd elected to wear a baseball cap and inexpensive reading glasses purchased at a gas station earlier to disguise my face, though I was still unsure if it had made it onto the news networks yet.

We checked our fastest exit routes, the most obvious being the four walkways radiating from the central hub, but we also took note of service and fire escape doors. It was lost on neither of us that Mercer might have decided it was too risky joining forces with us, and deeming us enemies, he'd laid a trap for us with the local PD, naming us as the perpetrators of last night's shooting at Suzanne Carter's house. Rink sat alone on a bench situated for the convenience of weary shoppers, while I moved fifty feet away and stood as if checking out the tasty wares through the window of a shop selling cookies and brownies. I used the reflective window to look for counter-surveillance and spotted nobody suspicious. We'd arrived twenty minutes prior to the agreed meeting time, allowing an opportunity to check for a trap before Mercer showed up. There was nothing alarming but I still remained at high alert.

Apparently Mercer had also decided to arrive early, probably for the same reason we had. I caught his reflection in the cookie shop window. He approached at a right angle from where we'd arrived. He was dressed in the same attire I'd spotted him in yesterday, now looking rumpled. He'd probably slept in his car, as we had in ours. His silvery hair stood up from being finger-combed by nervous fingers. His head darted about as he checked all places of concealment or possible ambush. He saw me, and paused in step, but only for a second. He held something tightly to his body, a folded magazine, and I guessed it was there to conceal a weapon. He could have shot me then, but didn't, which was a promising start.

His attention jumped from me to where Rink sat in the open central hub area. Rink was overlooked by a number of early shoppers, and those taking breakfast at the adjacent food court. Mercer's right hand crept under the magazine, and I steeled for the worst, but then Rink faced him directly and gave him a nod and placed his open hands on his thighs. Mercer's hand appeared, empty. Mercer stopped walking, a few feet from me. I turned from the window and appraised him. This close I could see he was shaking gently, vibrating like a plucked guitar string. He stared at me a moment, then gave a tiny jerk of his chin. 'You've aged, Hunter.'

'Haven't we all?'

'You want to keep on aging, let's keep things civil, shall we?' He tapped the glossy magazine, emphasizing what was concealed beneath.

'Making threats isn't the best way to begin a civil conversation,' I said.

'Just so you know, if this is some plot to trap me, I'll take both of you down with me.'

'Good job it isn't then,' I said, 'otherwise Sue will have nobody left to recue her.'

He tilted his head in response. For a moment his vision appeared unfocussed. He snapped to, and again checked on Rink. His tongue snaked over his bottom lip.

I said, 'Are you sure you're up to this, Mercer? You look fit to drop.'

'Yeah, you can blame Rink for that.'

'We have to move on,' I said, and without checking that he was following I walked towards my friend. I could tell by Rink's gaze that he was observing Mercer's progress. It was now or never. If Mercer had come with some preconceived notion of exacting revenge on Rink, he'd go for it now. It'd be a rash move to shoot in full view of all those witnesses, but rationality isn't always the overriding mood of someone bent on killing.

I halted ten feet out from the bench and faced Mercer. If he drew on Rink...

Two little girls charged past, whooping with excitement. A parent called out to them, but they didn't slow. They ran between Mercer and Rink. Mercer's shoulders slumped and his features softened. He was a better man than we'd once been led to believe: he wouldn't willingly shoot where there were innocent children at play. I nodded in understanding, then stood aside so he could approach. He sat alongside Rink on the bench. Neither looked at the other.

Standing over them — while keeping a regular look out — I waited for them to break the ice.

'Saying sorry would be a start,' Mercer finally said.

'Saying sorry would be accepting my culpability,' Rink said. 'I pulled the trigger, yeah, but I was a soldier obeying a command. Your beef isn't with me, Mercer, it's with the ones that gave the order.'

Mercer's right hand crept to the scarred flesh behind his disfigured ear. Again I noted the trembling of his fingers — Sue had told us how it'd taken him years to recover his health, but he was still a long way from being the warrior we once knew. He turned to appraise Rink's profile. 'For years,' he began, 'I've dreamed about getting my own back on you. You sent me to hell and it's been a rocky road back. I wanted you to feel even the tiniest part of the agony I've endured. I'm sat here now, fighting the urge to shoot you like a dog, the way you did to me.'

'If you were goin' to shoot, you'd have done it by now. Let's say the moment's behind us and move on.

The Fourth Option

We weren't stringing you a line, Mercer: if Sue has any hope of survival, it's on the three of us to make it happen.'

Mercer gazed up at me.

My lips formed a tight line as I nodded down at him. 'What do you say, Mercer? In or out?'

'I'm here…what do you think?'

'I think you need to put away your weapon and listen to what we've planned.'

Mercer allowed himself a tight smile as he rolled up the magazine and set it down beside him. There was no gun concealed in his belt.

'You came here unarmed?' Rink's mouth was downturned, but not in a show of disappointment.

'I'm armed,' Mercer said, 'just not as openly as I wanted you to believe. I'm pleased neither of you reached for your guns; if you had, well, I might've turned around and walked away.'

'Or got a bullet in your back,' said Rink.

'If what you've said is true, you're not the kind to shoot a man in the back of your own accord.'

There was logic in Mercer's statement. Rink grunted. 'You're either nuts, or you have balls of steel.'

'Whichever it is,' I added, 'we are going to need a bit of both from you once I make the call.'

Before, when we'd arranged our meeting, I'd again gone over the circumstances leading up to Sue's abduction. I'd also told him what we knew about Stephen Vincent/Vince Everett, and how Walter Hayes Conrad had allegedly lost his power of influence over him. However, I'd also mentioned how I'd believed that

Walter still had a direct line to the punk. Hiding out in the woods atop that chalky ridge, we'd thrown ourselves at Walter's mercy, and called him for help. He'd agreed to be our conduit to Vince, if not to Vince's superiors.

'It's asking a lot from me,' Mercer said, 'but for Sue's sake I'm willing to go along with the plan. I just need some kind of assurance that you won't abandon me as soon as you have Sue back. This head of mine might be a bit messed up, but it's the only one I've got; I don't want it cut off by any damn guitar string garrote.'

'There's not much more we can say to convince you, you're going to have to judge us by our actions. You have my word, Mercer,' I said, 'join us and I'll fight as hard to keep you safe as I will for Sue.'

Mercer rocked his head, and then looked again at Rink. 'What about you?'

Rink eyed him, and with a curl of his lip said, 'If I meant you harm, I wouldn't need a skinny-assed punk like Vince to cut your ugly head off for me.'

There was vinegar in Rink's response, but it had the opposite effect. There was a few seconds of silence while his words were absorbed, and then Mercer surprised us by guffawing in laughter. A few seconds after, Rink and I were infected by his humour and we laughed too.

'Isn't that the *damn* truth?' Mercer cackled, his face red. He stood, sat down again, clapping his hands on his thighs. He hooted again.

The Fourth Option

We were attracting attention, but nothing to be concerned about. Diners in the food court were smiling, grinning inanely, or even chuckling at Mercer's antics. He received several headshakes as he tried to control his laughter, but already people were returning to their breakfasts. Mercer got a grip — after a few phlegmy coughs and hiccups — and then sat staring at the floor, blinking as if his attack had left him confused. Maybe, I decided, his laughter was the release of years of pent up frustration and several hours of anxiety.

'So?' Mercer finally asked. 'How are we going to do this?'

Rink stood. 'First we get outta here, reconvene somewhere more private and Hunter will call the old fart. From then on Vince holds the cards…'

'But not all of the aces,' I reassured Mercer.

25

Jason Mercer wasn't the first loose end Vince had pursued on behalf of Arrowsake. Several years ago he had traced a knife wielding maniac from North Carolina's Barrier Islands, into the Deep South, and then almost to the border with Canada where his quarry had holed up in a hunter's cabin in Minnesota's Land of Ten Thousand Lakes. The madman, who'd gone by a number of pseudonyms, but most notably the Harvestman, had proven a dangerous enemy. Vince had come close to killing him, but the wily killer had had a contingency up his sleeve, and escaped. The three assassins that had accompanied Vince didn't survive the brutal encounter, and Vince hadn't come out of it unscathed either. He'd been stabbed through his right knee, and would have bled to death if not for the Harvestman's whimsy: Vince had woken from combat with his serious leg wound tourniqueted by way of his own garrote, and with his skeleton mercifully whole. The Harvestman was named for his penchant for taking bone trophies from his victims. In a note left for Vince at the scene, the maniac had explained his reason for allowing him to live, but with the caveat that should they meet again, he would reap his due. Yeah, well if it ever happened and they faced off again, the loon wouldn't find Vince lacking: he also wanted his due, and wouldn't be satisfied until the Harvestman's head was at his feet.

Unlike his simmering hatred for the Harvestman, there was nothing personal involved in the task of finding and killing Jason Mercer; it was just a contract to him. Not unless he counted the inclusion of Joe Hunter in the search. If he'd to put a finger on why he disliked Hunter, he'd struggle to admit it without sounding envious. Theirs had been a complicated relationship, one born of conflict but ending in an uneasy alliance. He knew Hunter still held a boner for him over the fact he'd throttled him unconscious with his garrote but that was due to a misunderstanding. He'd known that sooner or later — unlike he expected with the Harvestman — there'd be some kind of showdown with Hunter, one that'd draw blood but not necessarily in the taking of lives, but that was before this shit show threw them back into conflict. To Vince this was just another job, but Hunter had a different opinion, the noble fool being misguided by some kind of loyalty to Sue Bouchard. He couldn't understand why Hunter would stick up for a woman he owed nothing to, and who had for years assisted an enemy of Rink.

Actually, he could.

Hunter was a throw back to earlier centuries. He conducted himself like a night errant out of time and place: the first hint of a damsel in distress or a dragon to slay and he was on the job like stink on shit. He was surprised that Hunter's archaic behaviour didn't find him coming unstuck more often in this modern politically correct world. It was partly why he disliked the Englishman: Hunter could be a sanctimonious prick at times. But his disliking didn't end there. There was the need for Vince to prove his worth...no, strike that. There was a need to prove his *superiority* over Hunter.

Hunter was old school, as archaic as his questionable moral code, and had rightly been put out to pasture. And yet, Vince always felt his efficacy was compared to Hunter's and found wanting. They had both shared a handler in the form of Walter Conrad, and Vince had gone out of his way to impress the CIA director, although he got the sense that his best was never good enough. Walter, a man who should be above emotional ties, loved Hunter like a son, whereas Vince felt akin to an unwanted bastard foisted onto him: Walter tolerated him when he was around, used him when it was convenient, then ignored him like a shameful family secret at earliest opportunity.

Vince owed Walter nothing.

When the old man contacted him last night, pleading leniency on behalf of Hunter and Rink, Vince promised he'd do what he could do. His words held double meaning, because if killing them both was achievable, that was exactly what he would do. Their discussion had been brief: Vince had already missed his chance at wiping out his rival, but he knew how dogged Hunter was and that the opportunity would arise again. He didn't update Walter that he'd already captured Sue as the old dodder was out of the loop on this mission. He wanted to gloat: but he took secret pleasure in the fact he'd one-upped Walter's Golden Boy, and taken the woman from him. When he found out, Walter would be disappointed, but he'd have to eat humble pie too, when he realised he'd put all his faith and energy into supporting the wrong son all those years.

The Fourth Option

Vince grimaced at his thoughts.

They sounded like those of a spiteful child, green-eyed with sibling envy. Walter was a surrogate father figure to Joe Hunter, to Vince he was…well he was *nothing* really. He was unsure why he sought Walter's validation, his *approval*, especially now that the old bastard had lost his toehold in Arrowsake's upper echelons, and was fast tumbling into the void of obscurity. Walter had used him in the past, and Vince had reciprocated, taking from the old man too while he ascended Arrowsake's ranks, but now that Walter no longer had anything to give…

He turned his attention to the others in the room.

He had lost three of his team in the fight to win the prize, two men at the hotel and latterly Brian Cayton, sacrificed in order for Vince to escape with Sue. He had three remaining male helpers, Gary McMahon, Johnny Scott and Wayne Davis, and one female, although Pam Patrick was currently sleeping on a couch in a room next door, her bandaged leg propped up. She'd taken a bullet to the thigh, and a couple of nasty cracks to the skull when ambushed by Hunter in the parking garage: adrenalin had carried her through the ensuing chase and abduction of Sue, but once they'd arrived at their safe house she'd gassed out. Vince knew how debilitating a leg wound could be; it'd taken surgery and months of rehabilitation before he'd gotten back to health, so he gave her a break, as much to get over the concussion as anything. McMahon was napping too. Between them Scott and Davis could be trusted to watch the captive until their colleagues spelled them on guard duty.

Scott was a big, rangy guy, square of shoulder and chin, his dark hair worn in a high and tight military buzz. He put Vince in mind of a young Stallone, circa the first Rocky movie, but he lacked Balboa's wise guy charm. Davis was squat and burly by comparison, fair haired and freckled with an almost boyish face. They didn't comport themselves like soldiers, because they weren't. Once upon a time, Arrowsake gleaned its intakes from the cream of Special Forces. In essence it was still a counter intelligence service, funded by the blackest of black budget money, but for the sake of complete deniability, it now chose its recruits differently. Some of its assets were ex military, others private security contractors, and some of them were hired guns, recruited locally where some crap had to be swiftly dealt with and cleaned up. Take for instance the asshole they'd sent to Sue's house in Panama City: he was a street punk offered a cash payday to go and keep tabs on Sue until Vince's team could be mobilised and get their boots on the ground. Whether he was trying to impress his paymasters, he'd ignored instruction and gone in with all guns blazing — or at least that was his intention — and had royally fucked things up. He'd gotten himself killed, no loss there, but he'd also spooked Sue and her noble rescuers into running. The only saving grace was that there were no comebacks concerning the dead man, who it'd be impossible to trace back to Arrowsake.

The Fourth Option

The assault on the hotel in Mexico Beach hadn't gone the way Vince had hoped. It had been his intention to storm Hunter's room, overwhelm their adversaries with numbers and firepower, and take Sue without having to fight a running battle. There's an old adage in the military that if anything can go wrong, it will: how could he have predicted that Hunter would've left the hotel, and spot the team as they arrived, and warn Rink and Sue to run? Had things gone to plan, the execution of Sue's rendition would have taken minutes, and there wouldn't be the complication of corpses and wrecked vehicles to cover up afterwards — Arrowsake was on the case right then, using its influence to encourage a different narrative with the local PD, and wider law enforcement agencies: all anyone needed to know was that the shootings involved rival criminals engaged in a turf war, the gunmen choosing their moment to attack while the city, and the PD, was in disarray following the hurricane. The story wouldn't pass deep scrutiny, but Arrowsake would ensure the investigation was superficial at most. As the city began to rebuild, the deaths of three criminals would be buried alongside all the other trash being carted away to landfills.

Thankfully, despite the initial assault going wrong, an exfiltration route had been made in anticipation, and after capturing Sue, the surviving team members had made it to the rendezvous site at Cape San Blas and boarded the boat waiting there. The SUV they'd abandoned at the dock was currently en route to a crusher — it could've been forensically cleaned, but there was nothing that could've been done to conceal the bullet holes Hunter and Rink put in it during their final skirmish. Replacement vehicles had been sourced for his team on arrival here, so they could still go mobile if necessary. For now Vince's orders were to stay put, extract any helpful information from Sue, and await further orders.

Having sped north, the boat had docked at a private country estate on the western shore of Fanning Bayou. They stood within striking distance of Panama City where, according to intelligence passed via Walter Conrad, Jason Mercer had originally resurfaced. It was possible that the fugitive had bucked town, but also that he was lying low in an area he knew well. Apparently Sue Bouchard had also lived in Panama City for several years, and would know all of his hiding places. Similarly as with Mercer, Vince had no personal beef with Sue Bouchard, all she meant to him was an asset to be wrung until her usefulness dried up. He wished her no personal ill, but then again, neither did he have any qualms about hurting her.

He flicked his fingers at Scott. 'Do your stuff, Rocky.'

The big guy had been waiting. He picked up a semi-opaque roll of thick polythene and opened it, like an ancient mariner unfurling a scroll map. Its dimensions were approximately two by three feet. He walked across the room, as if studying what was written on it, though there was nothing: he was checking there were no perforations.

The Fourth Option

From where she sat, secured to a ladder-backed chair by zip-ties, Sue watched Scott. From the nervous tic tugging at the side of her mouth, she fully anticipated what was coming next.

'Things don't have to be tough on you,' said Vince, and her gaze snapped to his.

She said nothing, but he noted how she steeled her shoulders. It wouldn't help her.

'All you have to do is tell me where to find your boyfriend, and this can all end.' Vince had discarded his ball cap. Locks of his hair, often slicked up and back in a rockabilly pompadour had fallen loose and hung over his eyes. He liked the look, it added to his rakishness. 'C'mon, Sue, tell me where to find him and I promise you won't be hurt again.'

Sue clenched her fists, and gnashed her teeth against the pain in her joints. Her forearms were strategically secured horizontally on the armrests, in order that her captors could easily work on her hands. Earlier, Vince had Wayne Davis wrench back each of her fingers in turn almost to the point of dislocation. Davis might look like a sweet boy, but he'd the nasty penchant of a sadist for inflicting pain. She'd resisted that torment, so now Vince preferred to up his game, and use a method more likely to get results.

Vince cocked his head on one side, peering down at her with a frown of mock pity. 'You don't have to be afraid,' he said, 'I'm not a total bastard. Give me something, and you'll be rewarded…'

'You're a coward and a bully,' she rasped.

Vince smiled at the words. They were filled with condemnation, but they were a step in the right direction. Before now Sue had been steadfast in her defiance, refusing to answer. But now he'd gotten her to speak, he knew she'd find it more difficult to stop.

'I'm only doing my job,' he said. 'I only need a few answers to my questions, and that's all. Tell me what I want to hear, and put an end to this horrible experience.'

'You're a coward, a bully, and a *liar*.'

Vince pushed back his unruly locks, and set his jaw. 'Last chance. Tell me where your boyfriend is.'

'Jason isn't my boyfriend.'

Vince grunted. 'Then why protect him? He obviously doesn't care about you. I mean, take a look around. Do you see him hurtling to your rescue?'

Sue said nothing.

'Maybe you're expecting somebody else? The big bold Joe Hunter perhaps? Now wait! A little birdie told me you and Rink once had a thing going. Is that who you're expecting?' He shook his head in regret. 'You can forget about either of them helping you, Sue. There's only one person that can help you.' He pointed at her chin, waggled his finger. 'Only you can help you. And you can do it by telling me where to find Mercer.'

'I have no idea where he is.'

'Untrue. See, I believe you had an escape plan, with a prearranged meeting place agreed. I think you were in the act of fleeing there when Hunter and Rink stuck their noses into your business and spoiled your plan, and you only went with them out of necessity. I also think that you planned giving them the slip at your earliest convenience, and running back to your boyfriend, but then we threw another wrench in the works by capturing you. It doesn't change the fact that a meeting place was arranged, or that Mercer is there now, waiting for you to show up.'

'There was no meeting place. Mercer's gone, he's in the wind, and I can't help you find him.'

'And you had the audacity to call me a liar.'

Vince shrugged, flicked his a fingers a second time.

Wayne Davis who'd been sitting across from Sue, smiling amiably throughout the discourse, stood up. Sue clenched her fists tightly again, trying to glare defiantly at him, but the boyish thug only clucked his tongue and turned his back on her. While she scowled in frustration, she was unaware of Scott looming behind her. He dropped the polythene sheet in front of her face, and then yanked it backwards. The plastic was tough, but it perfectly moulded to the contours of her features.

Sue was blinded, but that was not the worst of it. The polythene sealed her airways. She could neither draw in breath, nor expel what was already in her lungs. Instant suffocation occurred. She fought for her life, kicking and jerking at her restraints, the chair jumping on its wooden feet, but Scott hove in on her, jamming the back of her head to his abdomen and pulling the plastic tighter. Panic engulfed her. Vince knew that the pressure in her skull would feel as if it was about to burst open, the way in which a victim of his garrote felt. It was the second time that Sue had endured similar torture since he'd grabbed her, and wouldn't be the last.

He flicked at Scott and the big man relaxed the pressure and lifted away the polythene.

Sue gulped for air, streams of saliva dripping from her mouth, bloody mucus running from her nostrils. The sclera of her eyes was pink.

Vince asked, 'Where's Mercer?'

'Go to hell,' she gasped.

He didn't bother instructing Scott again, the big man was aware of what was required. The polythene dropped over her face again and was wrenched tight. Vince observed as Sue fought for freedom, watching a concavity grow and deflate over the open oval of her mouth. She shivered and jerked, but her strength was diminishing swiftly. She made a noise in her throat like a wailing banshee and bubbles of escaping oxygen writhed beneath the plastic shroud. Her tremors grew more frantic by the second. Vince silently counted to ten, then quirked an eyebrow at his henchman. Scott withdrew.

Sue threw back her head, mouth open, her tongue squirming. It took a moment to get her lungs to work. She dragged in air, then her head fell forward and Vince was certain she was on the verge of blacking out. He backhanded her across the cheek. Saliva flew as she woke with a start.

'How long must we keep this up?' Vince demanded. 'You know you can't resist, Sue. Do yourself a favour and end this. Where is Mercer?'

The Fourth Option

He gave her a few seconds to compose an answer. She looked at him, and the pink in her sclera had deepened, a blood vessel had broken in the corner of her left eye. Her voice was hoarse and thin. 'I don't know.'

'Again,' he said to Scott.

'No, no, for God's sake!' Sue's face contorted in horror. 'It doesn't matter how many times you ask, I don't know where he is!'

Vince stared at her, and she tried to show how earnest she was by mouthing a silent plea. He pirouetted slowly on one heel, one hand clenching his pompadour as he thought. He faced her once more, bottom lip protruding. He lowered both hands at his sides. Thought some more.

'Nah,' he concluded, 'I don't believe you.'

Scott yanked down the polythene a third time and bunched his fists at the rear of her skull. He pulled her back so hard that Sue's neck craned painfully over the back of the chair. The plastic moulded to her face. Through it she looked skull-like. This time she lacked the strength to fight; only her frantic gulping and shivering indicated she was still trying to live. Then she fell still.

'She's out, Vince,' said Scott needlessly in a thick New Jersey accent.

'You'd better let her breathe then,' Vince said. 'She's not much good to us dead.'

Scott relaxed his grip. The polythene sucked off Sue's dampened skin. She made a compulsive gulp, but didn't rouse. 'I don't think she knows anything,' said Scott.

Vince held up a warning finger, though he was beginning to suspect the same. There were few people that could withstand such torture. If Sue knew Mercer's location then she would've been singing like a bird by now. Probably she didn't know exactly where he was, but Vince was convinced she'd agreed a rendezvous with Mercer, and he wanted to learn where. To hunt somebody you needed a starting point from where you could pick up the scent. 'I'm only asking the wrong questions. Wake her up, Scott.'

Scott wasn't gentle with his instruction. He grasped Sue's hair, rolling his fingers into a tight fist to exert more pressure and shook her head savagely.

She awoke with a yowl. Scott held her head steady as Vince approached and crouched in front of her. He faced her on her level, staring into her face. The broken blood vessel in her eye spread a scarlet wash across it. Blood dripped from her nostrils and was smeared across her top lip and cheeks. She was sweating profusely and white as snow.

'Welcome back,' said Vince, and he turned up one side of his mouth in a snarky smile. 'Are you ready for round two?'

Her answer came as a surprise. 'Look at me you goddamn idiot.'

'Huh?' He bent at the waist, jutted out his chin as he scrutinised her. 'I see you.'

'No. What you see is your own future.'

He straightened up, chewing the interior of one cheek.

The Fourth Option

'That's right,' she went on. 'This is what you can expect, possibly sooner rather than later, when your worth to Arrowsake is finished and *they* want rid of *you*.'

He laughed at her prophecy, but he didn't sound genuine.

'You know I'm speaking the truth. Sooner or later you'll be disavowed, and they'll send some other sadistic equally blind fool to torture you, that's if they don't just put a bullet in the back of your head like you're a sick dog.' Sue turned her condemnation on the others in the room. 'What do you think is going to happen to you once your value to them has ended? Do you think Arrowsake are going to allow any loose ends to live? Mark my words, sooner or later you'll feel Vince's garrote around your necks too. Save yourselves. Let me go and I can help you all disappear!'

'You didn't make a good job of disappearing yourself, did you, Sue?' Vince aimed a wink at each of his lackeys.

Wayne Davis grunted in disbelief, but behind her Scott swallowed and coughed, as if he had something important he wanted to ask. His fingers in her hair had relaxed incrementally. She tried to crane, to beseech him Vince guessed, and Scott's fingers unfurled completely. But only so he could grasp both ends of the polythene sheet again. He snapped it over Sue's face and squeezed his knuckles together.

'First she won't speak, now she won't shut the fuck up!' The big guy grinned savagely at Vince.

The numbskull wouldn't be smiling if he realised how close to the truth she was. Vince bared his teeth in reply, but then snapped up a hand. Sue again gagged and fought to breathe after the plastic was dragged off. Scott shoved her head roughly as he backed away a few steps. This was no act of mercy on Vince's part; he only wished silence while he answered his phone. It had begun vibrating in his hip pocket.

He frowned at the caller display: Walter H. Conrad. He swiped to answer. 'I told you already, whatever it is you want, you're wasting your time asking,' he announced.

'What if I can offer you something instead?'

'Unless you can deliver Jason Mercer to me gift-wrapped with a goddamn bow on his head, you're wasting my time, Walt.'

'Who else would I be talking about, Vince?'

'Say what?'

'I have Mercer.'

'You mean your goddamn Golden Boy has him?'

'If you're talking about Joe, then yes. He has Mercer, and he's willing to trade. Just so we're clear, he means Jason Mercer in exchange for Sue Bouchard.'

'Bullshit! What kind of cockamamie trap do you expect me to fall for?'

'You're fearful of a trap? Vince, you have the numbers, the guns and the hostage. What's to be afraid of? Hunter, and especially Rink, doesn't give a crap about Mercer's ass, but he does care about what happens to Sue. He's willing to trade, but if you've hurt her—'

'She's fine.'

The Fourth Option

Walter didn't halt. 'If you've hurt her, then all deals are off and you face all out war.'

'I told you she's fine.'

'I need proof of life.'

Vince held out the phone to Sue. 'Say hello.'

Sue said nothing.

'Fuck sake!' Vince slapped her with his other hand. Sue yelped, then swore at him. 'There you are, Walt. Satisfied?'

'I want to speak with her.'

'What? You think I have a random girl here I can smack around just in case I need to convince someone my hostage is still alive?'

'I want to speak with her,' Walter repeated.

Vince stabbed the phone at her. 'Don't make me hit you again.'

Sue craned towards the phone. 'H…hullo,' she croaked.

'Sue? It's Walter Conrad. I don't know if you remember me but—'

'I…I remember.'

'Good. Now listen to me. Are you hurt?'

'Just…'

Vince butted in. 'She's fine, I told you.'

Walter said, 'Sue, I need you to stay strong. I will get you out of this. Do not argue, do not fight, and do not try to escape. Obey all instructions given to you by Vince and you'll get out of this alive. Do you understand?'

'Yes.'

'Okay,' said Vince snatching away the cell phone, 'that's enough. You've spoken with her, Walt, and you've had your proof of life. What now?'

'Now we agree where, when and how we make the exchange,' said Walter.

'I didn't say I was willing to exchange,' said Vince.

Walter clucked his tongue in disappointment. 'Son,' he said, stressing the term so it sounded like endearment. 'Make the deal, it's for your own good.'

Vince laughed in denial. 'I'm not afraid of Hunter.'

'I'd prefer to say there's no need to be afraid, but you know I can't. Make the trade, Vince, for your sake. Return Sue safe and uninjured, and Hunter will give you Mercer. Do that and he'll take her and walk away. I've already warned you about the alternative.'

'It's a deal,' Vince said after a moment's rumination. 'But I need some time to think.'

'You know how to get me. Don't take too long, this is a time sensitive deal, son, and the clock's ticking down.'

Walter ended the call.

26

It was dusk of the second day when Rink drove us along a woodland trail bearing the ubiquitous name of Confidence Way. We had left behind the outlying burbs of Southport into a tract of uninhabited land jutting at the confluence of North Bay and Newman Bayou, about a mile and half across the sea from Panama City. There were no streetlights, no people, no other cars on the road; it was hard to believe we were so close to a major conurbation, but easy to believe why Vince had chosen the location to exchange captives. The possibility of any of us being observed was approaching nil, and that suited all parties.

Rink proceeded warily. We could be driving into an ambush. I had my gun ready, and another sitting between my knees ready to toss to Rink in the advent we must defend ourselves. I watched the car's sat-nav screen. 'We're a thousand yards out,' I announced and Rink brought the car to a halt. There was a soft clunk and the car rocked on its chassis. As Rink started the car crawling forward again, I glanced over my shoulder at our back seat passenger. As instructed, Jason Mercer had lain down across the back seat — we didn't want him shot from a distance before we got eyes on Sue. He wore a pillowcase over his head, and his hands were duct-taped before him. He shivered violently, and beneath the thin fabric of his blindfold I could see his head jerking spasmodically. 'Keep it together back there,' I warned him.

Mercer began uttering his mantra, counting down from twenty under his breath.

Rink and I exchanged glances.

'It isn't too late to turn around,' Rink said.

Surprisingly it was Mercer that replied. 'Sue's life is more important than mine.' Again, his words sounded like some sort of confirmatory mantra.

I checked the sat-nav. The countdown was on five hundred yards.

'It's too late to turn back now,' I stressed.

A thin strip of woods separated us from the water. The sun was low enough that it cast the long shadows of the trees over the car. Amber light flashed in an annoying strobe between the tree trunks. I deliberately averted my gaze inland as not to compromise my vision.

'We're here,' I announced, just as the sat-nav's robotic voice chimed that we'd reached our destination.

There was a passing place in the narrow trail, barely a wide spot in the dirt, marked by deep tire tracks at the soft verge. Rink drew the Ford to a halt. About two hundred yards ahead the trail took a tight left turn, and I assumed Vince's team had parked their vehicles out of sight beyond it. We sat for a few seconds, taking stock of our surroundings, and then Rink killed the engine. I passed him his pistol, and he got out. I did too, then opened the rear door and helped Mercer crawl out and find his balance. His right elbow was held by my left hand; there was no way I was going to relinquish my SIG, though I kept it down alongside my thigh.

The woodland wasn't thick with undergrowth. The ground underfoot was sandy, dotted by small pale fragments of rock. A beaten down path worked its way between the trees and we exited into a wide lozenge-shaped glade, sparse of vegetation. Small ponds of murky water dotted the area, and I guessed it was prone to flooding at high tide, the reason why trees found it difficult finding any footing there. Before coming here, we'd checked satellite imagery of Vince's suggested exchange place, so I knew this was the largest of a trio of similar open glades he could've chosen. He'd picked this one as it forced us to approach from a distance, with no hope of concealment.

Vince had posted up at a point adjacent from where we entered the glade. He was dressed in dark clothing and a baseball cap. He raised an open hand in greeting as if we were old pals, and there was a danger we hadn't recognised him. In his right hand he held a pistol. It was angled across his waist, positioned to put a bullet in Sue's spine should things go against his instructions. Two guys flanked Sue, one of them tall and dark, the other shorter and fair: they both toted firearms. Beyond them, half-concealed by the bole of a tree lurked another figure, with a rifle held ready, though the barrel was pointed at the earth, non-threatening for the time being. The way she held her weapon was at odds with the woman's face; even at the distance and the lowering gloom I could see the death stare she aimed at me. It was the woman I'd shot then knocked out back at the hotel.

There were four of them.

The math didn't add up.

It didn't surprise me that they'd kept at least another gunman in reserve, out of sight, probably now with us in his rifle's cross hairs. If we had the numbers, it's what we would do.

Mercer walked a pace ahead of me. I steadied him with a hand on his elbow. Although the ground looked relatively flat it was actually potted with holes and drainage channels. Rink fanned out to the side so we didn't form a single unit, or more correctly a single target. As we walked, Vince urged Sue forward and they met us pace for pace. I checked Sue out. She was gagged and her wrists were cinched, but she had the benefit of vision over Mercer: even then one eye looked darker than the other. Her face was puffy and her hair stood out in wild tufts. She'd taken a beating, and that made my blood run cold. She staggered as she moved closer, and it wasn't down to the uneven surface. Vince didn't lend her a supportive hand. He took delight in her floundering, a cocky grin lighting up his narrow features.

At one point a foot went in a deep pothole and she collapsed to her opposite knee. Her hands caught her from going face down in the dirt, and she pushed up again, gigged onward by a snarky round of laughter from her trio of captors.

Despite her cumbersome progress, Sue's gaze barely left us. At once it was on Mercer, blindfolded and restrained, then on me and Rink, and there was a look of deep betrayal in her stricken features. Her desolation said that all she'd gone through had been for nothing. She'd withstood torture, only for us to hand Mercer over to the men intent on murdering him. I returned her look with steely aloofness.

Vince brought her up short with approximately twenty paces separating us. I told Mercer to halt. He shook where he stood.

'Keep it together, Mercer,' I whispered, doing my best ventriloquism act I could manage.

'Is...is she here?'

'She's here,' I said.

'How does she look?'

'Worse than she should.' I stepped up alongside him, and raised my chin a little to stare down my nose at Vince.

'It's been years, guys,' Vince called, 'and then we bump into each other a few times in the last couple of days. Who'd have seen that coming, huh?'

'Quit your bullshit, Vince,' I said. 'I'm as happy you're back as having a recurring boil on my arse.'

It didn't matter how hard I tried insulting him, he always took my words in jest. He grinned, looked across at his big dark haired pal as if to share the joke. The thug was too intent on watching Rink, though, his square jaw set and eyebrows lowered. The fair-headed mug was equally staring at me, his tongue rolled in his bottom lip: he looked stupid rather than intimidating.

Vince said, 'Things don't have to be awkward between us, Hunter. I mean we're old pals, and can be again if we keep things nice and easy. Lookit, I've got you a gift like it's Christmas, and I see you've got one for me. Let's swap.'

'You were warned that Sue must be unharmed. Who did that to her face?'

Vince shrugged. 'You saw how unsteady she is on her feet just now, clumsy girl fell and bashed her face on a door.'

Sue didn't react to the obvious lie. She was too intent on checking out Mercer; staring so hard she might peel back the layers of his hood to reveal the face underneath.

I didn't comment further on her injuries. I didn't have to. As Vince had replied, the big guy's gaze had slipped from Rink to Sue, and I'd noted a muscle bunch in his jaw. I shelved away the knowledge of who was primarily responsible for her injuries for later.

Vince raised the barrel of his pistol, but only to use as an indicator. Understanding his request, I turned enough to grasp Mercer's hood and pull it off. Mercer blinked wildly as he took in the scenario. He breathed heavily; he'd stopped shivering though.

Opposite him, Sue's eyes widened, and I guess she would have called his name if not for the gag tied tightly between her teeth. Mercer straightened a few inches, and a low-pitched whine escaped from between his teeth. I clutched his elbow once again, holding him back.

'Steady on,' I warned.

Vince aimed his pistol directly at Mercer's chest.

The Fourth Option

'This job was only ever about finishing the job you started on him,' Vince said. 'Why not cut all the dramatics and let me get things over with and we can all leave this place as friends again?'

'Shoot him before we have Sue,' Rink growled, his pistol now aimed at Vince's head, 'and I'll blow your brains all over this place.'

All of Vince's lackeys sought targets.

Vince smiled, unfazed by the threat. 'Just saying.'

'Send Sue to us, we'll start Mercer walking to you,' I said.

I was totally aware that the woman at the glade's edge had settled her rifle into her shoulder, prepping to drop us at Vince's gesture.

'Tell your bitch to stand down,' I warned Vince, 'or the deal's off and we start shooting. Are you confident you won't be the first to die before we do?'

Vince seemed agreeable with my instruction. He flapped his fingers at the woman. 'Pam, Pam, take it easy, will you? We're ol' pals here.'

She scowled, but lowered her rifle, if only by an increment.

The setting sun now rode the horizon, a fiery orange ball. I'd swear that the temperature had dropped several degrees in as many seconds.

Vince moved so he was directly behind Sue. He said something to her I was unable to hear, but in response she straightened her shoulders, preparing, no doubt, to advance with the threat of a bullet in her back if she tried to run before she'd crossed paths with Mercer.

'We're good to go at this end,' Vince called.

'Then start her walking.'

'Mercer first.'

I nodded. Jabbed Mercer roughly on the shoulder. 'Get moving, arsehole,' I growled. As he began his march across the glade, I stepped sideways, to keep Vince and his lackeys in view.

Sue came on, still unsteady, but gaining speed with each step.

Mercer matched her for pace, although he staggered once when he trod in sucking mud. He pulled loose, kicking dirt out of his shoe, but kept going.

As they got to within a few feet I knew if things were going to go bad it was now.

I couldn't see Mercer's face, but Sue's had folded around the gag in horror. She was making muffled noises, probably trying to imbue how sorry she was that we'd betrayed him for her sake.

They passed within a couple of feet of each other, Sue never taking her eyes off him. Mercer though proceeded with his eyes forward, now staring grimly at Vince, whose face had taken on a devilish grin. Vince angled himself so that Mercer was between him and Rink's gun, while he aimed his pistol at me. He'd no intention of shooting yet though, his other hand flicked an instruction, and from the edge of the glade a rifle barked.

27

In warfare, plans often work only until the first bullet flies. Following that split-second everything changes, and then it's down to the fluidity of what happens next that determines the winners and losers. Often the end result is determined not by numbers or firepower but mostly by who is the most aggressive, or on who is most determined to survive, and not a little bit on luck.

It seemed Vince's plan was to wait until Mercer was in range of a shot, then his riflewoman would drop Rink and me, and then he'd take back Sue, and end her too. Whether or not he intended shooting Mercer the instant he'd given the woman the signal to shoot or not, things didn't go his way. Chaos exploded around him, giving him few options: kill Mercer immediately or save his own arse. He chose the latter, even before the sound of the rifle shot had faded. He dropped to a wide crouch, gun up, but he didn't fire. He was too busy plotting an escape route.

Several others jostled for their lives in the next second.

Jason Mercer ripped free of his restraints. Unbeknown to Vince and the others, I'd secured his wrists with ample duct-tape, but then cut through them, and re-secured the sundered sides in place again with single squares of tape: they looked formidable but all Mercer needed do was twist and yank apart his hands and he was freed. Hidden in his waistband was his pistol. He grabbed it, even as he lurched backwards, one arm extended to grasp and force Sue down to safety, while he chose his target. He fired, and blood puffed from Vince, even as the assassin spun away and scrambled for the relative safety of the trees.

In synchrony Rink and I fired, even as our opponents tried to kill us.

Rink's bullet punched the big guy in the chest, while mine hit lower down in my sturdy blond target. Neither man died before they got off shots of his own. I felt a bullet fan the air near my face, and I dipped away, out of line of a second round. I shot again, and this time the fair-headed thug sunk to one knee. My bullet had hit him in much the same place as the first. Blood at his gut shone wetly in the sun's dying rays. I too went to a knee but it was because the ground was treacherous. I settled myself and saw the thug blink in pained bewilderment at me, and this time I sent a bullet into his chest. He keeled over backwards and didn't move. All the while, Vince continued scrambling away, heading for where the riflewoman lay dead among the trees.

Rink's opponent wasn't dead. He had his left palm plastered over a bleeding wound in his chest, but his other hand was steady as he fired at Rink. My friend paid a toll in the shape of a nick of skin from his right forearm, and it also pulled off his aim as he returned fire. The big guy, mouth open in a shout of rage, came at Rink, as if the few extra feet would ensure him a cleaner shot. Rink shot him, again plugging the man's chest, and even if he didn't die in the next few seconds the wounds were fatal. The big guy understood his life was numbered in minutes, but it seemed he wanted to spend each second in destruction. He yelled a challenge, and fired again at Rink, though his shot went wide. Rink blasted him a third time, and this bullet halted the man in his tracks. His shattered jaw hung awry, but still he wasn't dead.

Rink could've finished him. I should have let him. But I'd noted the bastard's flicker of guilt when I asked who was responsible for hurting Sue, so I took some pleasure in shooting him in the temple. He toppled sideways like a felled tree, splashing into a drainage ditch filled with scummy water.

Immediately my attention went to Mercer and Sue.

He was on top of her, shielding her with his larger body, while he sought a target.

There wasn't one.

Vince had made it to the trees, and he hadn't halted there. Even armed with the dead woman's rifle, he knew he was the one now outgunned, outnumbered and outmanoeuvred. He kept running, and we let him go. Rink and I moved to cover Mercer and Sue while they scrambled to get up. After helping her drag the gag down her chin, Mercer enfolded Sue in an embrace, and kissed her face and lips repeatedly: Sue looked a little stunned by the familiarity, but didn't shy away either. In fact, after a few seconds, and a brief glance at Rink, she returned his kisses. Rink grimaced in mock disgust, but then he exchanged a look with me, and snorted.

'There's no accountin' for bad taste,' he said.

'Each to their own, I guess.'

Rink shoved away his gun and clasped the bleeding wound on his forearm. 'I'll tell you what gives me a worse taste in my mouth. After all these mutts died here, Vince has gotten away scot free.'

He was correct. An engine roared from somewhere beyond the trees, but surprisingly not that of a vehicle hidden further along the trail. This engine sounded different. Vince was out on the bayou, making off in a speedboat.

'That sumbitch has more lives than a damn cat,' Rink growled.

'His luck won't last forever,' I assured him.

Still holding each other, Mercer and Sue now looked at us. Sue's expression had morphed from one of deep betrayal to stunned gratitude. She said, 'You all worked together to free me?'

'Yeah,' said Rink. 'We all had our parts to play, and thankfully it worked. It wouldn't've if Mercer hadn't helped.'

Mercer blinked in shame. 'Vince escaped. I was supposed to shoot that evil son of a bitch. I'm sorry…my aim isn't what it used to be.'

Rink frowned at the implication, but this wasn't a poke at him. 'You did well, Mercer. You got him, chased him the hell away, and that's good enough for now. Things might've gone different if Vince had gotten a clean shot at any of us.'

'I can't believe this,' Sue said, a look of amazement now predominant, 'we're all here, alive, and—'

Standing out in the open, I thought.

The Fourth Option

And the math surrounding Vince's people still didn't add up.

I said, 'Let's get out of here before—'

But my warning came too late.

Mercer jerked, and Sue stiffened with a faint grunt.

The sound of a distant rifle shot followed a half-second later.

I was already moving, as was Rink.

He tumbled both Mercer and Sue to the ground so they were hidden in a shallow ditch. I crouched, offering less of a target, seeking the source of the shot with the barrel of my own gun. Over that distance, my pistol might be ineffective, but it was all I had.

Another shot sailed over my head, displacing air with a whine. I dived to the earth, scrambling to find cover.

Three sharp cracks sounded, one following on the back of the other. Then there was silence.

No. That wasn't the accurate truth.

I could hear Rink speaking urgently, Mercer emitting a sound it's hard to describe other than it was inhuman, and a series of short rapid gasps. But the gunfire had fallen silent.

I raised my head, seeking danger.

The sun was now down, the sky a fiery nimbus on the western horizon, and the shadows had deepened all around us. There was no movement from where I'd judged the shots originated. I rose up by increments, ready to go to ground again if the rifle fired.

It didn't.

I climbed further into a crouch, still alert to danger, but one ear on the unfolding drama behind me.

At the far left of the lozenge a figure appeared from the gloom. Some final fingers of light picked out the shape, and it was tall and amorphous at first. I levelled my pistol, but wasn't overly concerned. When telling Mercer that Vince held the cards, but not all of the aces, I'd been referring to this man. He was one of our aces. As he began a slow jog forward, a rifle canted across his chest, his costume billowed, and he threw back his hood. Those last rays of sunlight danced on his bald head where he hadn't bothered plastering camouflage paint.

He approached, slowing, and came to a more measured pace as he negotiated some wet channels in the earth. He was wearing a hunter's Ghillie-suit, at odds with the expensively tailored attire he usually favoured, and yet even in ragged net and fake foliage Harvey Lucas struck a sharp figure.

As he joined me, his painted features were set in a grim frown. He checked out the two corpses sprawled nearby, then the dimmer figure just inside the treeline.

'I got that first shooter,' he said with a nod at the dead woman, 'at the get go, but was unaware of a second sniper til he opened fire. Shot that fucker dead too, but I was too late. I'm sorry, man.'

I gripped his lean shoulder and gave it a squeeze. 'None of us knew there was a second shooter,' I said, but it wasn't the entire truth. I'd been spinning the sums around my brain, trying to equate the numbers of dead with how many of Vince's team had arrived last night in the SUV's. I'd been worried that there was another one we'd missed, at least.

'Vince escaped?'

'Yeah, but he's injured,' I said, as if it were a consolation prize.

Harvey chewed his lip, took another sidelong glance at the woman Vince had called Pam. He looked away. As far as I knew, she was the first female he'd ever been forced to kill and it might not sit well with his conscience.

'If you hadn't got her she'd have slaughtered us all,' I said.

'Yeah.' He rocked back on his heels a bit, and I followed his gaze to where Rink stood over Mercer and Sue. My big friend's shoulders were rounded, his head hanging low. He reached down and cajoled Mercer to stand. I felt sick to my stomach, because Sue didn't get up, and those short rapid gasps had faded to nothing.

28

We abandoned the bodies where they'd fallen, all but for Sue's.

Leaving her behind was the sensible move but Mercer wouldn't hear it, and to be fair it hadn't crossed any of our minds either. She deserved better than to be food for the birds and critters before Arrowsake inevitably dispatched a clean up crew. If he'd been able, Mercer would have carried her to the Ford himself, but he was too injured, and also wrung out with grief. The same high-powered round that'd slain her had first cut a chunk out of his side on its way to drilling a hole through her chest. He was bleeding, and possibly had broken ribs, and had to be assisted from the glade by Harvey's steadying arm. Between us, Rink and I carried Sue with as much dignity and respect as befitted a fallen comrade at arms.

When travelling to the glade it'd been a squeeze fitting four burly guys in the Ford, especially considering Harvey was toting a rifle, and Mercer had been pre-prepared to resemble a hostage. That time when Rink halted the car and Harvey slipped out with his gun, it had been a relief for Mercer to pull the pillowcase over his head and stretch across the back seat for the remainder of the journey. Leaving we had one extra passenger, and none of us countenanced the idea of stuffing her into the trunk. We did the best we could for her, seating her between Harvey and Mercer in the back, where the men could support her, but also conceal her from the view of other road users. As it were, for most of the drive south, Mercer held her against him, her head on his shoulder, as if she were a lover fallen asleep in his embrace.

We were all heartsick at her loss, even Harvey who Sue was a total stranger to. He felt guilty he hadn't killed the second sniper before he'd taken his fatal shot, but Sue's death wasn't on Harvey. If anything, we owed our lives to Harvey, because pinned down in the glade we'd have been dropped one after the other by the sniper. He described how he'd stolen in through the woods after we'd dropped him off, and set up, placing the woman, Pam, in his sights, deeming her the immediate threat as we'd approached. He'd fired the instant he saw her prepare to gun us down at Vince's signal. Unbeknown to him, Vince's other sniper had snuck up barely a hundred feet away, unaware of where Harvey's shot had come from, and stayed undetected until after our brief battle curtailed and he squeezed his trigger. As the rifleman then fired on me — and thankfully missed — Harvey had pinpointed him by his muzzle flash, and then as my would-be killer got me in his sights a second time, Harvey had sent a close grouping of shots into him.

Our rescue plan had been risky, and always there was the possibility some or all of us wouldn't get out alive, but it's one thing going into battle in that knowledge, something else coming out of it. We'd gone there in the hope of saving Sue's life, and ultimately failed. The only saving grace was that we'd thinned our enemies down massively. Not that it was much solace, because Arrowsake had plenty of other guns for hire they could send after us. Once Vince found time to catch his breath and rally, I fully suspected a second team of reinforcements would be fielded to assist him.

Best-case scenario?

Mercer's bullet had flown true, and even though Vince had fled the field, his wound was a bad one and he'd succumbed to it. It was a pleasant thought that he could be out there on the bayou still, the boat going round in circles, him lying in the bottom, the hull awash with his blood, his dead eyes staring at the uncaring moon above.

No, that wasn't the best case, at all. It was too easy a death for the bastard, and wholly unsatisfactory for me. Although Harvey didn't have a personal stake in ending Vince's life, Rink and Mercer did. Perhaps I was being greedy imagining personally throttling the life out of him with his guitar string garrote.

We'd driven north, taking trails and seldom-used roads, and were approaching Vicksburg, though it wasn't our intended destination. We were at a loss where to go next. Rink and I discussed holing up in a motel somewhere until we could dress our wounds and plan our next move, but it would be difficult getting Sue inside without anyone noticing. Harvey, at our summons, had driven in from Arkansas, so had no real idea of where he was, let alone where to go next. It was Mercer who came up with an idea. He'd been sitting as if wallowing in grief, but he'd also been thinking hard too, and listening to what we were discussing. He said, 'Sue returned home to collect some stuff…'

'You're talking about the property dossiers?' I asked. 'The ones with your network of safe houses?'

'Uh, so you know about that?'

'We figured it out,' Rink said, 'but maybe you can fill in some gaps.'

He ruminated a moment, possibly deciding on how much he could trust us, but after everything that had come to pass, what about us was to be distrusted? 'Our business was a front for a 'relocation service',' he admitted. 'We helped people like us — people afraid for their lives — on the run, needing somewhere to hide, people requiring a new identity. Sue had successfully faked her own death—' he swallowed at how ironic that statement now sounded '—and after tracking me down, she helped me stay hidden from Arrowsake for years. Using her experience, she saw an opportunity to earn a living and to help others in similar positions. Don't get me wrong, not all of our clients were assassins and spies on the run from their own agencies or enemies; there are many reasons why people choose to disappear, or begin a new life, mostly banal, so our business became quite lucrative. We amassed a decent property portfolio. Mostly our clients are genuine renters; they have to be, so that we don't attract too many awkward questions. We have empty properties: if I had access to Sue's files I could find us somewhere to hole up.'

'Easily rectified,' I said, 'they're in the trunk.'

'Let's stop somewhere and check then?' he said.

There wasn't a handy spot to pull off road yet.

Rink, despite the painful wound to his forearm, had taken the wheel again. He used to joke that, with me being a Brit, he didn't trust me to stay on the right side of the road, usually arguing semantics with "how can the left lane be the right lane?" His reason for driving again was because it helped keep his mind engaged and off Sue's senseless murder, but it wasn't working. I could tell from the way he chewed his bottom lip that he was hurting. Out of the blue he asked Mercer a question: 'You and Sue, you were an item?'

Seeing Mercer's face was unnecessary to tell it had set off another stab of grief. Behind me, I heard him shift, and assumed he was using the pretence of moving her to a more comfortable position to control his emotions. Finally he croaked out a reply. 'It…it was never like that for me before. I loved her, but not the way you think. I thought of her more like a little sister. But, well, when I saw her alive, after thinking…she was so happy to see me…I…'

Rink changed the subject as abruptly as he'd brought it up. He pulled the car on to the shoulder of the road and popped the trunk. 'This isn't finished, Mercer. Not by a long shot. You loved her; it doesn't matter *how*, only that you did. Tells me you probably want to avenge her every bit as much as I do. Then let's get her somewhere safe, and then let's get on with it.'

29

A few hours later a limousine worked its way slowly down a track with its high beams cutting filigree patterns through the low hanging branches of the trees on either side. The track exited the woodland into a wide meadow, and continued its serpentine path around low hummocks of grass and boulders deposited there during the retreat of the glaciers, millennia ago. It paralleled a river for several hundred yards, before the track swung away once more and led arrow straight towards a sprawling fisherman's lodge. A long time before it drew to a halt on a crushed gravel hardstand, the car's approach had not only been noted but also monitored. It had been tracked all the way from where it left the road and through the gate, electronically unlocked for it by the security detail inside the lodge.

The driver stayed seated within the limo, but a tall, suited man got out the passenger side and his gaze darted, taking in and noting his surroundings, and any perceived threat. The door to the lodge stood open, and a short, elderly man had stepped out onto the raised porch in greeting. Bald but for a strap of white hair over his ears, and bespectacled, the old man wore a plaid wool shirt tucked into jeans, held up with suspenders, and sturdy boots. The tall man had no idea, but anyone familiar with Walter Hayes Conrad IV would've known these informal clothes were at odds with his usual attire: ordinarily he wouldn't be seen out of a tailored suit, complete with vest, and most often paired with a western-style necktie at his throat.

No words passed between them, but Walter gave a slight lift of his chin. The invitation to enter was not for the tall man. The bodyguard turned and opened the back door, and then stepped aside to allow another man to get out. This man was as tall as his minder, but lacked the steely strength beneath his similar dark suit. He had neat grey hair parted on one side, and metal-rimmed spectacles perched on an aquiline nose that wouldn't look out of place on the bust of a Roman Emperor. He was a man at odds with his height, and carried his long head on a thin neck and rounded shoulders. Bony wrists and large hands with long pianist's fingers extended from the sleeves of his jacket. When he walked, his gait was peculiar, as if he stepped over a series of low, invisible objects. He didn't appear formidable but he was a powerful individual. He was Spencer Booth, a former Assistant Secretary of Defense for Intelligence, and currently one of the cabal of grey men and women behind Arrowsake.

The bodyguard escorted Booth to the door of the lodge, and that was as far as he was permitted to go by Walter's duo of guards. Walter's security detail halted the bodyguard there, then moved outside on the porch with him, while Booth stepped over the threshold. Walter had already gone further inside and he beckoned Booth to join him. It was the first time Booth had visited Walter's Adirondacks retreat, and he peered around taking in its rustic charm. It had been converted from an original log cabin, and retained much of the original features, but with additions that made it almost impregnable to attack both physically and electronically. It was furnished for comfort, even slightly chintzy with the inclusion of a feminine touch here and there in the flowery material on the chairs and tablecloth. There were also stuffed trophies, several of them fish caught by Walter during his frequent angling trips here over the decades.

The men didn't greet each other formally.

Walter waved at a chair, and said, 'Get you a drink, Spencer?'

'I'll pass.'

'Worried I might spit in it?'

'I'm worried you might spike it with something more poisonous than saliva.' Booth offered a withering smile, before perching on the edge of the proffered seat. He studied the room. 'We can speak freely?'

'Totally,' said Walter. The lodge was regularly swept for surveillance devices, and was also protected from satellite spyware by what amounted to a Faraday shield concealed within its walls and roof. 'But if you'd feel safer, I have a panic room in the basement we can retire to.'

Walter wasn't kidding. After a crazed enemy had once assaulted his fishing lodge, he'd had the secure vault constructed as a last resort bolthole.

'I'm satisfied with your assurance we can't be heard,' said Booth. He sat back and crossed his legs, settling his cupped hands on the uppermost thigh. Hi skinny ankle stuck out four inches from the cuff of his pants.

'What we are about to discuss can't be shared with anyone,' he said needlessly. 'For all our sakes.'

'I think what you actually mean is your sakes, Spencer.'

Booth sniffed in admission.

Walter chugged two fingers of bourbon into a glass tumbler. 'So what is it you don't want anyone hearing?'

'It concerns us that you are actively assisting our enemies in thwarting us,' said Booth.

'In what way? Sure, I acted as a middleman to arrange an exchange of hostages, a role sanctioned by Arrowsake, I should remind you. Tell me, Spencer, how does that equate to me assisting your enemies? You wanted your hands on Jason Mercer, and I made it possible. That the op went sideways has no bearing on my involvement.'

Spencer exhaled sharply.

'Your team,' Walter went on, 'were the ones intent on disregarding the agreed terms. They attended with the purpose of taking the lives, not only of Mercer and Bouchard, but also of Hunter and Rington.'

'You're aware of the outcome, that they were outmanoeuvred and most of our team died?'

Walter didn't answer directly. In the past hour he'd been updated with the sorry details by Joe Hunter, but wouldn't share his information source with Booth. He took a slow sip of his bourbon, watching Booth over the glass's thick rim. 'I warned Vince what would happen if he made war with my boys.'

'You say your boys? That's the problem here, Walter; you seem to have an issue with whom you owe your loyalty.'

'I've no issue with it.'

'You choose to back Hunter and Rington over your own people?'

'Hunter and Rington *are* my people. You forget, Spencer, I was their handler, their sponsor, their teacher, since they were wet behind the ears. They were like my own kids.'

'They were assets,' Spencer scoffed. 'As expendable as all the other assets you sent to their deaths.'

'Soldiers died on my watch, and it never sat well with me, but I never sacrificed any of them.'

'Keep telling yourself that, Walter. Maybe one day you'll even convince yourself.'

'I don't need any convincing.' Walter fought the urge to look away, to conceal the lie, but Spencer caught it and again offered a withering smile.

The former ASD(I) uncrossed his legs and settled his feet flat, leaning forward to stress a point. 'Need I remind you that you were the one that sent Jason Mercer to his death…albeit we now know his death is a misnomer?'

'I conveyed the details of the mission to him, with no prior knowledge of the sanction he'd come under next,' Walter sniffed, but once again he was lying. He knew Booth also knew he was lying, or at least he must've understood how it would end but had chosen not to let Mercer's inevitable death register in his conscience. It had registered of course, no less knowing he was responsible for the stain now on Hunter and, especially, Rink, who'd been lied to and ordered to execute him.

The Sierra Leone civil war had raged on for more than a decade, and several outside interventions had failed to stabilize the country. Following the Lome Peace Accord, control of the country's diamond mines was handed back to the Revolutionary United Front in return for a cessation of fighting. A UN peacekeeping force deployed to monitor the disarmament process, found the rebel RUF uncooperative, and worse. Soon the rebels were again advancing on Freetown and it was apparent the war might continue for many years to come. This was where Arrowsake came in, dispatching its assassins to target key RUF militiamen and their supporters. Such was its nature that the mission had to be totally deniable, with no connection to the UN peacekeeping force's involvement in the country. Under the guise of a South African private military operative, Jason Mercer slew a Libyan intelligence operative assisting with the training and arming of RUF forces: Mercer had a single target but was instructed to cause obfuscation surrounding his death by taking out several other men and women at random. Mercer had carried out his orders to the letter — slaying the Libyan alongside a good number of innocent villagers. This was during a conflict noted for its atrocities, and should have stayed buried, but as the British were preparing to launch Operation Palliser under a new UN mandate, their actions had to be kept above reproach to the international community, and Mercer's actions were disavowed as those of a free agent, a psychopathic mercenary. Walter had even assisted in the formulating of disinformation that would damn the former loyal operative, and, worse, had chosen two of his most capable assets to execute the kill order.

'So you were only a middleman then, and only a middleman now?' Booth sneered. 'You're as culpable as the rest of us, Walter. That's the very reason why you should be as eager for Mercer's death as we are. If the truth comes out that we were actively conducting wet work in Sierra Leone, under UN mandate, and then clearing up our crimes by murdering our own people, it won't only cause great political embarrassment to them, it will also be damning of the wider intelligence services. Heads will roll, and I'm not just talking metaphorically.'

Walter swished some dregs of bourbon in the tumbler. 'Is that a threat, Booth?'

Booth shrugged at the inevitability. 'A warning,' he said, and crossed his wrists, before drawing out his closed fists to each side.

'I'm surprised you have any confidence in Vince, considering his ineptness in his mission to date.'

Booth turned down the corners of his mouth. He was reminiscent of one of the sad-faced trout decorating the lodge's walls. 'We still have faith in where Vince's loyalties lie. I'm sorry the same can't be said about you.'

'It also surprises me that you're affording me forewarning,' said Walter.

'My visit isn't primarily for the purpose of threatening or warning you, Walter; it's with the hope of bringing you back into the fold. We are not completely devoid of understanding, we know that on a personal level you care for Hunter, but what you must do now is think long and hard about who you most value.'

Walter had a granddaughter Kirstie, and a great grandson, he cared deeply for, but those were not to whom Booth referred. He thought he had Walter's measure, that when all came to all, Walter would choose his own needs over those of a surrogate son.

'It's in nobody's interest for Mercer to spill his story, or for you to help him to do that,' Booth went on.

'That's the thing, Spencer; Mercer didn't just resurrect from the grave yesterday. He has lived off your radar for almost two decades. If he'd intended causing trouble for Arrowsake, he would've done it by now.'

'His only reason for staying quiet before was to protect his anonymity. Now that we know he survived his bungled execution, I see few avenues of recourse for him. He'll run and hide, and will remain a future threat to us, or he'll sing like a choirboy at his first opportunity. We can't allow either scenario to happen. As I said, Walter, you are equally culpable, and our mutual destruction is assured. It's as much in your interest to see Mercer dead as ours.'

'My problem is that you won't stop there. By now my boys have learned the truth too and will be targeted for termination.'

'They'll listen to you, Walter. Convince them that it's in all our interests for them to hand Mercer over to

The Fourth Option

us. In fact, we are prepared to sanction them to complete the hit they started back in Sierra Leone, with an assurance of reward and also amnesty from reprisal or persecution.'

'And you genuinely believe they'll buy your crap?'

'It depends on how well you sell it to them Walter.'

'You want me to sell them down the line? No fucking deal.'

'Think about what you're saying, Walter.'

Walter shook his head in disappointment. 'You expect me to lie to them, to betray them, in order to save my own ass?'

'If I was in your shoes, I'd sell them out in an instant.' Booth sneered at the admission, but it was a given fact that Walter was already fully aware of.

'Yes,' said Walter. 'I believe you would.'

He turned back to the bourbon bottle and poured another shot into his glass. Facing Booth once more, he swigged the liquor down in one, and reached back to deposit the empty glass.

'I don't see as how I have any other option,' Walter said.

Booth nodded his head at the inevitability of Walter's decision, allowing a smile of triumph to creep in place.

Walter added, 'Seeing as you'll then have to tie up all the other loose ends.'

A crease formed between Booth's eyes, and Walter saw how the grey man's eyes widened in understanding. Booth's mouth opened, and he struggled to rise.

Walter hadn't discarded his empty tumbler. It was still cupped in his palm as he swung it. The glass impacted under Booth's right ear, with all of Walter's burly weight behind it. The glass shattered into razor sharp chunks, biting into Walter's fingers, but it was a small price to pay in flesh compared to what was levied from Booth. Walter ground the broken tumbler into the man's neck, feeling hot blood jetting over his hand.

Walter stepped back and Booth dragged his ungainly body to his feet. The man's spectacles had fallen off during the assault, and his eyes now appeared beadier, but still round with shock. Booth's long pianist's fingers were ineffective in staunching the blood as he staggered away from Walter, crying out for his bodyguard.

Walter said, 'I told you we can't be overheard, but go ahead, open the door, call for your man.'

Booth — with blood raining in his wake — stumbled towards the door and grasped at the handle. He wrenched at it to pull open the door, and half fell over the threshold onto the porch. He fell to his knees before he reached the steps. Blood gouted between his fingers, and in desperation he croaked his bodyguard's name.

The tall man didn't respond. He couldn't as he was already dead, as was the driver of the limousine who'd also been shot dead by Walter's security detail the instant Booth had entered the lodge.

Booth lost the strength to kneel. He sprawled on the porch, his slick hands sliding down the steps. Somehow, he found a way to turn his head so that he could see Walter out of the corner of one eye. Walter stood over him, squeezing his fist to stop the blood oozing from his fingers.

'Do…you…know…what you've done?' Booth gasped.

'Yeah,' Walter said, 'I just declared war.'

Spencer Booth died.

Walter's security men had served him for many years, and he trusted them impeccably, but what he'd asked of them was a lot. By throwing in their hand with him they'd probably signed their own death warrants, but they were men that understood inevitability. Had Walter done as Booth asked, and betrayed Hunter and Rink, he'd be the next loose end to be tied up. Somebody would come for Walter, and the chances where his security detail would be murdered during the attempt. At least this way they had a fighting man's chance at survival, and a hefty pay-off apiece from Walter to help set them up with new identities and lives. After tonight, he'd say goodbye to his loyal guards, as he would to the fishing lodge that he loved so much.

'Lock the bodies down in the panic room for me, fellas,' he said, 'and then you'd best be on your way.'

'What about the limo, Walt?'

'I'll handle it.' He already had a spot in his favourite fishing hole picked out for it.

30

I'd later learn that at that time, corpses were being sealed in a secure vault underneath Walter Conrad's Adirondacks fishing lodge. Locked behind several inches of steel, they would go undisturbed without a concerted effort made to find and liberate them. The same couldn't be said for Sue Bouchard's body. We did our best for her, and with as much dignity as possible too, but Sue was laid out on a trestle in a tomb smelling of cement dust, damp cardboard and engine oil. Jason Mercer had scrutinised Sue's property dossier, then decided that a ranch-style house at the verge of a wildlife management area alongside the Apalachicola River offered us most anonymity. The ranch was remote, but within an hour's drive of Panama City, and maybe twice that to Tallahassee, it was still a handy staging post should we need to travel anywhere fast.

Mercer chose the house for an extra feature: it had a drive-in and lock-up parking garage separate to the main house, so it was somewhere private and self-contained where we could lay out Sue's body. We wrapped her in a plastic tarp, and raised her off the floor on the trestle workbench, to protect and preserve her as best we could, until we could arrange a proper internment of her remains. Mercer stayed with her a few minutes after the rest of us retired to the house, and we allowed him, so he could say what he needed to say out of our earshot. We found the key in a secure lock box, to which Sue's notes gave us the access code, and let ourselves in. Mercer joined us, red-eyed and shaky, very shortly, as he was in dire need of medical assistance and rest. The wound to his side had stopped bleeding, but he'd lost a fair amount of blood, and his broken ribs made breathing difficult. I had availed myself of the bathroom by then, and Rink was in the process of washing and dressing the wound on his forearm when Mercer stumbled inside. Harvey was nearest to him. He'd taken off the Ghillie suit before getting back in the car at the glade, but his ebony features were still smeared with camouflage grease paint. At six-feet five tall, built of lean muscle, he looked every inch a warrior, rather than a nursemaid. His fearsome appearance contradicted the care with which he caught and supported Mercer over to a large couch that dominated half of the ranch's main living space. He helped him to lie down, whispering soft encouragement for Mercer to show him his wound.

Mercer's shirt and trousers were stiff with dried blood. His side was smeared with the stuff, but on inspection the bullet wound amounted to a shallow groove and the two ribs either side were cracked but not shattered: he was fortunate he was turning as the bullet flew at him, or the projectile would've pierced his ribs and torn out a large part of a lung too. In his current agony he probably didn't deem himself the luckiest person in the world, and besides, his salvation had been Sue's damnation. I'd bet that in his mind he wished she'd lived rather than he. Harvey, having a decent knowledge of field medicine from his years as an army Ranger, cleaned and dressed Mercer's wound, and then his patient promptly fell asleep.

We were all in need of rest. Except for a couple of hours of uncomfortable slumber in the car last night, I hadn't slept for any length since my last undisturbed night in the hotel. Rink had suffered a similar lack of shuteye, and even Harvey must've been weary after our summons had seen him set off from Little Rock in the pre-dawn. We needed rest, and equally we had to eat and drink, or we'd lack the strength or brain function to react if our enemies attacked us again. It still concerned me that my face might be on a wanted poster by then — and the news feeds — and the cops might also expect me to be accompanied by my business partner and best pal, Rink. Therefore Harvey was the best man to send out on a supply run. Despite him having killed two opponents earlier in the evening, nobody had seen his face or was aware he was the shooter that'd saved our necks back in the glade. We had called on Harvey's services before, so it was only a matter of time before Arrowsake pieced together who had assisted us, though I doubted they'd share that knowledge with regular law enforcement agencies.

There was a nearby community called Dalkeith, but it was unlikely any services would still be open this late in the evening, so Harvey offered to drive ten miles towards the town of Wewahitchka and see what supplies he could drum up. Earlier we'd driven through the small town, and found it buzzing with evening activity, the very reason we hadn't slowed for fear anyone noticed Sue's condition.

The Fourth Option

Before Harvey could go anywhere he had to remove his grease paint and get cleaned up. He'd fetched a grab bag, some snacks for the road and his rifle before setting off on a ten hours drive across four states to join us in Florida. He showered, and even ran a razor over his jaw, and dressed in fresh clothes before he deemed he was presentable enough to face the checkout girls in the Wewahitchka branch of Piggly Wiggly. Harvey wasn't vain; he simply had personal standards he adhered to. His car had been left in Panama City, so he had to take the Ford, but we were reasonably confident his trip would go without a hitch: the cops might be on the lookout for me and Rink, not a lone African American.

After he headed out, Rink and I tiptoed our way around Mercer and set up in the ranch's kitchen, so we wouldn't disturb him. The basic furnishings in the living space didn't extend to the kitchen, but there was a cooking range and microwave oven we could put to use on Harvey's return. I could've killed a coffee or three by then, but we lacked the makings. Rink rummaged through the cupboards but came up with nothing appetizing. Whoever had stayed at the ranch previously hadn't left us as much as a tea bag we could've run under a tap and wrung out between us. We drank cold water from chipped mugs left by the previous occupier on the draining board.

We were killing time, waiting for Harvey to return, but more realistically keeping our minds off Sue's regretful death. I barely knew her, but I still ached at losing her. Rink hurt worse, but he controlled his grief admirably. We set to planning our next move; unbeknown to us that Walter had already gotten things in motion with his slaying of Spencer Booth and his security detail. I'd telephoned Walter earlier, filling him in on our failed attempt to rescue Sue, and warning him of the consequences of Vince's escape. He'd taken my words more sanguinely than expected, and I should've suspected then that he was not a man to go quietly. In common with us, Walter was an advocate that attack was the best form of defence.

We sat on the kitchen counter, discussing our options for a long time, and maybe at some point we'd forgotten we had a man slumbering next door and raised our voices. We heard Mercer's halting approach as a series of scuffs and scrapes, and then he appeared at the door, one hand steadying him against the frame. His other arm was clutched across his injured ribs. His face was as pale as a fish's belly. He gave us a look that suggested he hoped that this was all a dream and we were figments of his worst nightmare. When we didn't fade from view, he shook his head and groaned in abject misery: it was true, Sue had died.

'You need to go and lie down, buddy,' Rink said.

To Mercer it must have sounded like an instruction, that perhaps he wasn't welcome to join our conversation. He moistened his lips with his tongue before speaking. 'I woke through there with no real memory of where I was for a moment. It happens sometimes, it's because of…well it doesn't matter. I thought I'd been abandoned but then I heard your voices and came looking for you.'

The Fourth Option

Rink shrugged noncommittally.

I said, 'You're welcome to join us, it's just there's no comfortable place to sit. Tell you what, now that you're awake, we'll come back in the living room with you. That way you can rest, and still be part of the planning.'

My offer was to help reassure him: maybe now that Sue was dead and he was no longer needed to help rescue her he might have thought we'd dump him, or worse. He began shivering, and his eyes darted between us, before they practically zoned out. His mind was somewhere in the past or future, but not with us in that moment. His knees gave several jerks as if he was on the verge of collapse. I jumped down from the counter and took two hurried steps towards him. He snapped out of his fugue, alarm now in his refocused gaze. 'C'mon,' I said, taking his arm, 'let me help you.'

He gently withdrew from my grasp. 'I'm okay; I'm not about to fall again. Is there anything to drink, I'm parched?'

'Will lukewarm water from the faucet do ya?' Rink shook droplets from the mug he'd used, and then ran it under the tap.

I walked with Mercer across the kitchen, ready to grab him if he dropped. He winced with each step, his wound tormenting him. He set his back to the counter, and accepted the mug from Rink. He gulped down the water as if he'd just stumbled in from a desert trek. He held out the mug for Rink to replenish it.

Before following the request, Rink eyed his former enemy. 'I asked before if you were ready to avenge Sue, and I'll ask again. See, you don't look up to the job to me.'

'I'm hurt, yeah, but I'm not an invalid,' Mercer responded. 'Once I've rested up and healed some—'

'We don't have time for healin' up. You're hurt, but still on your feet. Either you're good to go, or you ain't.'

'Rink,' I cautioned, but he shook his head at me.

'This bullshit has to stop, Hunter,' he growled, although his sentiment was aimed elsewhere. 'We're all hurtin' in our own way. It's time to tighten our bootlaces and man up, or it's time to curl up and die.'

As pep talks went it was a bit brusque, but I understood it was as much about getting his head in the game for Rink as for the rest of us. He dashed water into the mug and shoved it towards Mercer, with a terse command to 'Suck it up, buttercup.'

Mercer glared at him, his upper lip curled, but after a second or two he nodded sharply. 'I'm good to go.'

'That's what I need to hear,' said Rink, lightening up a little. 'Now you listen up, 'cause it's the last time I'm gonna say this. You still have doubts about us, and that's understandable. You've probably carried what I did to you all these years, hatin' me ever wakin' minute of every day, and that's fine. The feelin' was kinda mutual. Back there, you probably suspected that we were willin' to sacrifice you for Sue's sake, but you were wrong. We gave you a gun, made it so's you could help us get Sue safely away from Vince and those other bozos, when we coulda hogtied you and tossed you to them instead. We got her away from Vince, and you helped, and then things went sideways. If I thought you'd be no good to us now, I'd have put a bullet in your bread pan, there and then and had done. I didn't. We brought you with us. You're still with us now, d'you get me?'

It was quite a mouthful coming from Rink, but it was necessary to get his point across. I waited with him while Mercer absorbed his words.

'I get you,' Mercer said.

'So stop worrying about us abandoning you, or doing you harm,' Rink went on. 'Get your head back in the fight. That girl out there, she didn't deserve what happened to her, and I'm going to make sure somebody pays for killing her. Vince is a royal prick. But he's just a prick following orders. It doesn't excuse him for what happened, and he'll be made to pay, but it won't — *it can't* — stop with him. If we're gonna survive this, *and* make Arrowsake pay, there's only one way I know how: we take the offensive.'

'I second the motion,' I said, and gave Mercer an in.

He didn't come straight to the point. 'When we got Sue back, she scolded me for risking my life to save hers. She said how she'd resisted torture, refused to lead them to me, so I didn't come to harm from those bastards. She even took the bullet intended for me. Damn right, I think we should take the offensive!'

He stood breathless after his outburst. But I was glad to see that he was standing stronger and clearer of eye. His injury was painful, but no longer crippling. There was no hint of a tremor in the hand holding his mug, or in his pupils.

Rink stuck out a fist. After a moment, Mercer released his side, and returned the gesture, and they bumped knuckles. Fist bumping wasn't really a custom of mine, but I offered my 'welcome aboard' to Mercer with a clap of his shoulder.

31

'You're just gonna have to start wearing your hair longer on the sides,' Vince told his reflection in the bathroom mirror, and laughed.

Jason's Mercer's wild shot had come close to killing him. It had struck the top of his right shoulder, and ricocheted, taking off a chunk of his ear and scouring a small furrow towards the back of his head. Travelling another quarter inch deeper it would have completely ruined his day, instead of his rakish good looks. He could be ebullient about his near miss now, but by God, he had been unhappy at the time. As he'd scurried like a rat for the cover of the woods, his skull felt like a beaten piñata, and he'd fully expected to find it laid open to the grey matter by the amount of blood gushing from him.

His mission had been to kill Mercer, and he had a contingency in place in the shape of Gary McMahon and a high-powered rifle, so hadn't hung around trading rounds with Hunter and Rink. There wasn't any value in it after Scott, Davis and Patrick had bought it, but he'd had faith in McMahon's ability as a sniper. Even as he ran, he heard the rifle shots, and took it that Mercer had died, but then he'd heard another barrage of shots and doubted McMahon would be collecting his paycheck. Hunter and Rink had brought a wildcard to the game — the sneaky sons of bitches — and whoever it was they were a good shot: it hadn't been any of the men standing before him that'd dropped Pam Patrick before she could gun them down.

His head wound had been the most worrying at first, but it was the one to his shoulder that proved worse after he'd tumbled into the speedboat and tried to get the outboard motor going. Twice he'd fallen on his ass when his grip failed him, and there were minutes of frustration when he thought he'd never get it going. The bullet had struck his muscle a glancing blow only, but the kinetic force had travelled deep, and his arm had gone numb to the tips of his fingers. Thankfully, as a deep haematoma had later blossomed the feeling had returned to his extremities. His shoulder ached like a bitch but the pain was bearable. Besides, the pain in his head and neck kind of diverted his attention from it. By the time he'd guided the boat the mile or two back to his temporary base his jacket was awash with his blood, and he was lightheaded and stumbling. He'd made it inside, and collapsed into a chair, and sat there bleeding some more. Scalp wounds were notorious for bleeding, but the quantity of loss never matched how bad it looked. He fought the temptation to sleep, and instead went in search of medical supplies. He found a kit in the bathroom and staunched his head wound, and tried to make something of the ragged chunk of cartilage hanging from his ear. Adhesive sterile strips patched his Frankenstein monster ear back together, but failed miserably when it came to the cut in his scalp. He applied a cumbersome gauze pad and bandage, but he looked hick-stupid and pulled it off again.

The Fourth Option

Having returned to the bathroom again, hours later, he decided he didn't look as bad as he'd feared. He'd worn his hair in ducktails for so long now they'd become part of his Vince Everett identity, but, after all, he was really Stephen Vincent, and the hair unimportant to him. It was time for a fresh look, he decided, and growing it longer to conceal his scars wasn't a bad thing: he'd once styled his looks on a young Johnny Depp circa that *Cry Baby* movie and these days Depp was more into grunge than a man in his mid-fifties normally got away with, and he'd almost two decades on Vince. He teased the longer locks of his pompadour out, trying to conceal the weeping gash on his temple, and smiled sourly. 'You look like a complete dick, man.'

He pushed his hair back into place, chiding his vanity, and looked down at the porcelain sink. It was blotched crimson, as if some redneck hunter had gutted a kill in it. When he looked back at his reflection, all trace of humour had left him. Other than surviving a supreme ass kicking, what had he to be happy about? Earlier, he'd reported to his bosses, claiming with 99.9 per cent confidence that Mercer was dead, despite the sudden and eternal loss of his teammates, and had been applauded for his success. However, within two hours, his handler had gotten back to him with an alternative report. A team dispatched to clean up the battleground had found Vince's fallen comrades — including McMahon, gunned down several hundred yards away — but no other bodies. Until he could show them Mercer's corpse, the job was incomplete, and he was on warning that his continued failures would not be tolerated much longer. Earlier in the day, while squeezing Sue Bouchard for information on Mercer's whereabouts she'd made a foreboding prediction that'd given Johnny Scott a moment's pause: Vince had brushed it off, but not entirely.

There was once a time when Stephen Vincent had set his sights on a career in federal law enforcement, and as a FBI special agent he'd distinguished himself in the field of undercover work. Having assumed several mantles, he'd excelled as a white trash, racist hillbilly cat, who had proven invaluable to Arrowsake who required an inside man to help manipulate a domestic terrorist plot to suit their agenda, and he'd been recruited. As Vince Everett, he'd played fast and loose with the FBI motto of "Fidelity, Bravery, Integrity," adhering to each component only when it suited his mission, but he still felt he was imbued with each of those admirable traits. See, as Vince, he had the capacity to switch his morals on and off as befitted the task at hand: in the guise of Vince he did bad things, usually to bad people, but it didn't make Stephen totally bad. Maybe it would have been better if he had totally separated himself from his former identity during this mission, rather than allow Stephen Vincent to creep back in. As Vince he disliked Hunter. As Stephen he envied him, but also held the man in high regard: he wouldn't want to attain credibility by superseding Hunter if he didn't respect his abilities. There was a tiny, he grudgingly accepted, spot of hero worship in his heart for Hunter, and it was this that had caused him to stay

Vince's murderous instincts whenever they'd met before. Now, given the alternative, he must put aside Stephen's pussy ways and get Vince's head firmly back in the game. The point being, whose head did he value most?

'Yours, my man,' he concluded, as he met the dead-eyed stare of Vince in the mirror.

He left the bathroom, returning to the room where he'd earlier overseen the torture of Sue Bouchard. The chair in which she'd been restrained, and the polythene sheet Johnny Scott had used to smother her were still in evidence. None but the keenest eye would identify the room as a crime scene, but teamed with the blood he'd dripped all over the house, and left puddled in the bathroom sink, it'd raise the pecker of even the most jaded of detectives. He made a mental note to have Arrowsake dispatch their cleaners here to scrub away every trace of his and Sue's presence in the house. In the meantime he began collecting whatever belongings left there by his team he could use, including a spare shirt and jacket belonging to Wayne Davis to replace his own. After dressing and tucking the voluminous shirt into his jeans, he shrugged into the jacket, finding it roomy too, but useable and nearest his size. Dressed in either McMahon or Scott's clothing, both much bigger men, he'd feel like a child playing dress up in their dad's suit. He took any items that would readily identify his dead team, but with no intention of using them; he'd bin them in a trashcan many miles away. He holstered his pistol, shoved ammunition into a backpack, and rewound his garrote around his left forearm, having taken it off while dressing and cleaning his wounds. The steel string, weighted at each end, was a comforting weight under his sleeve. Lastly he retrieved the satellite phone used during his communications with Arrowsake, and stuffed it in the backpack. He'd only summons a clean up team once he was on the road, and well out of reach of anyone else they might decide to send along uninvited with the cleaners.

32

I took my turn on stag duty, watching over my friends as they slept. Having gotten around three hours of shut-eye, Rink spelled me and I dragged my weary butt to bed. Bed wasn't a comfortable divan, but a bare space on a bedroom floor of the ranch house, but it didn't matter: I slept like the dead and didn't rouse until summoned by the aroma of freshly brewed coffee. I found Rink and Harvey in the kitchen, presiding over the remnants of the supplies Harvey brought back from his trip last night. There was no sign of Mercer, but from another room I heard a flushing toilet and assumed it was he. I needed a leak too, but more so, I needed coffee.

'Get your laughing gear around that, mate,' Rink said, in a fair impression of an English accent. These days my Yank buddy could approximate something that sounded less Dick Van Dyke more Jason Statham.

Grateful, I accepted a steaming mug of coffee from him, and drank deeply. It was strong and black and unsweetened, just the way I liked it.

'Top me up?' I asked, after less than ten seconds.

Rink wielded the jug, sloshing more coffee into my cup.

'I hope you've saved some of that for me.' Jason Mercer entered the kitchen. He moved gingerly, but was apparently finding moving a tad easier than before. His shirt hung open, and underneath was a compression bandage where somebody had strapped his damaged ribs: I assumed it was Harvey's handiwork.

I made room so that Rink could serve him a steaming mugful. Mercer dumped in several spoonfuls of sugar and a glug of half-and-half from an open carton. He drank as eagerly as I had my first cup. Then he joined me in digging into the food Harvey had brought. As crude as it sounds, most soldiers follow the maxim to sleep, eat, drink, piss and shit whenever you could, because you didn't know when the opportunity might arise again. As soon as I was sated, I headed off in search of the toilet.

On my return to the kitchen, I found another round of coffee on the go, and took a third mug, then joined the other guys at the counter. They were making an inventory of weapons and ammunition. Between us we had four pistols — I still had the gun I'd discovered in Sue's tote bag after Vince grabbed her — and a rifle. We had enough bullets to stage a gas station robbery, but too few to go to war: a situation that must be rectified soon. We discussed our next moves, unsure what or how we were going to do anything without compromising our liberty. We judged the merits of staying put and using the ranch as a base to moving on to somewhere where we could launch a counter strike against our enemies. Then and there, most of those ranged against us were unknown, faceless entities, except for Vince. Killing Vince was on several of our agendas, but he was but one enemy among who knew how many others.

The Fourth Option

Over the years, Rink and I had come into contact with some of the men and women behind Arrowsake, and we'd noted their identities should we ever be pushed into a similar situation as this. I thought some of the older ones could have passed on by now, or be too feeble politically to cause us any problems, but we lacked intelligence on the current crop. It seemed inevitable that we must go again, cap in hand, to Walter, to beg the names we needed, and hope he'd steer us correctly. I was the one elected to make the call, but before doing so, I joined the general kafuffle, milling with the others around the kitchen as we avoided the elephant in the room, or more correctly our murdered comrade in the parking garage.

Mercer went a bit quiet. At first I thought it was because he felt out of odds with the three of us, old pals, with plenty to talk about, but that wasn't it. I watched his eyes grow glassy, and a faint tremble in his hands appear, and realised that he was contending with more than a gunshot, and grief, he also was suffering from his older wounds. He hung his head and fell silent. Then began a slow shamble, elbow pressed to his ribs towards the door.

I matched him for a couple of steps until he became aware of my presence.

'I'm gong to go out and check on Sue,' he said.

There was the opportunity for a quip about her not going anywhere, but it would've been in bad taste at any time. I thought he just needed some space, and visiting Sue's body was an excuse. An excuse was unnecessary. 'Sure thing,' I said, and walked with him through the living room to the exit door. We were safe there, for now, but someone should watch his six. Outside, I checked around. It was the first I'd seen of the exterior in daylight. Beyond the ranch was a wilderness of trees, grass and bogs, and further on the river. To the front the lawns had been kept short, somewhat parched now by the sun, and more trees bordered the drive up to the house. At a glance the ranch was off the beaten track, but wasn't as far removed as it looked. Traffic noise could be heard from FL-71 just beyond the close horizon, and something bigger, an agricultural behemoth of some type, worked in a field somewhere closer. There was no hint of a strike team about to launch an attack, but who knew if there was a sniper laid up with us in his gun's sights? If that was so, there was nothing I could do about it. I didn't progress beyond the front stoop, only watched Mercer climb down off the porch and angle across the front yard to the large parking garage. The shutters were down but there was a regular access door to one side, to which he headed. I watched until he was safely inside.

As a bird flew, I was probably no more than twenty miles from Mexico Beach, but the little town I'd called home felt out of reach at that moment. There, up against the Apalachicola River, there was no sign of the hurricane that had recently devastated my community. This could be another land entirely separate from the vistas of sand and twinkling waters of the Gulf I was used to seeing. Standing there, in the morning warmth, surrounded by the distant noises of innocent activity, it was hard to imagine that the last two days had consisted of running battles and violent deaths. If there were a benevolent God, perhaps He would look kindly on us for a while and allow us to exist a little longer in this peaceful, safe haven. No. What was I thinking? Better for us if He was a wrathful, Old Testament war-god who'd give us the strength to strike down our enemies and tear down their tyrannical empire.

I took out my cell phone and brought up Walter's number.

As per usual, my call was bounced around before connecting, and I listened while the phone rang and rang. I was on the verge of hanging up when Walter picked up.

'Sorry, son, you've kind of caught me on the hop.'

'Are you okay?'

'It's good of you to ask, Joe. I'm fine. Not sure how much longer that'll last.' Walter told me about his visit from Spencer Booth, and how the former Assistant Secretary of Defence for intelligence had made him an offer he couldn't refuse: Booth gave Walter the choice between betraying us and saving his own life, to which there could only be one outcome. 'I killed that motherfucker dead,' he announced with uncharacteristic venom.

'Jesus, Walt,' I said.

'The sanctimonious son of a bitch tried to convince me I was as guilty as the rest of them for what happened in Sierra Leone, and the only way I could protect my ass was to help them brush it all under the carpet. That in simple terms means silencing Mercer, Rink and you, son, and I mean permanently. He must have thought I just fell out of a stupid tree, because there's no cleaning house without silencing me too, or the rest of *them* for that matter. I got things started with him, and good riddance.'

'What happened?'

He told me in broad terms, without embellishment. 'Let's just say he's no longer a threat. Booth and his security detail are tucked up nice and secure in the panic room under my fishing lodge. They'll stay there for now, out of sight and mind.'

'You killed his security detail too?'

'Had to,' he said, 'out of an act of kindness. Couldn't have them dying of thirst locked down in my bunker, could I?'

He was attempting to lighten the mood, but it wasn't working. I could tell he found the deaths of Booth's bodyguards regretful, even if necessary to his — and our — survival. I changed the subject.

'Tell me you're no longer there.'

'I already did. I said you'd caught me on the hop. I'm currently twenty thousand feet in the air above Pennsylvania en route to Langley.'

'You're going to CIA headquarters?'

'Safest place I can think of to be right now,' he said. 'Besides, there's some stuff I need to get my hands on there, that might prove useful to us in the coming days.'

'Surely you're walking into a hornet nest?'

'You forget, son, I'm CIA first, Arrowsake second. In fact, can't say as I've anything to do with them now, seeing as they made my position clear. Don't worry about me, I've more allies in Langley than I have enemies.' His logic made sense. It was unlikely that anyone would try to harm him while he was at the heart of CIA headquarters.

Back when I was drafted into it, Arrowsake was a top-secret coalition taskforce, primarily funded by black budget money, but there was always a layer of congressional oversight involved. In later days, it morphed into something else. Black budget funding was still its mainstay, but it also garnered funding from several anonymous multi-billionaires, and as such was now a private rather than governmental unit, with its own autonomy. Government projects are subject to scrutiny, and freedom of information requests, whereas private entities are under no obligation to share their secrets. It has been said that when diplomacy and military intervention fails, the third option is the intelligence community. Arrowsake offered a fourth option: complete denial. This was where they had gone wrong, because with no oversight or fear of reprisal, they had come to believe they were untouchable. These days they were more about the interests of their leaders, the destabilising of competitors, the procurement of the almighty buck, and their methods went beyond criminal: blackmail, coercion, and murder by proxy of dangerous mercenaries and assassins. It had surprised me to hear that Walter had taken such extreme action against Spencer Booth, but not that he might strike out to defend himself. Before Walter was a mover and shaker in the CIA, he had been a field agent, and had operated in wars ranging from Vietnam up to the first Gulf War. Beneath his slightly comical exterior was a hardened operative who could kill as easily with an innocent piece of crockery as with a smart bomb. His killing of Booth was a reminder to Arrowsake not to prod a sleeping wolf; killing Booth was akin to ancient times, when sending back the head of an emissary showed the terms offered were unsatisfactory.

I could have almost gotten teary-eyed over Walter choosing us over them, but I was under no illusion, this was mostly about him. Not that I held it against him, because at base level, when their survival instincts kick in, many individual's believe their life is more important than anyone else's. Walter was fleeing back to the bosom of the CIA because there were people within its ranks who'd help him, people that might enjoy the dissolution, the destruction, of the untethered beast that Arrowsake had become.

I'd told him earlier about our failure to rescue Sue, and told him now how we wished to avenge her. I also asked that he send someone to collect her body, and see to its safe and dignified storage until a proper funeral could be held for her. After finishing up, I added, 'I understand you need to protect yourself, but we also need to know you've got our backs in this fight, Walter.'

'We are on the same page, son. It's in all our interests that the threat from them is permanently off the table. Here's my promise to you: whatever's mine is yours.'

The Fourth Option

'It's good to hear,' I said, and meant it. 'So, here's what we need from you, Walt.'

33

Three days and eight hundred plus miles later found Rink, Mercer and I seated in a panel van near Williamsburg, Virginia. We were alongside a tributary of the York River, not far from where it spilled into Chesapeake Bay. Earlier we'd been smuggled in via a landing strip on a Naval supply flight, organised for us by Walter: Yorktown Naval Weapons Station dominated a good stretch of the land east of Williamsburg. Further up river there were state parks, several golf courses, and a proliferation of small churches, vineyards, farms and even a county jail. We weren't interested in any of those, but had done recon so that we knew the lay of the land, and possible exfiltration routes.

It was dark. We were parked at the head of a hiking trail, off the approach road to a private residence seated on the bank above the York River, which I scanned with a pair of infrared binoculars. The house was an ultra-modern feat of architectural excellence, complete with indoor and outdoor swimming pools, a huge sun deck, and glass walls, some overlooking the riverside to make the most of the views. It sat at the northern end of several acres of manicured lawns, one of which incorporated stables, paddocks and a gymkhana. To the south there was a large fishing pond, bordered by the wilder expanse of a national park. There were outbuildings, one of them a huge parking garage, while another housed a bar, a lounge and a games room for when, I guessed, the frequent parties held there must be taken inside. There was also what amounted to a bunkroom that housed the on-site staff. There was ample outside parking space for dozens of vehicles, although right then there were only four cars and a van not dissimilar to ours in evidence. Also there was a helipad, on which sat an executive level Airbus H145.

The presence of the chopper made me regret sending home Harvey. He still took on private investigation work for pocket money, but it was his second income these days. In the 75th Ranger Regiment he'd flown everything from MH-6 Little Bird's, through Blackhawks and up to MH-47 Chinooks and now in civilian life he had made a sightseeing business out of shuttling tourists around Little Rock in his personal helicopter. If the shit hit the fan and we needed rapid exfil, Harvey in the pilot's seat of that H145 would've been ideal. However, this was our battle and not Harvey's: he'd already given more to us than what we'd asked and we would ask no more of him for now. Nobody in the enemy camp knew of Harvey's involvement back at the hostage exchange, and we'd rather things stayed that way. Harvey, being a generous and loyal friend, had argued against leaving us but in the end he saw sense, and understood we were thinking about the best for him. As it were, we weren't totally without Harvey's back up. Along with Raul Velasquez, he was now a recipient of copies of the "stuff" Walter had gotten his hands on, and would make use of it should our more hands-on plan to destroy Arrowsake go pear-shaped.

We could've gone ahead with Walter's initial plan to bring down Arrowsake, but doing that would also condemn him — and probably us too — to a similar prison term as most of the other key players, and to me that outcome was both undeserved and unpalatable. I'd come up with a more ballsy solution to our shared problem. If it worked we'd all be free of Arrowsake, which as an entity would self-implode and we'd fully avenge our fallen comrade, Sue Bouchard. If it failed, well, we'd be dead, and Walter could fall back on Plan-A. If Vince, or another of their killers got to Walter first, then that was where Harvey and Velasquez would come in.

Rink was in his customary position behind the steering wheel. I sat up front beside him, while Mercer was on a bench in the rear. He had Harvey's rifle resting across his thighs — if it ever came to it, he'd swear he was the one to shoot dead Vince's snipers back at the glade, keeping Harvey out of the equation. At his feet sat several canvas bags containing weapons and various other tools we might require. Rink and me had already gotten equipped with silenced sidearms, combat knives, equipment pouches on our belts, and walkie-talkies. The van was also equipped with a radio tuned to the same band as ours. All three of us were dressed in matching attire of black boots, black cargo pants, and black hoodies, looking like paramilitary cat burglars. Mercer had more mobility now than a few days ago, but wasn't fully fit to join us on our assault of the private residence, but he'd dressed as we had should he need to abandon the van and require stealth. Once we got out, he was under instruction to get in the driving seat and keep the van ready for when we needed him.

The Fourth Option

Only as a last resort might we need him to cover us with the rifle.

Through the binoculars I studied the grounds as much as I did the buildings. From what I'd counted there was a security detail of six people patrolling the exterior, and perhaps as many again inside. There was even the possibility of more security operatives inside the bunkhouse because I guessed the team had to be on some kind of shift rotation. It was best, I'd contend, to over- rather than under-estimate possible enemy numbers. Those I could see through the augmented night-vision of my binoculars weren't openly armed, but I'd bet my house — if it were still standing — that they were. Thankfully there weren't any dogs, though we must take care not to spook the horses, as they'd make as much racket as any barking mutt.

Inside the house, various lights were dimmed and in two rooms were extinguished completely. We'd waited for that moment, allowing those inside to settle down for the night before making our move.

'Good to go?' I asked Rink.

'Ready, willing and able, brother.'

I checked with Mercer. 'Keep the engine running and come when you hear the signal,' I said. It was a needless reminder, but I wanted him to feel part of the team, and that he was making a contribution towards vengeance for Sue.

He began clambering into the front even as we exited the van, bringing the rifle with him. I handed him the binocs; they'd be more useful to him than me once I got moving. I exchanged a look with Rink, and caught his solemn nod. We threw up our hoods and then I slipped away towards the approach track, while Rink went into the trees alongside the tributary. It was necessary to either circumnavigate the exterior security detail, or neutralise them. I had no intention of sticking to the road; my route was going to be alongside the bank of the fishing pond, where I could employ the natural contours of the land, and the shrubs afforded there, to cover my advance.

Up to a point there was public access along the road, but the private property was clearly marked by signage and a demarcation fence. The fence was barely two feet high, made from thick wires strung between posts, and was more a visual than physical deterrent. Once I'd crossed the road and gotten down towards the pond I stepped over it. If this had been a totally secure facility, I'd be wary of pressure and motion sensors but was unconcerned: this place was private but not a no-man's land, paying guests were invited to fish the pond, and at the house regular photo-shoots and executive or celebrity gatherings occurred there.

Keeping to the brush at the edge of the pond I passed a couple of jetties to which rowing boats and even a flat-bottomed skiff were moored. From my lower vantage I could see neither hide nor hair of the house, but the same could be said of me for any watcher. I made swift progress and once at the far end of the pond began to angle towards the nearest paddock. It was night but some of the horses had been left out to graze. They knew I was approaching before I ever moved into view, but they were obviously accustomed to strangers on the land, as beyond a few soft wickers and snorts the horses didn't react. Nevertheless I was careful not to spook them as I crept over the rise in the earth. I was then at an approximate ninety degrees angle from the house, and able to use the fence around the paddock to help conceal my approach. Unlike the wire one at the perimeter this fence was sturdy and comprised of thick upright wooden posts and cross beams. My silhouette was darker than my grassy surroundings. I crouched so my height was relative to the posts and moved from one to the next without revealing my shape in the open.

I advanced until I was equal with the helipad, and crouched lower as I spied over at the chopper. It looked like a wasp, sleek and dangerous, but it wasn't the helicopter I was bothered about: I ensured there was no crewmember still aboard the craft that might spot me lurking and raise the alarm. I could see no one, yet I waited a little longer, to be sure.

Ahead, and to my left, a pair of guards patrolled. They were deep in conversation and totally unaware of my presence. If I wished to, I could've shot them both dead and they'd be none the wiser, but the same might not be said of the horses. Even the suppressed gunshots could set them stampeding around the paddock and bring other guards to investigate. Maybe I should've let the horses do my work for me and bring the others into my line of fire, but no, I wasn't there for the purpose of cold-blooded murder. Rink and me were both in agreement, we wouldn't kill any of the guards or other staff unless absolutely necessary. Our resolve made our task more difficult, but easier to swallow.

I allowed the duo of guards to continue in blissful ignorance, watching them sauntering almost nonchalantly out towards the pond I'd just come from. I wondered if they were sneaking out of sight of the house to perhaps loaf about for a while or have an illicit cigarette. Luckily they hadn't chosen their stroll to the pond while I was still down there. Once they were over the rise and out of sight, I left the cover of the fence and jogged as swiftly as I could without making much noise towards the house. I was within spitting distance of it when I heard somebody cough. Immediately I dropped to one knee and brought up my pistol. There was no sign of whom the cough had originated from, and I couldn't even be fully certain of which direction it had come: maybe, I considered, the cough had come from one of the horses. I was wrong. A second cough erupted, this one louder, and this time I followed the sound to its source and spotted a figure on the far side of the external swimming pool, peering out across the slope leading down to the river.

The phlegmatic guard was a tall, burly man. His size alone made up my mind for me, because I didn't want that guy sneaking up and jumping on me from behind. I rose up and made to skirt around the swimming pool, this time padding slower and noiseless. He was lost in thought. At one point he dipped down and teased a stone from between tufts of grass and weighed it in his palm. He then swung and released the stone towards the river. The stone plonked in the water, and from his stance, head cocked on one side, I could tell the guard had heard it land. He bent to choose another stone; unbeknown to him he was assisting me as his digging around covered any sounds I made. I closed the gap, all the while casting glances across the pool towards the house. If anyone were stationed at one of those huge windows, they'd spot me about to launch at the guard. I could see nobody inside.

The guard stood straight, then torqued his body to let loose another missile into the river. As his arm came back, I moved in at a rush. Clutching tight my pistol, I swung under his outstretched arm, then hooked it in the crook of my elbow. At the same instant I swept my hip in tight to his buttocks and jammed out my right heel so that it halted any backwards movement by him. A bump of my hip, and a yank of his arm and he very nearly completed a reverse cartwheel. I drove forward and down, and his neck and shoulders impacted the earth with stunning finality. He'd gotten out a croak of consternation, but not loud enough for his voice to raise the alarm. My pistol was free of him simply by the way he'd fallen. He was dazed. I could have shot him in the face or heart and had done, but that wasn't the plan. Instead I slammed the flat of the gun's frame against the side of his jaw, and he went out like a doused match. I couldn't count on him staying asleep long enough for me to complete my mission. Immediately I rolled him belly down, dragged around his hands and secured his wrists with zip-ties from my equipment pouch. Moments after that I'd secured his ankles, and also slapped a duct-tape gag over his mouth. Rather than leave him out on the lawn where somebody might spot him, I dragged him to the edge of the riverbank and rolled him down onto a sandy embankment. There I liberated him of a pistol holstered under his armpit, and I heaved it out into the York River. It made a satisfying plonk as it hit the water, as the stones he'd chucked had moments ago. I left him breathing in short sharp rasps through his nostrils. As I moved back towards the house, I gave the man a second thought: he suffered from a hacking cough, hopefully he wouldn't choke to death on a build-up of phlegm behind his gag.

I couldn't concern myself with his welfare; I'd done what I could to spare his life and had time to do no more. I crept back to where I'd first knocked him out and surveyed the house. This time I did spot movement, a blur beyond the thick glass. Some kind of technology I was unfamiliar with allowed the walls to become semi-opaque, probably for the sake of privacy after dark, but from the sylph-like shape and the high-pitched giggle recognised it as a tipsy young woman who was tripping her way along a second floor landing. A guy carrying a bottle pursued her.

I moved, allowing her distraction to attract anyone else, and went around the far edge of the swimming pool. There were several deckchairs and low tables littered with empty glasses and bottles, testament to a party that had happened there before being carried on inside. It just showed the arrogance of our enemies that they would believe themselves safe from us enough to continue their debauched ways. Picking my

The Fourth Option

way around the litter, I used the shapes of some topiary nearer the house to disguise my shape. The door was open on the ground floor. Just inside a man was seated in a low chair, bent over a table. He frowned down at something on the table, and chewed on the end of a pen: oblivious to what was going on around him, the guard was perplexed by a Sudoku or crossword puzzle. Something must have inspired him, because he took the pen from his mouth and scribbled on the puzzle. In that moment I'd checked that the area was clear of more astute guards, and I was safe to move. I transferred my gun to my left hand and approached him, and he didn't acknowledge me at first. Only when I halted beside him, and he became aware of my presence did he look up. He wasn't alarmed for about a second, and then realisation struck that I wasn't a stray partygoer, or his phlegmatic pal that'd returned from his rounds. As he began to rear back, he was more inclined to open his mouth in question than reach for a weapon. Suited me fine. I hit him with a snapping right cross to the chin, and he sank back down in the chair.

From up a grand flight of suspended marble stairs I heard a giggle, and thought it was the same girl as before. Something smashed with a high tinkle. The giggle grew more drunken and a man's deeper guffaw joined in. It was all fun and games, up there. No wonder the guard I'd just knocked unconscious had kept his head down, he was trying to stay well away from the drunken antics: I kind of felt bad for whacking him so hard now. But it was necessary, as was securing him so he wouldn't again become a problem.

I took away his pistol, leaned out of the door and under-armed it into the swimming pool. Returning to him, I pulled zip-ties from my belt pouch and bent to the task of tying him up. All the while I kept one ear, and regular glances, aimed upstairs. I almost missed detecting a soft footfall on the floor behind me. I twisted to the left, transferring my pistol to my right hand, and aimed it backwards under my left armpit, even as a heavy hand clamped down on my opposite shoulder. From there, I could put any number of bullets through the giant's torso as he loomed over me, but I'd a split-second or less to do so.

__34__

'Take it easy, brother, it's only me.'

Rink's whisper stalled my natural reaction to being crept up on, and I immediately released pressure on my pistol's trigger.

'Shit,' I replied, equally low, 'I almost shot you.'

'Nah,' said Rink. 'I wouldn't've let ya.'

Rink peered over my shoulder at the sleeping guard.

'How many?' he asked, meaning how many of the guards had I neutralised.

I showed him two fingers.

'Then he makes four. I put two to sleep.'

'Another two have gone off on a jolly down by the fishing pond,' I said. 'They could still cause us problems if they come back, but I'm guessing they're keeping well out of the way while their boss gets down and dirty with his girlfriend.'

Upstairs the girl was still giggling, but it was interspersed with other less identifiable noises.

I caught a frown from Rink.

'This is too easy,' he intoned.

'Yeah. I don't like it either, but maybe we're just getting a break for a change.'

He seesawed his head, while holding his pistol up alongside his right shoulder. He was on high alert for a possible ambush, but unless there was a squad of assassins hiding in the bunk house ready to assail us any second, I was doubtful. I'd only counted six guards during our recon, and though I couldn't be positive the man I was currently restraining was one of them, we'd thinned their numbers dramatically. We couldn't of course discount the fact that the man we'd come here for had houseguests, but it was unlikely they'd be elite combatants considering the amount of empty glasses and bottles of hard liquor I'd come across at poolside.

'Ground floor clear?' Rink asked.

'Haven't heard anyone else.'

Rink sloped off, his gun held ready.

I shoved my pistol in its holster on my hip. Grabbing the dozing guard under his armpits I dragged him out of the chair and across a room that was sumptuously decorated to another door. This one was formed of heavy oak and chrome fittings. In any other property it would have been an ostentatious entrance to a cloakroom. I pushed the guard inside, closed the door on him. There wasn't a visible lock, and it would be pointless trying to barricade it to keep him inside, as anyone spotting the piled furniture would be alerted to our presence as easily as by him screaming blue murder. Hopefully by the time he came around we'd be done here, and then he was welcome to shout as loud as he needed for release.

Rink came back.

No words were necessary.

We exchanged nods as I drew my pistol, and then headed for the stairs. Rink went up first while I covered him.

Once he was on the upper floor, I went up, taking the marble stairs slow and steady.

The Fourth Option

The woman's giggles had halted. Now she was making the types of over the top noises you heard from those pay-for-view videos available in seedy motel rooms. If she was charging for her services, our target sure was getting a bang for his buck. Similar — but less vocal — sounds emanated from other rooms on the upper floor: it sounded as if we were in a damn knocking shop.

'Sometimes the filthy rich are just plain filthy,' Rink quipped at a whisper.

We lowered our hoods. Not so we could hear better, but for appearance's sake. Now that we were confined to a narrow walkway towards the far bedroom, our silhouettes would present against the semi-opaque glass walls. Should the remaining duo of guards continue their walk and move away from the pond they might spot us, and wonder at two hooded dudes where they were expecting guys in informal clothes and women in skimpier attire. We kept our guns down by our sides for the same reason. There were rooms behind us: Rink again set off to clear them, whilst I headed for the furthest bedroom.

A figure stepped out onto the landing. He didn't spot me. He was looking back into the room he'd exited, in the process of assuring his bed buddy that he'd be right back. He was wearing an unbuttoned shirt and boxer shorts and a sheen of perspiration on his forehead. He pulled the bedroom door shut in an unexpected act of protecting his partner's modesty and turned towards me. He looked vaguely familiar: a handsome guy, with a square chin and too perfect nose. I didn't slow my pace. I kept walking towards him as if I'd every right to be there, and was rewarded with a drunken grin of camaraderie from the guy. It took another second or more for it to dawn on him that I was a stranger, and also dressed oddly for partying. By then it was too late for him to let out as much as a squawk. My pace never faltered as I stepped alongside him, gave his shoulder a nudge and spun him towards the wall. My right arm wrapped his neck, catching it in the vice of my inner elbow. I got behind him, and sat my gun hand over the crook of my left elbow, my left palm on the back of his head. A controlled squeeze cut off the blood flow to and from his brain. Under normal circumstances a man can be strangled unconscious in short order, but this man surprised me. As drunk as he was, he succumbed to strangulation the instant I locked the hold on, his legs folding and he almost dragged me down to the floor with him. I kept the hold in place for a few seconds to be sure he was fully out, and then allowed him to slither boneless to the floor. I shook my head softly in bemusement: his silly drunken grin was still plastered on his lips.

I moved on, alert to other doors that might open. None did. Behind me Rink had returned. He stepped around the sleeping partygoer, and paused momentarily at the door he'd exited. From within there was no hint his partner had heard anything untoward. Rink looked at the guy, then at me, and his mouth curled up at one corner.

Earlier we'd both expressed our concern that things were going too easy, and they were. We both got ready for the shit to hit the fan as I reached for the door handle to the master bedroom, and shoved the door wide. Immediately I followed the door, lunging in, my eyes going everywhere, and my pistol with them. I'd cleared the room of immediate threats before the two figures cavorting on the bed realised I was there. The middle-aged man was naked but for his socks. The woman sitting astride him still wore her dress, but it was pulled down below her breasts and up above her knees: evidently she wasn't wearing underwear.

As I advanced on the huge bed, the man's face lit up in alarm, and he grabbed the woman by the waist and literally heaved her aside. She bounced once on the edge of the mattress, then rolled off it to the floor with a yowl. The guy scrambled to get off the bed, reaching for a bedside cabinet. He got a drawer partly open, his hand digging inside as I stepped up and stamped the drawer shut on his wrist. He gave a sharp curse, but then my suppressor was pressed to the base of his skull. 'Drop it or die,' I warned him.

The woman was vocal, her ire at once aimed at her partner, then at us, before Rink swept across the room and grabbed her by the nape of her neck. He gave her a shake to get her attention. 'You won't be harmed, girl, unless you given me reason to hurt you. Now hush.'

Rink was bluffing. He wouldn't hurt an innocent for any reason, but she didn't know it, and her compliance was important. He more or less lifted her to her feet by way of the pressure on her neck then took her into the corner and made her sit. He touched the suppressor of his gun to his lips in a command she fully understood. She was young, barely out of her teens, and I briefly wondered what crap she'd endured during her young life to end up serving the needs of a piece of shit like my captive. I'd grabbed his trapped wrist and drew his hand clear of the drawer. Inside there was a shiny semi-automatic pistol with a mother of pearl handle that looked more about show than shoot. I shoved the guy back on to the bed, even as I dipped in the drawer and retrieved his gun. For safety's sake, I pushed it down the back of my belt.

'Who are you? What do you want?'

I pressed my lips tight at the man's questions.

He was sweating like a pig, and not from the exertion. He was splayed, starfish-like on the divan. Not a pretty picture. I grabbed his discarded trousers off the floor. Threw them at him. 'Put those on, and not another fucking word,' I growled.

He did as instructed, at least the former part. As he struggled to coordinate his legs with those of the trousers, he babbled in outrage. 'I don't know who you are or what you intend doing, but you won't get away with it. Do you realise the trouble you're in? Do you know who you're messing with? Do you?'

'Of course we do, otherwise why would we be here?' I said. 'Now stand up and put your arms behind your back.'

He stood, but still couldn't keep his lips zipped. 'What are you doing?'

The Fourth Option

It was pretty obvious. I snapped a set of prepared plasti-cuffs on his wrists, then grabbed him by his elbow.

His eyes were huge, almost protruding from their sockets, and his mouth hung awry. He glanced once at his girlfriend, but without an iota of care for her predicament, then back at me. 'Wh-what is going to happen to me?'

'That depends on whether or not you play nice,' I warned him. 'Now move.'

Rink again hushed the girl with the pistol to his lips, then left the bedroom ahead of my captive and me. It was unlikely we'd exit the house before she raised the alarm, but we could live with that probability. Rink had already keyed his walkie-talkie. 'Bring up the van,' he said as Mercer responded.

I propelled my prisoner along the walkway. We passed the drunkard I'd choked-out, and noted that he was beginning to rouse. He'd also urinated through his shorts: evidence that he was on the hunt for a toilet when we'd bumped into each other. We made it back to the head of the stairs before the caterwauling began behind us. It wasn't the girl Rink had warned but the partner of the drunken guy. She stood in the walkway, staring down at her dopey paramour, her nakedness barely concealed by a silk sheet wrapped around her middle. She squawked and hollered, demanding answers she didn't receive. Other voices than ours were raised in reply though, and from inside the ground floor cloakroom, I heard the puzzle-player yelling for help. Rink hurtled downstairs first, and I sent my prisoner down after him with my pistol jammed between his bare shoulders. We ignored the doors we'd entered via next to the swimming pool, going across the palatial living room for the main door. Up on the walkway, people were beginning to converge, but thankfully none of them armed guards.

As we left the house, Mercer came screeching to a halt in the panel van, the tires kicking up rooster tails of grit.

Shouts came from over by the pond, and before I'd pushed my captive all the way to the van, I spotted the duo that'd sloped off for a while come pounding over the rise. Neither guard had a prior clue what was happening, but the squealing arrival of Mercer in the van and the shrieks of alarm ringing from within the house told them enough. They drew their guns and came at a run. Rink used the front of the van for cover as he fired a couple of rounds at them. One man stumbled and fell, clutching his thigh, and then the second one thought better of being a hero and swan-dived at the earth. The horses stampeded wildly around the paddocks. I yanked open the van's side door and threw my captive inside, then clambered inside to force him to sit on the bench, out of grabbing range of any of the weapons or tools in the canvas bags. Rink piled in the front alongside Mercer and told him to hit the gas.

Our tires again tore up the ground as Mercer swung the van around and sent it hurtling back the way he'd just come from. I couldn't see what worried him, but Rink snapped a warning for Mercer to keep going, then hung out of the window to pop off a few shots at — I

The Fourth Option

later learned — some other guards spilling out of the bunkhouse. I fully expected return fire, for the back of the van to be filled with holes like a sieve, but our prisoner was evidently too important to risk hitting.

I checked on him.

He was outraged at his mistreatment, a little terrified, but also relieved to have survived. Exactly how we wanted him to be.

35

Pursuit was minimal. It amounted to a couple of guards chasing us on foot towards the exit gate, but it was a token gesture, as they'd no hope of catching the van as we sped away. If they returned to their vehicles to give chase, they never turned up in our rearview mirrors. I'd half expected the security detail to put to the sky in the Airbus H145 to hunt us down, but the helicopter must have stayed grounded: maybe the pilot was one of the drunken partygoers. Mercer did a sterling job as a getaway driver, handling the van like a pro, and Rink was comfortable in the shotgun seat. In the rear I was tossed around a little as the van took sharp corners or vaulted off mounds in the road, but I took no harm from it. Our prisoner wasn't as stable with his hands bound behind his back. He fell off the bench on a couple of occasions and was shoved back into place. After a third tumble, I decided to leave him where he fell, at my feet. I refused to answer any of his questions, my silence doing more to unnerve him than any threats or dire promises I could make.

Mercer took us through various small settlements and townships en route towards the Naval supply base. Back at the airstrip we boarded a private jet, crewed by a shady bunch of individuals that I suspected were either criminals or spooks, and perhaps both. We didn't ask, and they returned the favour, ignoring the fact with studied indifference that we shoved a restrained half-naked captive on board and secured him in a seat.

The Fourth Option

The flight south over the state line was short and sharp and we disembarked on a private airstrip somewhere near Alligator River in North Carolina. There was little to be made sense of our surroundings other than ploughed fields and a wilderness of tidal coastland. We weren't too far from Roanoke Island, where the first attempts at building an English settlement in North America saw all the settlers mysteriously disappear. Many theories had flourished over the centuries surrounding the "Lost Colony", but none had fully explained the disappearance of more than a hundred and twenty men, women and even the first Colonial baby born in America. The nearby location was apt in its way, as we were going to a place from where others had gone missing, never to be found again. The CIA, despite what they would admit to, once had a number of black sites dotted around the country, some of them secret locations to which rendered detainees were taken for enhanced interrogation. We boarded a covered Jeep with our prisoner and with Rink back at the wheel we headed out into the boonies.

We arrived twenty minutes later at a clearing near the coast. A swamp encroached on three sides of a field cleared of the short, tough little trees that dominated the landscape. To an outside observer they might have thought they'd stumbled upon some kind of electrical substation or pumping facility, as the only structure in sight was a square concrete building with a flat roof, on which a tall metal pylon reared thirty feet tall. There were thick pipes and several steel boxes disappearing inside or mounted on the exterior walls, and little else definable. The building was protected from trespassers by way of a mesh fence standing at least twelve feet tall: there were other hidden security and monitoring devices I guessed, but all invisible to the naked eye. Other than a steel vent positioned low on the front wall, the only other egress or entry points to the building was a scuffed red steel door. On the door "High Voltage" warning signs, and one claiming that entrance posed a "Danger of Death", told me that our spook friends had a wickedly dark sense of humour.

Rink pulled the Jeep alongside the only other vehicle that'd been apparent for miles. It was a black SUV with tinted windows: it kind of spoiled the hick subterfuge, but still, it was unlikely anyone would be out this way in the wee small hours. We got out of the Jeep, and I ushered our captive towards the fence with his own mother-of-pearl handled pistol. He walked gingerly on the rough ground in his socks. The gate had been left unsecured for us. Rink drew it open, then stepped aside as I prodded our prisoner forward, and then Mercer followed me through. As Rink entered and pulled the gate shut the door opened in the building with a swish of pneumatics. My prisoner halted, rearing back on his heels. He personally didn't know about this site's location, but he'd guessed at its exact purpose. I was about to prod him forward when a figure presented in the open doorway.

Walter eyed the man spuriously through the lenses of his spectacles, and it was a few seconds before he allowed a smile of triumph to paint his lips. He held out his arms, both palms up, like a magnanimous host.

The Fourth Option

To our prisoner he said, 'Welcome to my humble abode, Wyatt.'

It was the first time any of us had used his name since snatching him from his playboy pad, and the shock of hearing it made Wyatt Carling shudder. His knees almost gave out, and I had to grasp his cuffed wrists to hold him up. He groaned in abject dismay as I hauled him towards the door.

'No,' he cried, 'you can't do this to me! You can't!'

'So you keep on saying,' I said snarkily.

Wyatt Carling was so wealthy it was disgusting. He had so much money that he didn't conceive of the notion of price tags, so therefore had no comprehension of value. Whatever he wanted he got, and it didn't matter how outlandish or depraved his requests he was never told no, or can't. He was a man used to getting his way, so when he was refused he couldn't handle it. He began blubbering. He stank of sweat, alcohol and faeces as I manhandled him inside the concrete structure.

We encircled our captive. Beneath our feet the floor was steel. Walter stood at a podium, pressing buttons on a console. Behind us the door closed, again assisted by pneumatic servers. Walter pressed another button and the floor began a slow, steady descent, taking us deep underground. To Carling it must have felt as if all of his sins had caught up to him and he was on the final approach to hell.

36

It was never any of our intentions to physically torture Wyatt Carling. We only wanted him to believe that it was. We took lengths to deliver him to a subterranean cell where a bucket of filthy water was upended over him, then he was left in the cold and dark for a while, allowing him to contemplate his dilemma. Once we were certain he was ready, we dragged him from the cell, Rink on one side, and me on the other with our faces set sternly. He'd barely been in the cell for two hours but was already a broken wreck. Being dragged forth, he must have been filled with conflicting emotions, relief that he was out but also yearning to return, as the alternative filled him with more dread. We force-marched him through dank corridors smelling of stagnant water. This site had been decommissioned more than a decade ago, and the swamp was beginning to reclaim it. We deposited him in an archaic wooden chair reminiscent of something Torquemada might have recognised. Leather straps secured his wrists, ankles and throat, so there was no escape.

Walter and Mercer were already in the room. Mercer was grim and silent, and took an observer's role, leaning against a mildewed wall with his arms folded. Walter had discarded his jacket and tie and rolled up the sleeves of his shirt, so he looked ready for business. Beside him there was a small, wheeled trolley on which sat a large leather folder. As we strapped Carling down, Walter made a show of opening the folder to display its

The Fourth Option

contents: there were all manner of tools, ranging from pliers to scalpels to steel contraptions I couldn't identify. Carling eyed the torture implements, and in his mind he must have been conjuring the torment each could inflict. He shook, only partly from the cold. Rink stepped away, and I followed his lead: this was Walter's gig, and we were only supporting players. We posted up either side of the exit door.

Walter kept to a sedate pace. He mulled over the tools, then chose a set of pliers. He turned to our captive, tapping the end of the pliers gently against his chin as he assessed various points to twist or crush on Carling's body.

Carling wailed.

Walter continued his calm perusal.

Carling cried like a baby.

I'm all about fighting my enemies tooth and claw. But I was not at ease with cruelty like this, and my stomach was soured by the thought that Walter could inflict excruciating injuries to a helpless human being, and only the fact that this was currently an act stopped me from intervening.

Walter said, 'Dry your eyes, Wyatt.'

Carling had no comprehension of the command.

'Apparently,' Walter went on, 'you're not ready to bargain yet. Take him back to his cell, boys.'

Immediately Rink and I obeyed, pulling free the restraining straps, and hauling Carling up out of the chair. In our hands he felt insubstantial. He didn't possess the strength or will to walk unassisted, let alone fight back. We didn't drag him back to the dank cell, we allowed him to fall at Walter's feet and curl up in abject dismay.

Walter grunted. 'You really aren't cut out for this are you?'

Carling didn't respond.

Walter toed him, a nudge to his ribs. Carling contracted further.

'Look at him,' Walter said, this time for our ears. 'This is one of the men who'd choose to fund violence, when really he doesn't possess the stomach for it.' Walter directed his next words at Carling. 'Look at me, Wyatt.'

'Please don't hurt me,' Wyatt whined.

'What? It will hurt for you to look at me? Open your goddamn eyes you snivelling coward.'

Carling forced open his eyelids, as if doing so was a great strain. He turned his head so he could see Walter out the corner of his eye. He flinched at the sight of the pliers still in Walter's hand.

'You know who I am?' Walter asked.

Carling's head shook almost imperceptibly.

'What about these other fine fellas?' Walter swept an arm to encompass us all.

Carling's head shook harder this time.

'Sit up and take a better look.'

It wasn't as if Carling hadn't gotten a good look at all our faces since we'd grabbed him from his boudoir. But he did as commanded, making a meal of seating himself on the concrete floor. He kept his arms wrapped around his bared torso, as if they could save him from a brutal beating.

The Fourth Option

'Let me introduce my boys,' said Walter. He aimed the pliers at each of us in turn. 'The Brit is Joe Hunter. The hulking fella is Jared Rington. And this guy here is Jason Mercer. Tell me if any of those names ring a bell with you.'

Shaking his head, Carling took fleeting glimpses at us.

'None of those names means anything to you?' asked Walter. He clucked his tongue. 'Not even the latter?'

'I…I swear to you, I d-don't know any of them, or wh-why I'm here.'

'Ordinarily I wouldn't believe you. But I'm prepared to give you the benefit of doubt, and accept your word. Their names probably won't mean anything to you, because I understand how things work, and how layers of separation are put in place for the purposes of plausible deniability. So, allow me to enlighten you. These are the men whose deaths you have paid for.'

'Wh-what? Wait a minute! I haven't paid to have any of them killed.'

'Could the same be said of Henry Lauder?'

I had no clue whom Henry Lauder was, but apparently Carling knew from the way in which he flinched at the name. Probably for our benefit, Walter elucidated. 'Lauder was a councilman standing in the way of your business expansion plans. Had he been around to continue his objections there was a potential loss to your company in the region of tens of millions of dollars plus change. You will remember being approached by people that promised to make Councilman Lauder disappear, in return for your continued sponsorship in their future endeavours.' Walter snapped a palm out to halt Carling's bleats of denial. 'Corporate and industrial espionage is a component of Arrowsake these days, and clearing the way for their sponsors a mainstay of their fund-raising efforts. Although you might not be directly connected to the effort to murder my boys, you are one of those putting up the cash that pays their would-be killers.'

'I've never heard of…what did you call them, *Arrowsake*?'

'Of course you don't know the name under which they operate. Nevertheless, you know they exist, and regularly deposit large donations into the charitable institutes via which they launder payments. I understand your dilemma, Wyatt: you made a deal with the devil and now your soul is forfeit. You paid them to make a rival disappear, but are now being blackmailed into continuing to pay for their silence. You are a coward, a weakling, and you know you wouldn't survive prison should they ever release the evidence of your involvement in Lauder's murder, therefore you keep on paying. What's a few hundred grand here and there to a man now with a net worth of billions, huh? You regularly donate cash, and granted some of it does indeed find its way to the humanitarian causes it's intended, but some doesn't. Until now, you've been able to turn a blind eye to where that money goes, and are able to enjoy the fruits of your wealth despite the tarnish on your conscience. Look at these men again, Wyatt. You funded the people trying their outmost to kill them, and who recently murdered a companion dear to them. You came here fearing torture—' Walter deliberately dropped the pliers and they clattered on the floor '—when right now you've a worse fate to fear. Take a look at their faces; they are struggling against the impulse to rip you limb from limb. If I stepped out of this room and left you alone with them…'

I kept the emotion off my face, while Rink contained himself by sucking in his bottom lip and chewing down on it. Mercer, however, took a lunge towards Carling, his fingers working as if he was going to rend him apart: he wasn't acting either. Carling cringed in anticipation, but Walter halted Mercer with an upraised hand.

'I'm not going to step out, and these men won't do you any further harm. That is, if you agree to work with us to stop those bastards.'

'I'll do anything,' Carling promised, 'but I don't see how, not without condemning myself.'

Walter exhaled sharply. 'Wyatt, what you did is nothing compared to what they're guilty of. They'll be more concerned about saving their own asses than ruining you.'

37

'How do you feel about Walter lettin' Carling off the hook?' Rink asked me.

'I'm not happy about him getting away with the councilman's murder, but I guess I have to go along with it seeing as this was mostly my idea.'

We'd gone topside to get some air. It was probably 3 a.m. or there about. It was a cool night, with no breeze, and there was stillness over the nearby swamp. We stood in the lea of the concrete block and metal tower. Downstairs Walter and Mercer were going over what was expected from Wyatt Carling in the coming hours, Walter laying out the details, Mercer looming menacingly should Carling decide he didn't approve of what being demanded of him. I for one had had my fill of terrorising the man into acquiescence for now, whether or not he'd been complicit in the plot to murder a rival. The business we were involved in was murky however I looked at it. We'd killed rivals, and to their friends and dearly beloved we'd be seen as villains, murderers even. It was all a matter of perspective. In our narrative we were the good guys, despite our questionable tactics. Maybe it was preferable to think of us as good men doing bad things to worse people.

Unexpectedly Rink chuckled.

'What?'

'Just wonderin' how Carling's gonna straighten things out with his famous buddy once he gets home. The look on that guy's face was priceless.'

The Fourth Option

'The drunk guy I choked out?'

'Tell me you recognised him, brother.'

There was something familiar about his face, I just couldn't place where I'd seen it before. I shrugged.

'I'm surprised, the previous time you saw his face it was probably thirty feet tall on a movie screen.'

I got it, despite having never been near a cinema for years. 'He's that guy that does all those brainless action movies?'

'Jon Cutter,' Rink confirmed. 'He plays the super spy in the Death Before Dawn series. His stunt double's obviously the one that makes him look good on screen, cause he didn't do shit to defend himself when you grabbed him.'

'He was pissed up,' I said, making a concession for the ease at which I'd put the actor to sleep.

Rink chuckled again. 'I guess if they ever make a film about you, Cutter won't be gettin' a casting call.'

'As if that's ever going to happen,' I said. 'But, yeah, if it ever came to it I'd be putting a rider in the contract that he stays well away.'

'I don't think you need worry about Hollywood miscasting him, he's far too handsome to play you.' Rink grinned at my expense and then his mood shifted. 'I never did care for that asshole. There's somethin' sleazy about him, and that's before I saw him in his soiled boxers and the underage girl he was with. Mark my words, Hunter, that guy will be found out and get his comeuppance before long.'

Perhaps, I thought. But it'd have to be some other crusader for justice to bring him down, because right then Cutter didn't even register on my radar. He was barely a momentary distraction, something to lighten the mood and keep our minds off what was coming.

Rink scuffed at the dirt with his boot heel.

Out towards the river something screeched a death cry, probably prey to one of the alligators the river was named after.

I kept my pistol close, not for fear of alligators. I'd bet the woods were teeming with dangerous wildlife, bears, bobcats and who knew what else? We were secure enough behind the tall wire fence, but not from the most dangerous of predators: humans. Had Carling's security team been allowed to report his abduction, we could have been tracked here by law enforcement, or by Arrowsake, but once we safely had our prisoner off his property Walter had called and spoken with the guard in charge. In no uncertain terms he'd warned what would happen to Carling if we caught even a sniff of pursuit, and also that, if he complied, Carling would be returned unharmed in the morning. Trying to sound as if he was still in command of the situation, the guard had agreed to a twelve hour window in which he'd run damage control with those affected at the stud farm, but if Carling wasn't returned…

The guard had no bargaining power, but he needn't have been concerned — except perhaps for his job once Carling was returned home — as we fully intended taking Carling back unharmed, but fully coerced into our way of thinking.

The Fourth Option

We stayed outside for the best part of an hour. We talked through what had happened, and how we hoped to put right the wrongs done to us all, especially to Sue. We went over our plan to avenge her. We'd ridden the elevator platform up earlier. We heard it retreating into the bowels of the black site, knowing Walter had summoned it. There was nothing down there we needed to fetch, so we waited, ready to return to our Jeep and head back to the airstrip. The concrete building vibrated as the elevator platform made its upward march. Twenty seconds later, we moved to the door to greet the others. Mercer led Carling out first, and I could tell there'd been a paradigm shift in Carling's thought processes since we'd snatched him. He nodded at me as if I was an old pal, instead of a fellow conspirator. He hadn't been restrained again, but still stood barechested, in his damp trousers and socks. As Walter stepped out to join us, he laid a companionable hand on Carling's shoulder.

'Our friend Wyatt may be taken home now,' Walter announced.

I gave my old mentor a look, and he nodded behind Carling's back. It was all the confirmation I needed. The multi-billionaire had agreed to a shift of allegiance and would assist us in springing our next trap.

More confident in his place among us, Carling made an expansive outward sweep of his palms. 'Come on, you guys. Isn't there one of you going to offer me your jacket? I mean...look at me, practically standing here bare assed!'

'Just remember you're lucky to be standing at all,' Mercer growled at him, and gave him a shove to follow us to the Jeep.

Our drive back to the landing strip was made with me seated in the back with Carling. Mercer sat up front with Rink. It was best: the murderous glances Mercer had aimed at Carling as we led him to the Jeep told us there was still a possibility of him exacting revenge for Sue on the man who'd — albeit unknowingly — payrolled her killing. Walter had stayed behind at the black site to close it down and had organised a different mode of exfiltration once he was done. We were met again by the shady crew and boarded their jet for the flight back to Virginia. Our van was waiting for us at the Naval supply base.

Back at Carling's playground we drove directly in through the gates towards the big house. It was dawn, but we were surrounded by a hive of activity. As well as members of house staff, and a few lingering guests there were perhaps ten armed guards now acting far more vigilant than they had last night. They waited hard-faced and determined as Rink pulled the van to a halt next to the big house. The guards had spread out so that they didn't offer single targets; I recognised a couple of familiar faces, one of them from his bruises as the puzzle player. Hollywood golden egg Jon Cutter was nowhere in sight, and neither was the Airbus H145: apparently the fake super spy wanted no part of the real world of secret agents and assassins and had high-tailed it out of the way, but I didn't hold that against him. While we'd been in the air, Walter had again paved the way with a call to the head of security. Carling's supposed protectors had gathered in solidarity, as they'd all been equally at fault in losing their mark, and were determined to show they weren't completely useless when it came to taking him off our hands.

It could have been the moment for an FBI hostage rescue team to pounce, or even for a reckoning with Vince or other Arrowsake gunmen, but we were confident enough that Carling's people had taken heed of Walter's instructions. As I slid open the side door of the van and stepped down, some of those facing me shifted, and I watched a few itchy fingers reach subtly for weapons. But then Carling climbed out, and all eyes went to him. There was still the possibility that Carling could do something stupid like order his pack of guards to take us on, which would probably result in a high body count on both sides, but he didn't.

One man stood opposite us with mixed emotions flitting over his features. I knew him from his size and build that he was the one I'd dumped on his head and left tied up on the riverbank. He at first sent dire unspoken threats at me, then blinked at the dirt in embarrassment rather than meet Carling's eyes. I took it he was the one in charge that'd been taking Walter's calls.

'Somebody get me a shirt,' Carling announced. He looked down at his stockinged feet. 'And a pair of goddamn shoes.'

The head guard gestured to somebody behind him, then turned again open mouthed to Carling. 'Sir, I—'

Carling stalled him with the jab of a finger. 'Don't speak,' was all he said.

The guard immediately returned his glare to me. Not only had I dumped him on his head and tied him up, I'd done far worse damage in making him look inept to his employer. I didn't expect gratitude, but at least he'd woken to a sore head, and not submerged in the river where I'd sent his weapon. He stuck out his chin at me.

Carling scoffed him on my behalf. 'Back off, Ronnie. You aren't in this guy's league. If you were I never would've been taken in the goddamn first place.'

Cowed, big Ronnie again blinked at the dirt and his ears grew red.

I kind of felt sorry for him.

Carling turned to appraise me. 'You know, once this is over with, and things settle down, maybe you and your pals can come work for me?'

I held out an olive branch, though not to Carling. 'Lessons have been learned, and your own guys will do a much better job of protecting you in future.'

'To be fair,' Carling said, 'they're usually good at their jobs. Tends to be manhandling a few rowdy drunks or whores getting too insistent on how much they deserve, not taking on fellas with your skills.'

I scowled at Carling's choice of words, but understood that he was paying us a lop-sided compliment. 'Just do as you agreed and you don't have to worry about us coming back.'

He held out his hand.

The Fourth Option

I knew what the gesture was intended to mean, but I didn't accept it. I took his pearl handled gun from behind my back and slapped it in his palm. 'I'll keep hold of the bullets for now,' I told him.

A woman approached tentatively, carrying a shirt and a pair of leather loafers. She looked to be regular staff rather than any of the working girls Carling had shipped in to entertain his wealthy guests last night. Carling shoved the gun in his pants, and snatched them from her without thanks. He probably paid all of his staff a similar lack of respect given to any of the abused young girls. He was oblivious to my look of disgust as he wormed into the shoes and then pulled on the shirt. Maybe, I thought, I will come back sometime whether you do as agreed or not.

For the time being I kept my anger to myself, and returned to the van. Carling's people closed ranks around him, as he marched towards the entrance to his over-excessive home.

'Son of a bitch didn't even say goodbye,' Rink grunted to my amusement, before he hit the gas and took us back towards the airstrip.

38

With Spencer Booth and his security detail missing, presumed dead, and now one of their wealthy sponsors threatening to withdraw their support, those at the helm of Arrowsake must've been experiencing itchy buttholes. The main drive of my plan was to discombobulate them, get them arguing among themselves, but ultimately to get them to realise they were better off negotiating a truce rather than continuing a battle that'd only end up destroying us all. Walter would do the direct negotiating, because I wasn't interested in seeing any of their vile faces in person incase I couldn't control my urge to take retribution from them for Sue's murder. Rink was of a similar opinion, and there was no way we could allow Mercer a meeting with them, not without his hands restrained with unbreakable duct-tape this time.

We had returned to Florida, and set up in the ranch-style house near the Apalachicola River where we'd first taken Sue's body, allowing Walter time to deal with them. Walter was confident he could negotiate a deal agreeable to both opposing parties, if not to all of the supporting players. For years Walter had assumed this day might come, when he might have to defend himself against those he'd served loyally for decades. For an equal amount of years he'd been preparing. He'd built a fat dossier on Arrowsake's personnel and their nefarious activities, and it was damning. Yes, he too would be vilified if ever the contents of the dossier saw light of day, but he believed it would only add weight to the sincerity of his promise to keep it under wraps if Arrowsake agreed to our terms. He was gambling with our liberties too, as there was stuff in that folder that would bring us down as hard as it would anyone else, so we were as keen to see it buried as those we were trying to bargain with. It was akin to a dead man's switch: the button a suicide bomber holds down until he's in position — or gunned down — where taking pressure off the button detonates the explosives packed around his body. We'd all be obliterated in the explosion. Our friends Harvey Lucas and Raul Velasquez held digital copies of the dossier, ready to release to the media and a number of select prosecutors and trustworthy congressmen and women, if Arrowsake chose not to play ball and came after us. Walter was prepared to dangle Spencer Booth's unknown — but guessed at — fate before them, as well as how easily we'd gotten to one of their key funders to illustrate how easy we could come for any of them if they continued with acts of aggression. He truly believed the existence of his dossier — and also the evidence of their part in state sanctioned murder in Sierra Leone compiled by Sue — would ultimately prove the ruination of their organisation: knowing of its existence those at its highest level would soon seek to distance themselves from Arrowsake, and once they had fled, those few left behind would scatter or dissolve back into the muck where they belonged.

The coming demise of Arrowsake would be Sue Bouchard's enduring legacy to the world. It would be bloodless vengeance, but vengeance all the same, and we thought she'd prefer things that way. She once told me she thought she'd made her feelings on assassins clear, and I suppose she had.

It felt strange being back at the ranch. We ate, we drank coffee, and we took turns sleeping and standing stag duty, because until we got the all clear from Walter we weren't safe. We chewed the fat, laughed and joked, and after a while we fell morose and sought our separate places in the house. After the room I'd retired to begun to feel like a prison cell, I stepped outside for some air and found Rink had beaten me to it. He was sitting on the edge of the porch with his pistol resting on his thigh, watchful.

'Whatever happens today, it ain't the end,' he said.

'I know.'

I sat next to him.

'It can be for Mercer,' Rink added. 'He's got the connections through Sue's network to disappear and start afresh some place. The same can't be said for us, brother.'

Rink had a business to run, a stable home, and friends down in Tampa. Whether or not Arrowsake agreed to our terms he wasn't prepared to run away and leave those things behind, and I wouldn't either.

I steered the conversation away to another possible future. 'I've been thinking about your suggestion about flicking through Sue's property portfolio, seeing if there's someplace I can come to some agreement on with Mercer.'

The Fourth Option

He made a gesture indicating where we sat. 'You could do worse than taking on this place. It has everythin' you need and then some.'

I scowled over at the parking garage. I'd never think of the building in the same way again, forever it would remain a morgue, tainted by the memory of Sue's resting place. Enough ghosts haunted me without having to endure a reminder every time I went to fetch my car from the garage.

'Nah,' I said. 'The landscape's too flat here for my liking. It didn't have mountains, but I lived at Mexico Beach because of the sea and beaches. The views here would bore me in no time.'

Rink grunted in mirth at my attempt to feed him bullshit, and gave me a nudge with his elbow. We both laughed, but it didn't last. Rink turned his gaze towards the parking garage. 'Yeah, the view would bother me, too,' he admitted.

'I'm sorry she died, man.'

'Yeah, me too.'

'When I left you guys alone in the hotel, did you get chance to say what needed saying?'

He rocked his head. 'You weren't gone long before Vince and his goons showed up…but, yeah; we both got to say a thing or two, and I'm sure we ended up as friends again. Things could never be like they were before though. You didn't get to see when we rescued her and she fell into Mercer's arms. That guy loved her, and I think she'd suspected for long enough, but she still looked at me first for approval before she returned his affection. Wasn't my place to come between them.'

We fell silent again. I pictured how, barely a minute later, the bullet meant for Mercer had killed Sue, and Rink probably had a similar picture in his mind. We sat in companionable silence for some time, and together watched the sun lowering over the distant Gulf.

After a while, Rink stood, shoved his pistol in his belt and went inside. I stayed on the porch and watched the stars come out.

The ringing of my cell phone disturbed my ruminations.

'It's done,' Walter announced the instant I answered.

'They've agreed to all of our terms?'

'They understand that no good can come from them continuing this fight. They know that coming after any of us will destroy them too. I made it clear that I would bury the evidence, that it would never see daylight, unless they gave us cause to dig it up again. They also know I made copies that will be released the second anything untoward happens to any of us.'

'This includes Mercer?'

'Especially Mercer.'

'You trust them to uphold the agreement?'

'They are a bunch of lying hyenas,' Walter reminded me, 'but I believe they'll stick to their part. Hunter, son, while they're fighting us, they gain nothing and risk everything. They understand that now. In fact, keeping us alive and the evidence under wraps has become a priority for them. They've rescinded the hit on Mercer, and have also disavowed Stephen Vincent.'

The Fourth Option

'They've burned Vince? I thought he was their star pupil.'

'They're unhappy at the way he has handled things, and left a trail of bodies and destruction in his wake. They're pulling out all the stops to cover up what happened at Sue's house, and in Mexico Beach. They're using what considerable influence they have to change the narratives at each scene. Obviously their efforts in cleaning up gets you boys off the hook too.'

'What about the bodies left at the hostage exchange site?'

'Already cleaned. Thankfully the glade was remote and there were no witnesses to what happened. The people killed there were private contractors, and easily made to disappear. Vince's staging post was set up at a property nearby but their cleaners have been in and scrubbed every trace of their activities.'

'This was where Sue was tortured?'

'Yes.'

'They should burn the place to the fucking ground,' I growled.

'Burning it would attract unwanted attention.'

'I know. Shame they didn't find Vince there when they went in. Mercer shot him; I had hoped he'd bled to death.'

'Vince made himself scarse before they could arrive. His handlers suspect he'd guessed what was coming and skedaddled. He has kept off the radar since: they thought perhaps you had caught up with him already and solved the problem for them.'

'That's one problem I wouldn't mind solving, but it wouldn't be on their behalf.'

'It saddens me that it has come to this,' Walter said. 'There was a time I had high hopes for that boy, but…well, he was never going to be the man you turned out to be, Joe.'

It was supposed to be a show of endearment towards me, but I didn't react to it. Whatever man Vince had turned out to be had been influenced by Walter, and the thought gave me pause. Who was the real monster: Victor Frankenstein or his creation? I said, 'What about Spencer Booth and his men?'

'Still in situ in my vault.'

'How does Arrowsake feel about that?'

'They deem Booth's death collateral damage, and accept that forcing me to choose between them and you was bound to end badly. They're currently concocting a plausible scenario to explain his sudden disappearance. I've told them I'll give back the bodies. We'll probably hear in the next few days how he has burned up in a car wreck or downed flight or some other cockamamie story.'

'I've no love for the guy, but what about Wyatt Carling?' There was the possibility that withdrawing his monetary aid from them could give them cause to punish him. At our urging he'd encouraged rebellion among his other rich friends under Arrowsake's control, an act that could severely damage their cash flow and force them to shut him up permanently.

'He's been given special dispensation from retribution, and has been allowed to withdraw his involvement in their organisation without fear of penalty. Don't forget, they can't finger him for Councilman Lauder's murder without also coming under scrutiny.'

'They could still kill him.'

'They won't. Who will purchase their services in future if they think they might end up dead?'

'So what happens now, Walt?'

'We do the right thing for Sue Bouchard.'

'Yes, we should,' I said, as a proper funeral was overdue.

'And we watch our backs,' Walter added, because we still had an active enemy out there who wasn't constrained by the truce struck with his old masters.

39

A few days after fleeing Florida, Vince Everett — not Stephen Vincent — was hiding in plain sight. He stood at the bar in a trendy pub overlooking the George Washington Memorial Parkway, and the Potomac River. He was probably equidistant between the George Bush Center for Intelligence and the Pentagon, so was in the stomping grounds of both the intelligence services and the military, factions he must now consider as potential enemies. The bar wouldn't have been his first choice for a clandestine meeting: it was the domain of Generation Z students and sad sack Millennials desperate to cling to their youth. Vince could be mistaken for one of the latter, except he didn't conform to the adopted fashions in his leather biker's jacket, jeans and cowboy boots. Many of the guys there wore hairstyles similar to his, but their coiffed hair and perfectly groomed hipster beards contrasted with his stubbled face and wilder greased ducktails. They elected to drink gin, or margaritas or who knew what else, while he stuck to the piss water masquerading as drought beer from the pumps.

There was a bubble around him, where other guys in the bar didn't step foot, and it wasn't because they disliked his aftershave lotion. He'd attracted attention from a couple of women, attracted by his bad boy image, but he'd given them short shrift and sent them packing with a surly grunt, or blatant curse. He wanted to drink his beer and couldn't do that while fending off inane chatter or too familiar hands. He'd hooked his right heel on the brass footrest running the length of the bar and braced his right elbow on the bar itself, bending his mouth to his glass rather than lift it. Nobody could have guessed he was recovering from wounds to both limbs, his only visible injury the ugly scab on his ear.

Around him voices babbled, growing louder and higher-pitched in line with the volume of alcohol imbibed. Accents were many, and the clientele diverse, with numerous skin colours represented. A man brayed like a donkey at his own joke, an abrasive forced laugh that caused a tic to jump at the corner of Vince's jaw. He scowled over at the comedian, a mistake in hindsight. He turned back to his beer. The laugh, he understood, was not only at the joke but also at his expense. Vince didn't give a shit; his image often attracted derision.

His beer finished, he caught the eye of the bartender and ordered another. While he waited, he cupped his empty glass in his palm, and took surreptitious glances at the mirror behind the bar. He didn't know the face of the man he'd come to meet, but was certain he stood out enough that he wouldn't be missed. There were clusters of friends standing in groups, yapping and laughing. He noticed when somebody was moving against the tide and out of rhythm with his fellow drinkers. But this wasn't the person he'd come to meet; the joker was wending his way through the crowd, followed by a couple of his pals. The joker, a burly guy with a thick beard and shaved head posted at the bar beside him, invading Vince's space. Vince stayed put, mulling over his empty glass in studied indifference.

The bartender brought Vince's second beer. He let it settle on the bar, a ring of foam bubbling on the counter, while taking the joker's order. The bartender frowned a little, perhaps feeling the tension from Vince or the faux joviality from the joker and moved away.

'Say!' The joker had turned his attention on Vince. 'I haven't seen your face in here before.'

Without looking at him, Vince said, 'What does that tell you, buddy?'

'You ain't from around here, I'd guess.'

Vince checked out his reflection. The joker's two pals had set up behind him, one at each shoulder. One man was big, red-haired and freckled, the other a black guy, tall and athletic.

'You'd guess right,' said Vince.

'See, I'd say, if you were from around here you'd know that these things *here* aren't acceptable.' The joker's finger tapped at a patch sewn on the left shoulder of Vince's leather jacket. Vince didn't need to look to know what had gotten the guy's blood up: these days the Confederate battle flag had been adopted by neo-Nazis, and neo-Confederate white nationalists and other hate groups. For decades music fans had displayed it innocently as a nod of respect to the land where country and rockabilly music originated. Fitting his guise of Vince Everett his jacket sported a number of flags and banners paying homage to Dixie.

'Last time I checked Virginia was still in the South,' Vince said.

The Fourth Option

'Are you one of those racist motherfuckers?' The joker jerked a thumb at his black friend. 'My buddy Julan is offended by that flag. His ancestors were enslaved by white cracker motherfuckers waving the same flag as yours.'

Vince sighed. 'Don't get me started on slavery, man. My Irish ancestors were brought here in shackles too, as indentured servants. Call them what you want, unpaid servants, slaves, but they were treated as badly as any nigger.'

His final word was a deliberate trigger. He hadn't come to the bar looking for trouble, but it had found him, and he only wished it over with.

'You *are* a motherfucking racist,' Joker snapped.

'Man,' said Vince at the inevitability of what was coming, 'I'm not a racist. I only hate white apologist hipsters with stupid-looking beards.'

The blood drained from the joker's features. Vince recognised the effects as endorphins washing through the joker's body as he prepared to launch his attack. Behind Vince the other two guys postured, ready to jump to their pal's assistance. Vince beat them all to the punch—

Rather, he smashed the empty glass upside the joker's head. The glass shattered with enough noise to still everyone around them, all bar none shocked by the sudden violence in their midst. Vince filled the void with action. As the joker reeled away wailing and trying to hold together his gashed cheek, Vince jabbed an elbow into the black guy's sternum and drove him back. With enough space cleared, he spun and kicked savagely between the man's legs, and before he had folded to the floor, Vince rounded on the third man in the group.

'You want some of *this*?' Vince snarled.

The big, freckle-faced guy was torn. He glanced between his two injured pals, and was still deciding if retreat was the better part of valor when Vince capitalised on his indecision. Vince launched at him, spearing at the bigger man with his forehead leading the attack. The man got his hands between them, and grasped Vince's forearms, but it did nothing to stop the headbutt. Vince's forehead crushed the cartilage in the man's nose. Blood poured down his chin, but he still had a grasp on Vince. Vince butted him again, and then a third time, and the guy collapsed senseless to the floor.

A cacophony arose around Vince. People either scattered to avoid his wrath, moved to encircle him, or to help the trio of injured men. Vince was aware he faced the potential of further violence, but he turned his back on it, and reached for his second glass of beer. He downed it in one long swallow, and then set it down on the bar. Opposite him, the bartender looked on in horror. Vince wiped the froth off his chin with the back of a leather-clad wrist. 'I'll take another, please,' said Vince.

The violent clash had lasted seconds at most, but the aftermath would resonate much longer. The joker wasn't laughing now, he was bleating. Julan was gasping, while Freckles was making a soft mewling sound. The other bar goers were all strident, noisier even than

The Fourth Option

before. The bartender shook his head at Vince's temerity. 'You're outta here, man,' the bartender said, from the safety afforded by the bar separating them. 'Go on. Get outta here before I have to call the cops.'

'What is it with all this intolerance? There won't be any more trouble from me.' Vince took a stack of dollars from his pocket and tossed them down on the bar. 'C'mon, man, I'm beginning to get a taste for that Granny's piss you're selling as beer.'

The bartender shook his head again. His head darted around, possibly looking for the doormen who had failed to show up yet. Vince felt a hand clutch his elbow. He checked it out, and then followed the hand to its source. The small, skinny man facing him was either the most innocuous-looking doorman in town, or the person Vince had come to meet.

'You're David Paulson, I take it?' asked Vince.

'Are you trying to attract unwanted attention or what?' Paulson was genuinely unnerved by what he must have just witnessed.

'Don't know if you noticed, but I was just standing here minding my own business when these clowns decided to butt in.'

'Come with me. We're going to have to go somewhere else now.' Paulson jerked his head towards the door, and set off. Vince followed and noted that a path through the drinkers had cleared for him.

Outside, Paulson indicated up the street. 'I have a car.'

'Lead on, then.' Vince gave a little smile.

As they strode for the car, Paulson glanced at him, his face twisted with concern. 'The cops could've been called, man, and I don't want them sniffing around my business. What were you thinking, taking on those three dudes like that?'

Vince shrugged his shoulders dismissively. 'It was easy. I just pictured some other guys I want to kill, and couldn't restrain the urge.'

'These are the three you want my assistance with?'

'Yup,' said Vince. 'Just wait til I tell you what they did to Pam. I bet you'll want to kill them too.'

40

'How are you holding out?' I asked Jason Mercer.

'I'm as sick as a dog,' he admitted, and wiped a hand across his bloodless features, 'but I've managed to hold down my lunch for now.'

I clapped him on his shoulder.

My enquiry was actually about his emotional state, rather than his nausea, but I hadn't made it clear. While he was concentrating on not being sick, he wasn't dwelling on why we were out on a boat.

We had been on the water for a couple of hours by then, but were on the way back to shore. Earlier we'd been riding the swells, but the change in direction now put us at odds as the boat undulated from side to side with each wave we summited. I was feeling a little queasy too, but didn't let on. Rink sat cross-legged at the prow of the boat, almost Swami-like, gazing at the distant line of sand dunes denoting the state park on St. Joseph Peninsula — he was probably fighting seasickness too, concentrating on the horizon rather than the rolling sea.

The only other person on the small charter boat was a man who had been paid enough to ask no questions. The skipper was a military veteran, old enough to have fought alongside Walter in Vietnam, but we didn't ask and he didn't tell. Neither had he presided over the ceremony as we'd lowered Sue Bouchard's remains into the water; Mercer had spoken a eulogy for her, and me and Rink honoured her with a salute and whispered goodbye. Rather than a wreath, Mercer had scattered flower petals to dissipate on the current, so there would be no hint a burial had occurred. Afterwards, the skipper had turned the prow for the far away shore. The sun was at its zenith and there were other craft out on the Gulf, but none of them close enough that our actions had been witnessed. It was best that way.

Holding a burial at sea is legal, as long as certain requirements are met. There are designated areas where a burial can be performed, and distance and depth play a factor, as well as how heavy a coffin or shroud are weighted, to avoid a body being washed back to shore. Usually a retrospective permit is granted by the Environmental Protection Agency, and a registrar or preacher — the latter depending on the deceased's religion — or even a layman presides over the ceremony. I was pretty certain that Walter adhered to none of the requirements when arranging Sue Bouchard's burial: there was no death certificate, no holy man, and no report would be given to the EPA. But we did give Sue a dignified send off by sinking her remains to the bottom of the Gulf five miles out beyond St. Joseph Peninsula. We chose the maritime tradition of a burial at sea for Sue as it was in keeping with how she'd originally supposedly died. We were on the wrong side of the Atlantic from where she had reportedly drowned and been lost at sea off the coast of Tenerife, but it was still the same ocean.

The skipper delivered us safely back to Port St. Joe and we returned on rubbery legs to our car, Rink's company Ford, where we'd left it near the Cape San

The Fourth Option

Blas Lighthouse. I'd heard from Rink that he had made it to the same parking lot when chased from the hotel by Vince's team, and how he now regretted waiting there too long before returning to pick up me and Sue: had he returned sooner he believed Vince would never have snatched her, or been able to use her as a hostage, ergo she'd still be alive. I had to remind him that had he come back sooner, we wouldn't have been at the pick up point and who knew how that might have affected any of our fates. Maybe we all would have died in a gunfight with Vince's mercenaries.

It is a tradition to hold a wake in remembrance of the deceased, but there was none held there for Sue, not when her burial must remain a secret. We drove back from Port St. Joe up FL-71 towards the ranch that had by then been home for the better part of a week since agreeing our truce with Arrowsake. Due to their influence on the local police investigations I was no longer a wanted man, so the fridge there had been stocked with beer following supply runs I made up to Wewahitchka. We planned on downing a few bottles in Sue's memory on our return home.

Our plan went to shit.

We arrived back at the ranch around mid-afternoon. A mountain of clouds had piled in from the eastern horizon, dark blue and steel grey and veined with purples and scarlet. There was a storm coming, but this was one of the electrical storms that often struck Florida as opposed to another hurricane: often there'd be a light and sound show but not necessarily rain or destructive wind, other times they came with the full kit and caboodle. This was one of the latter times. We parked and got out of the car just as the first heavy droplets began falling. The ground was dry, and the first raindrops kicked up puffs of dust. They drummed on the Ford, and on the roofs of the house and parking garage. Within seconds the rain became a deluge, forcing us to hurry for the shelter of the covered porch. Rink often followed the maxim that you must embrace the inevitable but even he jogged to avoid a soaking.

Mercer came up short on the porch, breathing heavily, one hand clasped to his side. Ten days after being shot he was physically on the mend, but the unexpected run had taken a toll on his injured ribs. He sucked in oxygen and I could see that it pained him. I wiped rain off my face. Rink had the house keys on the same ring as his car key. He moved to let us inside. He stopped with the key poised before the lock.

Lightning forked across the heavens.

Rink exchanged a squint with me. We both looked at the damaged keyhole and heard the *ker-chunk* of a pump action shotgun.

'Get down!' I hurled my body into Mercer, taking him in a graceless tumble to the decking, even as Rink span with a dancer's grace in the opposite direction. We were each a split-second clear of the buckshot ripping through the door. Inside the house, another shell was racked into a shotgun, and a second blast blew out another portion of the door, scattering shot and splinters in the front yard.

I reached for my gun nestled in the small of my back; even to a funeral I'd gone armed. Mercer also had a pistol, but right then he was under me and it was out of easy reach. I rolled off him, freeing my own gun and came up sharp against the wall of the house. Mercer took a roll in the opposite direction and went off the edge of the deck, and I heard him thump on the ground two feet or so lower. For the moment he was safe from further gunfire from within the house, whereas all I had between the gunman and me was a thin layer of planks and plaster. Above my head there was a living room window over which were fitted security bars. The bars didn't do much to stop the blast of shattered glass cascading over me as another shell was discharged. I screwed my eyelids tight and averted my face, feeling the bites of several shards of glass that hit me. Something sharp jabbed my cheek, and tiny slivers invaded my collar and got down inside my shirt, but thankfully nothing vital was severed. I spat sharp bits off my lips as I scrambled on all fours to get away from the window. More glass crashed, and as blinded and confused as I was, I still understood the gunman was knocking a wider hole in the window so he could get a cleaner shot at me. I raised my gun, firing blindly at the window even as I crawled for my life. From elsewhere another gun barked, and I am unsure whose.

The shotgun fired again.

I was stung by shot on my back and butt, but thankfully I was spared the full bore that tore a hole in the deck to my left. I had no option other than follow Mercer's example, so I took a dive over the edge of the deck and fell into mud. Rolling onto my back, I aimed my pistol between my knees as I checked for a target.

There was none. I couldn't see where Mercer or Rink had gotten to either. Raindrops battered my face, but I could live with that inconvenience.

Again I heard the crack of a pistol, and this time understood that Rink had made it off the porch at the far end and was defending himself. It was impossible to tell who he was exchanging bullets with, but apparently the gunman inside wasn't our only enemy. I was in an untenable position where I was, because where there were two attackers there could be, and probably was, more. No sooner had I began to scoot backwards on my ass for the corner of the deck than a third gunman presented, this one from over by the parking garage. He fired, and I felt a thud to my right thigh. I was hit, but I'd no idea how badly, and had no time to take stock. I rolled on my side, my injured leg in the mud as I returned fire, forcing the gunman to take shelter behind the garage. I kicked my way along the earth, churning through bloody dirt and got to the edge of the porch. Even getting around it, I was still open to more fire from the man that'd shot me. He leaned out from the garage wall and got a bead on me. He was a skinny little guy, the type of enemy I'd normally backhand into submission, but then and there with a pistol in hand he could kill me as easily as anyone else could. I fired at him first and he jerked back under cover. I'd earned a few seconds respite at most.

I couldn't capitalise on those few seconds, because the roar of an engine brought me about. A grey SUV tore down the approach towards the ranch. No part of me believed those inside were hurtling to my rescue. It

The Fourth Option

came to a juddering halt behind Rink's Ford, and doors were thrown open. Gunmen piled out, at first taking cover behind the open doors as they took stock, sought targets, and then one of them ran at a crouch for concealment behind the Ford. I counted three more guns, military grade M4 carbines, and decided my best option was to get the hell out of their way.

I could do nothing for Mercer or Rink if I got gunned down.

Scrambling up, I'd to throw my left hand against the side of the house to support me. My right leg was a lead weight, feeling heavier at that moment than those we'd attached to Sue's burial shroud to help draw her into the ocean's embrace. My entire trouser leg was soaked, hopefully not all of it with my blood. Pushing off I limped away, gathering pace and fortitude with each lurching step. I was out of view of the newcomers, but an open target to the skinny guy that'd put a hole in my leg. I passed my SIG to my left hand, so I could aim better should he show again.

Out of my sight, an M4 chattered on fully automatic fire. God help either of my friends that were its target. I heard Rink's pistol fire in response. So far my big buddy was still alive and in the fight. Mercer was yet to join in, and I hoped he wasn't already dead.

A bullet punched the wall behind me. Another smacked the wall several feet ahead. The skinny guy must have shifted location. I snapped a look at where I thought he'd gotten to, but couldn't see him, so didn't waste any more bullets. I ducked around the back of the house. From within, the shotgun blasted a hole the size of my fist through the back wall: the son of a bitch must have been tracking my ungainly race to cover, but he'd overestimated how far I'd moved. It was tempting to stick my pistol through the hole and return fire, but that would be madness. I threw myself at the dirt just as another part of the wall disintegrated exactly where I'd been a few seconds earlier. The pain in my thigh had caught up with me by then; it was red raw agony. I clenched my teeth, cursing under my breath, as I was forced to scuttle like a rodent through the mud. I made it to the smaller rear porch and came up against one of the support posts. It didn't afford me much cover, but it was all I had. I shoved up to my feet, my spine braced against the support, and aimed at the back door. There was no point in shooting through it, because the gunman wouldn't be stupid enough to stand directly behind it. I quickly measured where his last two shots had perforated the wall, and judged his position to be somewhere still inside the kitchen at the back of the house. I aimed and shot out the back windows of the living room and kitchen, drawing fire, and he obliged. Glass hurtled outward on a hail of lead, glistening like the falling rain. I realigned and fired, then moved a fraction more to the left and fired again. Whether I hit him or not didn't matter, I just wanted to keep him from getting a clear shot at me as I turned and threw my back into the door. Before leaving the ranch that morning, I'd gone around and ensured the doors were locked, but hadn't bothered adding any extra layers of security. My entire weight against one mortise lock was an unfair competition: the lock and its retainer burst free with a shard of doorframe and I rammed inside the house full of spit and vinegar.

There was the tiniest of vestibules that opened into the kitchen and before the gunner had time to reload, I was inside the room and firing at him. The son of a bitch was wearing a bulletproof vest, but it didn't save him from the bullets I put in his face. As he fell, his shotgun clattering on the floor, my only regret was that the face wasn't that of Vince. However, I fully expected Vince was the one behind this ambush; I just hadn't a clue where he was.

I'd probably expended more than half the bullets in my magazine by then, and needed to reload. My stuff, including extra ammunition, was in a closet in one of the bedrooms I'd commandeered as mine, and it was at the far end of the house beyond the living room. I bent and grabbed the shotgun off the floor. The corpse had a belt ringed with extra shells. I unbuckled the belt and slung it around my hips, and rapidly set to filling the shotgun with 12 gauge buckshot cartridges. This was no duck hunter's gun; it was a Mossberg 590A1 tactical weapon. Its firepower didn't match the carbines I faced, but with a killing range of around one hundred and thirty feet it helped make me feel a little less overwhelmed.

I quickly nudged the backdoor closed, and threw a retainer bolt to stop anyone sneaking inside, then lumbered through the house on my injured leg towards the front. The living room window was mostly shattered, only a few large chunks of glass still clinging to the frame, and the front door had all but been obliterated, but I still didn't have a clear view outside. During the fight I'd kind of ignored the storm, but the rain thundered on the roof and gushed from the eaves. I was looking through sheeting rain where human figures were fleeting shadows. At least I was indoors. It was no castle of stone, but the ranch afforded me some protection from both the weather and flying bullets. It also gave me an option to take the fight back to our ambushers.

I let loose with the Mossberg, firing through the shattered window at the SUV. Sixty feet or less away, each load of buckshot put holes in the metal and shattered the windshield. There must have been some kind of bulletproofing beneath the outer shell though, because my shots didn't make it through to those using the open doors as shields. I aimed lower, blasting at the feet of one of the attackers. A yell of pain rewarded my efforts, but I couldn't tell how badly I'd injured the shooter. In the next instant another one opened up with his carbine and the ranch around me began dissolving. I lurched on my damaged leg as fast as possible, chased through the house by a stream of bullets. At the far end, my bedroom was being similarly chewed to pieces by gunfire. I turned around and raced for the only stable structure that'd take a few rounds, and concealed myself up against the stone chimneystack. There I was open to a shot through the broken window in the rear, and I didn't trust that skinny guy not to sneak up on me. The only option open to me was to crawl into the large inglenook in the fireplace and take cover. Bullets cut through the house largely unimpeded, and some ricocheted off the stone chimneystack, but for a few more seconds I was out of danger. I fed fresh cartridges into the Mossberg.

Where was Rink? Between the rattle of assault rifles I caught the occasional answering pop of a pistol, but from where I hid it was hard to determine its source. I was still yet to hear anything from Mercer, and now feared the worst for him. He'd been silent since rolling off the porch in the first few seconds of the assault. Rink and Mercer were both grown men, both of them with training and experience in warfare. Instead of worrying about them, I should have concentrated on my own arse, but if I've to be honest, their welfare right then trumped mine, as I was at least behind shelter.

Abruptly, the carbines stopped targeting the house.

I had an inkling why.

Boots scuffed the front porch, and I assumed somebody had closed in to check if I was still alive, as I hadn't returned any of their shots. At the same time, a face showed briefly around the edge of the window frame at the back of the house. The visage was that of a ferret: it was the skinny guy who'd shot me. He didn't spot my hiding place. A few seconds later he appeared again, popping up over the window frame and this time taking a longer scan around the room. He had his pistol held alongside his chin, and it was angled down, expecting to find me bleeding on the ground. He spoke, I guessed, through a throat mike, and he heard a response in his earpiece. He rose up taller, and peered harder into the room. His face for a moment was turned away from my hiding place. I aimed, pulled the trigger and blew him away.

Killing the skinny guy gave me no satisfaction or sense of revenge for nailing me. He simply needed killing so that I could live to help my friends. But in shooting him I alerted the one on the porch, and I again came under withering fire. Chips of stone flew, and something scorched my knuckles. I couldn't stay in my hidey-hole. I swarmed across the floor on my belly, but the mostly unfurnished room offered no other hiding places: the couch Mercer had slept on was already riven apart by carbine fire. I swung onto my side, aiming along the barrel of the shotgun, waiting for a hint at where the shooter was and tried not to think about the bullets cutting the air all around me.

Somebody followed my bullish tactics from earlier, busting their way inside through the back door. I had an enemy approaching from the kitchen and also the immediate threat of the man on the porch. If I shot one I was at the mercy of the other. They were coordinating their attack via radio, and I'd no idea who was going to draw fire first. I assumed the man coming through the kitchen was supposed to engage me, while the other shot me dead. I sent several loads of buckshot through the wall towards the kitchen to slow him and immediately swung my gun back towards the front window. The shooter was already there, silhouetted against the bucketing downpour, his carbine to his shoulder. He was a millisecond from blowing me apart when he performed a crazy little dance to the beat of a gun, and his carbine flew up and wasted his rounds in the ceiling. He was wearing a bulletproof vest like the first man I'd killed, but it wouldn't help him at this close range. I fired into his central mass and watched him get knocked off his feet and pinwheel off the porch.

Whoever had come to my rescue had done so in the absolute nick of time, but it didn't help me with the gunman in the kitchen. I scrambled to get to another position because lying on the floor I was an open target from the kitchen door. Not making enough ground, I pushed up, and was plummeting forward at the same instant an arm came round the doorjamb and tossed something into the room.

It was a grenade, and I'd no cover whatsoever.

41

Jason Mercer had Joe Hunter to blame for another cracked rib. Then again, when Hunter tackled him and knocked him on his back, he'd also saved his life, so he didn't hold the fresh breakage against him. He'd have been in a far worse position than having a painful chest if he'd taken the full load of buckshot through it. As they broke apart, and Hunter returned fire at the bastard who had tried ambushing them, there was only one place for Mercer to go. He had rolled and allowed gravity to suck him out of range of the shotgun blasts. He'd landed in the dirt, rain pummelling him, with his brain trying to play catch up with the chaos erupting around him. The shotgun's boom contested with the sharper crack of Hunter's SIG, and then a third gun had joined the fight. Somehow, Mercer had commanded his hand to grab his pistol and he'd dragged it out, but his hand was shaking so wildly he couldn't have hit an elephant standing twenty feet away side-on to him, let alone kill the elusive attacker over by the parking garage.

Mercer had done what he thought best.

He crawled under the porch into the domain of spider webs and windblown litter. No sooner had he gotten under cover than Hunter thumped in a graceless heap on the ground a few yards away. His first thought was that Hunter had been gunned down, but then the Englishman was butt crawling away with his pistol raised between his knees. That sumbitch by the garage shot at him again, and then Mercer's attention was snatched away by the roar of an approaching vehicle. The big car came to a juddering halt and doors were thrown open. From his position Mercer had no idea how many gunmen got out, but even one was one too many. He squirmed back deeper into the crawlspace under the deck until the brick foundations of the house stopped him. Nobody but the guy by the garage could know where he was, and judging by the gunshots being exchanged, he was in a contest with Hunter. For the time being Mercer was out of mind and out of sight, and that was the best he could hope for. Adrenalin had replaced the ache in his ribs with a wave of nausea, and he fought it. Equally he fought the shaking in his hands, because he understood it was his neurological impediment causing the shake and not fear itself. He'd hidden, yes, but not out of cowardice. He fully intended taking the fight back to their attackers once he had some control of his goddamn shooting hand.

Things escalated rapidly.

Assault rifles began to join the fray, and the shotgun laid down a steady backbeat. A pistol fired from further off and Mercer was glad that Rink had survived the first encounter…funny, he thought, how once over he'd wished for the direst end for Jared Rington, and yet now he was cheering him on. Misery, he'd heard, acquaints a man with strange bedfellows.

From inside the house the shotgun continued booming. Hunter's pistol replied. Another boom was accompanied by shattering glass. Mercer felt things sifting down on him, and heard the echo of a door being barged open. It sounded as if Hunter was determined to come to close quarters with the shotgun man. The SIG made a drumroll of three shots and then silence followed. Actually, it was anything but silent, because the rain fell harder and formed an angry buzz of white noise. Drips off the porch found their way between the boards and struck Mercer's face. He shook his head to clear his vision, and understood again that his eyes were juddering uncontrollably. Of all the times for his eyesight to fail him—

From only a few feet behind him the shotgun boomed several times. At first he feared Hunter had failed to kill the gunner, but who then was shooting out through the living room window now? A pained curse drifted from near the newly arrived car, and Mercer gave a silent cheer: Hunter had liberated the big gun. His cheer was short-lived. Assault rifles let loose on the house, and even deep under the porch Mercer wasn't safe. He cringed as ricochets plowed through the planks on each side of him. He squirmed onto his back, holding his gun tight to his sternum, trying to pinpoint a target, but the rain coming off the deck was like a waterfall.

The barrage of gunfire on the house was too much for Hunter to contend with. His shotgun fell silent, and after a few more bursts from the assault rifles so did they. Mercer eyes were open again, and he could see clearly. He watched somebody race forward and hop up onto the deck. It had happened too fast for him to target, let alone shoot the feet out from under the attacker. A voice begged a question, and the tumult of rain made it too difficult to hear the words, but Mercer thought the gunman was on a radio, coordinating with another. The first man crept along the porch, and Mercer noted a change in shadow play as the man tread slowly along the porch. The guy came to a halt directly overhead. Mercer held his breath for fear he'd give away his hiding spot. There was more indistinguishable whispering, but it was obvious a trap was about to be sprung.

Boom!

The shotgun blasted somebody to hell, and then the house rumbled as — Mercer assumed — Hunter scrambled to a new position. Again a door was kicked in, and Hunter blasted away at the home invader, and directly above Mercer, the first gunman swung around the window frame to cut Hunter apart. Mercer couldn't hit an elephant twenty feet away but there was no missing the man standing directly over him. With his gun butt jammed against his chest, he fired repeatedly, and heard the drumming of boots as the man's legs and groin were torn to pieces. Hunter served the coup de grace and knocked the gunman flying off the porch. Mercer peered between his feet at where the gunman lay. The corpse steamed in the bucketing downfall. Mercer grinned rictus-like at his handiwork feeling not altogether useless for a change. Again his reason to be happy was short-lived: a grenade detonated and the concussion almost burst his eardrums and he barely heard the collapsing of the wall behind him. Boards tumbled on him, pounding him.

42

That lucky son of a gun has more lives than a goddamn cat, thought Vince as Joe Hunter took down Jason Mercer in a flying tackle that saved them both from the blast of 12 gauge buckshot. Vince, more bemused than disappointed at Hunter's seeming invulnerability, watched as Hunter avoided several more attempts on his life until he tumbled off the porch and came under fire from David Paulson. It looked as if Paulson winged him, getting Hunter in a leg, but unsurprisingly to Vince it also galvanised Hunter into seek-and-destroy mode. As Hunter disappeared around the far side of the house, Vince adjusted his binoculars, scanning for what had become of Hunter's pals. Rink had darted along the porch and hurdled the railing, and must have gone to ground out in the taller, coarse grass at the edge of the grounds, where it met the untamed wilderness next to the Apalachicola River. Mercer had also disappeared in the time that he'd concentrated his binocs on Hunter, but couldn't have gotten far.

Vince licked his lips in thought, then keyed his throat mike. 'Bravo team. Move in. Pin those bastards down.'

'Copy that,' came the reply.

The sound of a revving engine heralded the approach of the second three-man team. Vince didn't hang about until the reserves were in place. He rose up from concealment where he'd set up between the V formed of some tree trunks a hundred yards away from the house. As Bravo team roared into battle, he used the distraction to jog from his hiding place to the longer grass to the right of the house. Rink was out there somewhere, and a danger to Vince, but he was confident the man was currently trying to find an advantageous position and wouldn't have spotted him approaching through the pummeling rain. Besides, Vince had another of his Alpha team set up out there, and Rink would be kept too busy to contend with Vince too. Vince lowered to one knee, so that the tall grass mostly concealed him. Bravo team had arrived and was getting in position.

Inside the house, the shotgunner was trying to make up for the failed ambush by blasting out windows and walls. These were the best hired guns that Paulson could rustle up? Up until now Vince was unimpressed. When all was said and done, it didn't really matter to him how the battle was fought, only that he was the ultimate victor. Slightly irksome was the fact the gunner had waited a second too long before shooting, and the fool must have given some kind of warning to his prey as they stood in a bunch outside the door: had things gone to plan, that first shot should have at least taken out one of them, and perhaps disabled the others. It would've been a simple task to then move in and mop up the others, but now Vince had a full-on siege to contend with. He wasn't put off by the thought of a prolonged battle, and now that a lightning storm had blown over them, he was happy that their gunshots would be confused with thunder and go unreported.

'Paulson,' he said into his mike, 'what's going on back there?'

Paulson came back: 'Hunter's inside, I think he's taken Durrell out. I'm getting no reply.'

Harry Durrell was the shotgun man. Yeah, Vince thought, because he'd heard the volleys of competing shots ringing out, and the last to be heard had been from a pistol. Durrell was down and out of the game.

'Have you got eyes on Hunter?'

'Negative.'

'So what are you waiting for?'

'He needs softening up first,' said Paulson.

From somewhere nearby came pistol fire, answered immediately by an assault rifle, causing Vince to duck lower. Rink had engaged the gunman out in the tall grass. He would prefer to be the one to end Rink's life, but he'd be a bonus prize at most, while Hunter was the trophy he really wanted. He might yet get to kill Rink. If he were a betting man he'd still place Rink with a pistol at higher odds than a punk with a carbine. No, he shouldn't think like that. In the past he'd paid Hunter and Rink far too much respect, and doing so had been to their advantage. There'd be no more looking up to those old timers, and no pity shown either. He'd come here to kill them, and must focus on that alone.

A shotgun boomed repeatedly from within the house. Durrell wasn't the one to pull the trigger. The target was the SUV that a couple of Bravo team sheltered behind. He heard one of them curse in pain, obviously hit, but still in the game.

The Fourth Option

'Light him up boys,' Vince commanded.

Two carbine's let loose on the house, the bullets shredding the walls and what remained of the windows, and probably everything else within. From their earlier recce of the house, after Durrell's forced entry of the front door lock, they'd discovered the home largely devoid of furniture, only a sunken old couch, a few bedrolls in the bedrooms, clothing and sundry belongings in various others. There was nowhere Hunter could hide from the flying bullets, to which the wooden walls would prove little impediment. Vince was happy to see that the two gunners had the sense to target the house from one end to the other, ensuring there was no hiding place. The third man, the one wounded by Hunter, joined in, and emptied an entire magazine through the front window in a single sustained pull on his trigger.

There was a lull in the fighting, if not the storm.

In his earpiece, Vince heard Paulson ask for a situation report from Allonby: Allonby was the guy that had engaged Rink. His negative response probably meant that the odds Vince gave him against winning had proven true, or maybe that he'd killed Rink with his dying shots. There was no sign or sounds of life out in the long grass, only the constant susurration of water through the tall blades.

Neither was there any hint of life from inside the house.

Vince ordered Paulson to check, while also instructing the nearest member of Bravo team to move in to cover him.

He could detect the uncertainty in Paulson's response.

'What are you waitin' for, man? I thought you wanted revenge on these motherfuckers?' said Vince.

'I do, these fuckers killed my baby sister, and I want to see them all dead. But not at the expense of my own life,' replied Paulson.

It was the reason why Vince had sought David Paulson out. The ex CIA agent, and now private contractor, might not share a family name with Pamela Patrick, but he shared a birth mother. In the years before Arrowsake had disavowed Vince, he'd worked alongside numerous assets and had built a network of contacts in and outside of the organisation. He had discovered that Pam Patrick, the female operator killed by Hunter's sniper at the hostage exchange, and also wounded and beaten by the man himself during the assault on the Mexico Beach hotel, had an older brother she also contracted to on mercenary jobs. Vince had played on Paulson's desire to avenge his murdered sister, encouraging the man to pull in several of his assets to assist in killing their mutual enemies. Through his contacts in Langley, Paulson had learned of plans to deliver, on Walter Hayes Conrad's instruction, a secret package to a boat in Port St. Joe, scheduled — it was whispered — for a burial at sea. Langley, supposedly a place of secrets was also a place of human beings, most of whom suffered human traits: gossip and speculation was as rife there as anywhere else people gathered around the water cooler. Some further digging, and well-placed bribes, had discovered this ranch as a likely hideout of Joe Hunter and his merry men. It was a handy staging post from where Hunter, Rink and Mercer could leave from to attend the secret burial of Sue Bouchard. Initially Paulson had planned assaulting them at dockside, but Vince had argued that the remote ranch was a far more suitable battleground, where there was little fear of involvement from local law enforcement officers. Paulson's team had conducted surveillance on the ranch, confirming it was where their enemies were in hiding, and once they left the farm that morning for the funeral, had moved in to launch the ambush on their return. Despite losing Durrell and probably Allonby too, the plan hadn't been a complete bust. To all intents and purposes Rink was out of the fight, Hunter was down for good, and Mercer was barely an afterthought.

Vince asked Paulson: 'Who could have survived that shit storm we just laid on him? Take a quick look, confirm he's down and we'll go in together and finish him off.'

'You'll back me up?'

'Of course, man. I wanna be there to see the light go out of his eyes.'

Vince ordered the two backmost gunners to cover, and waved the nearest to approach the broken window along the porch.

'I'm on my way. What do you see, Paulson?' Vince said as he slipped around the side of the house.

'Nothing. Wait one, I'll take another look.'

Boom!

Paulson said no more, and it was obvious why.

Vince had to reappraise his earlier summation of Hunter. The lucky son of a gun had more lives than a clowder of goddamn cats!

Not to worry. Vince was still intent on proving his mettle, and finishing Hunter once and for all: he was armed with something that'd challenge a god's immortality. He spotted Paulson's corpse slumped under the furthest window away. There was little left of Paulson's ferret face. Vince had no intention of ending up blasted at close range too. He sought entrance via the safety of the kitchen door, presuming Hunter was still in the same room he'd shot Paulson from. He told the gunner at the front to get ready to shoot and then he kicked open the door and lunged inside, his gun up and ready. He spotted and instantly ignored Durrell who was splayed on his back at the centre of the kitchen.

He could hear the faint scrape of somebody shuffling in the adjacent room.

Through his mike, he said to the gunman on the porch, 'I'll draw his fire, you shoot that fucker.'

'Copy that,' said the gunman.

Vince was about to stick his hand out round the door and fire a few random shots into the living room, but Hunter beat him to it. Buckshot tore through the wall into the kitchen, each shot closer to Vince, who was forced to duck, then go to his knees to avoid them. There was a series of gunshots, lighter fire than from a carbine, and Vince assumed his plan to catch Hunter in a pincer movement had failed. Bits of tiles and splinters of wood dusted his back, as he returned to his feet. He shoved his pistol in its holster, and reached instead

The Fourth Option

for his belt. Unclipping a grenade and pulling the pin in one swift movement, he peeked around the doorframe and instantly spotted his foe scrambling away across the floor. Hunter had nowhere to go, nowhere to hide.

'Survive *this*, Golden Boy,' he crowed as he tossed the grenade into the room, then ran and took a flying leap out of the back door.

__43__

The device Vince tossed at me was probably an M67 fragmentation grenade, packed with six and a half ounces of explosive. Its effective injury radius was about fifty feet; anyone within fifteen feet would be literally torn to ribbons by the flying shrapnel. I was about ten feet from where it hit the floor and rolled. Its detonation mechanism was most likely fitted with a pyrotechnic delay fuse, meaning my life expectancy was no longer than four or five seconds.

All of this I mention in retrospect, because at the time I wasn't thinking much beyond saving my arse. As soon as the grenade was in flight I rose up and launched towards the only escape route I could. The front door was still shut, and worse, it opened inwards, but it was my only possible egress. The first shotgun blasts had smashed holes in it, and the withering rain of bullets from the assault team's carbines had cut more holes through it. I threw aside the shotgun and hit it with a rounded shoulder, my elbows tucked tight around my head. At much the same instant the grenade detonated, and I went through the wooden barrier with a headful of nothing, trailing smoke and blood as I rode the concussive blast over the porch and onto the ground beyond.

I've no idea if I rolled once or maybe several times before I came to a halt, huddled in a ball and feeling as if I'd just gone ten rounds with Godzilla. My ears were ringing so hard I could hear nothing, and couldn't

The Fourth Option

think straight. I had no idea I was partly buried beneath debris blown out from the front wall and roof of the house, or that behind me the porch's deck had partly collapsed. I was completely unaware that two enemy gunmen armed with assault rifles were very close by, but who had for now taken cover behind the cars. Frag grenades can hurl shrapnel more than eight hundred feet, so it was possible some of the flying shards had come down around them.

Some cognizance came into my mind, and it was in the sense of pain. My left scapula felt as if it was on fire, and my leg, already in flames from the earlier gunshot throbbed with fresh agony. I'd not been fully spared the grenade's fury, but I welcomed the sensation of pain: it confirmed I was still alive. I unfurled, groaning in anticipation of further misery, but for now my beaten body couldn't hurt any more than it did. Pushing to my knees, I shed some of the detritus off my back, and then had to crawl forward on my palms through the mud to free my left leg from under something heavier. Shaking my head to clear it, I spat saliva on the ground, and was happy to find it wasn't bloody, so flying shrapnel hadn't pierced my lungs. I stood on wobbly legs, stretching out the muscles around my shoulder blade and felt a ripping sensation. The smaller intercostal muscles between my ribs contracted in protest.

Everything around me was blurry. It took a moment after lucidity returned to my vision for me to remember that it was bucketing down. I exhaled a heavy breath, and pulled in another whether my ribcage wanted me to or not. I was about to turn, to survey the wreckage of the ranch, when reality returned with a start. My ears must have popped, reacclimatizing to the air pressure, and the sounds of the storm returned. My attention snapped on different sounds; the two surviving gunmen had risen up, aiming their carbines at me. One of them glared daggers at me, and I took it he was the man whose foot I'd hit earlier. For a reason unknown to me yet, they both held fire, even though I was at their mercy. I caught where they aimed quick glances and tried to turn.

Vince's guitar string garrote dropped over my head, and instantly cinched tightly around my throat.

'Good-fucking-goddamn,' Vince snapped in my ear, 'if nothing else will kill you, let's go with the tried and tested method!'

He reared backwards, pulling apart his crossed hands so that the wire cut instantly into me. The only thing saving me from decapitation was that I'd reacted a second before he tightened the noose, shooting my left fist against the side of my neck and craning my head the other direction. The wire sliced into my fist and jaw, sparing my neck from being opened up. However you looked at it, I was still in a dire situation and it could only get worse. I was still weakened by my near death experience with the grenade and in no fit state to fight back, but instinct took over. I grabbed his testicles and squeezed.

Vince mewled in pain, but wouldn't relinquish his hold, but I'd forced him to bend his knees so I wasn't craned over backwards. I released his balls. Before he

The Fourth Option

could crank my spine once more, I threw my backside into his thighs and bent forward, pulling him off his feet. I swung my upper body, and Vince was carried with me, the centrifugal force throwing out his legs. My chin was sliced to the bone, an open gash that poured blood, but by swinging him off his feet I'd gained some slack. His wrists were no longer crossed, and before he could throttle me again he'd have to jostle for position.

I didn't allow him to find his footing, instead ramming my right shoulder into him and bearing him backwards at a run. I hoped to smash him against the Ford's hood, but long before we reached the car we both slipped in the mud and went down. Thankfully, for me, I was on top, and more or less facing Vince, so he no longer had the capacity to cut off my head. We kicked and rolled to the side, with Vince trying his damndest to keep me rolling so that he could get astride my back and finish the job. My left fist was still trapped, my right wasn't. I pounded him in the jaw. He gritted his teeth around an almost hysterical titter, while trying to readjust his grip. A few inches more and he'd once again have my throat encircled with the wire.

Desperation called for desperate measures. As cheap a shot as it was, I didn't care. I lunged in with my teeth and snapped down on his face. I bit deep, chewing down on the fattest part of his narrow cheek. Vince howled in abject agony, and perhaps a little terror at the further disfiguring of his features begun when Mercer shot off a chunk of his ear.

My unconventional defence forced him to drop one end of his garrote in order to insert a hand between us, to pry my teeth off him. The wire unfurled, so I released my bite and went with the roll he'd tried to force me into earlier. The mud and beating rain made getting any balance difficult, but I found space and kicked at Vince with my right heel. There was little force generated by my injured leg, but enough to shove him away for now. I came up onto my knees, facing him as he also scrambled to get his knees under him. He clamped one palm over the painful wound in his face: to my regret I hadn't torn a chunk of flesh out, but he'd carry the imprint of my teeth for the rest of his days. If he survived our battle, that was.

On our knees we faced off.

'What the fuck do you call *this*, Hunter?' He jabbed a finger at where my incisors had met in his flesh. 'Fucking biting like an animal? Grabbing my balls? That's some dirty, sneaky shit right there!'

'No dirtier or sneakier than trying to cut off my head with a cheese wire,' I snarled.

The two gunmen had observed our tussle, and had moved into the clear to get a better shot at me after we spilled apart. I faced them, wondering if I could reach for the SIG I'd tucked down the back of my belt, draw it and shoot them both before their bullets tore me apart. I'd already denied the Grim Reaper twice in the past few minutes, and didn't believe I'd make it a third time. I held out my palms to show I was no threat to them, blood dripped from the back of my gashed left hand. It was also running hot and freely from the wound in my jaw, pooling in the hollows of my collarbones. I probably looked less threatening than I did pathetic.

Vince struggled to his feet. He'd done away with his rockabilly look, and was dressed similarly to our other attackers, in paramilitary garb. He wore an antiballistic vest, and an equipment belt, on which was holstered a pistol, and another grenade. If he decided to use either weapon on me I would die, no question. I pushed to my feet, furling my fingers at him.

'We should finish this man to man,' I said.

'We should. You've fucked me over for the last time, man.'

'When did I ever fuck you over?' I asked, genuinely perplexed.

'When you broke your word at the hostage exchange and didn't hand Mercer over.'

'Oh, you mean when I had my pal shoot your snipers. Who planned fucking over whom, Vince? None of us were ever meant to leave that place alive, were we? Your guys were ordered to gun us down the second you had Mercer in your hands.'

'You think I'd have had you murdered in cold blood? Joe, man, it's me Vince you're talking to. We go back a long ways, we're old pals.'

'We were never pals, we only worked for the same man.'

'It's another reason we have to finish this,' he said, morose for a second. I thought I even read sorrow in his eyes. 'You turned Walter against me, man, when all I wanted was to make him happy. I did everything I could to please him, but my best was never enough. He chose you over me; do you know that? Yeah, of course you know it. After everything I did for him he still had Arrowsake burn me, and make *me* the hunted man.'

'So this here's about revenge?'

'What else?'

'Jason Mercer?'

'I could give two craps about Jason Mercer. He was a contract, man, and it ended for me the second Arrowsake cut my strings.'

'Then it's totally personal, between you and me?'

He nodded.

'So tell your boys to stand down. They don't have to die today.'

'Whaddaya mean?' It had perhaps slipped his mind that his two gunners still stood ready with their assault rifles aimed at my chest. Vince graced his men with a pained grin. 'Do you believe this joker? He's such a hot shit, he actually thinks he's going to defeat us all'

They laughed with him. The one whose foot I injured looked ready to tear me a new one right that instant.

'You were warned,' I said.

They sneered at my words, unaware that another figure had materialised out of the teeming rain behind them. I'd rarely been happier to see Rink in my life.

He could've spared them, but he still burned to avenge Sue's murder. Rink gave no warning, he gunned down both of the hired killers without remorse, using a carbine he'd liberated from another of their murderous number.

The Fourth Option

Startled, Vince wasted a few seconds, first watching his gunmen collapse in the dirt, then turning to face Rink, and then going for his holstered pistol.

'Don't be stupid,' Rink told him, and aimed the smoking muzzle of his assault rifle at Vince's chest: even wearing a bulletproof vest, he wouldn't survive a hail of rounds at close quarters.

'Twice now you've had goes at killing me with your weapon of choice,' I said, drawing Vince around to face me. 'Now it's my turn to kill you.'

'Are you really going to have Rink shoot me in cold blood, Hunter? Nah, you're a better man than that, right?'

'You're right. I'm not going to have Rink do my dirty work for me. Trust me, he'd happily blow you away after what happened to Sue. I warned you *I'd* shoot you in the face if you hurt Sue. But here's the thing, Vince. I'm going to give you a chance. You've a gun on your hip. Draw it.'

'D'you think I'm crazy? Even if I beat you to the draw, Rink will shoot me.' Vince kept his right hand well away from his holstered weapon; the left hand though was on the move.

'Rink,' I said, 'you'd better get back.'

Vince snapped the second grenade off his belt, deftly pulling out the pin with the opposite hand. He held up the grenade as if it were something to be admired. He peered at me with a triumphant grin. 'Try shooting me now and I'll blow us all to hell.' Vince performed one of those crazy pirouettes of his, spinning on a heel in the mud, threatening us both with evisceration.

'C'mon, you guys. Go for it. Shoot me if you dare, but then I'll let go of this and…BADOOM!'

Rink began backing away, staring back at me. I gave a surreptitious nod: I've got this, brother.

Our ploy to defeat Arrowsake had employed a metaphorical dead man's switch; perhaps it was ironic that Vince should employ a real one here.

I snatched the gun from my belt, aimed and fired, even as realisation struck Vince that his bluff was a complete failure. He tried to hurl the grenade at me but couldn't, not when my bullet had struck between his eyes and killed him. The grenade tumbled out of his hand and fell to the ground. He folded and then toppled forward.

Ten feet separated us, so I was in range of the explosion. But I also had about four seconds grace on my side. I was unsteady on a damaged leg, but it didn't slow me as I spun and charged away. Rink hightailed it for the cover of the cars. Five paces further on I took a dive into the dirt, and the bomb went off. The explosion didn't sound half as loud as the one in the house had, but then Vince had helped muffle it. He'd fallen atop the grenade, and pressed it into the mud beneath his armoured torso. Still, bits of him rained down on me while I lay in the dirt.

44

The rain stopped as abruptly as it had begun. Over our heads the clouds still boiled, all manner of shades of grey, purple and yellow, and lightning flickered through them, though soundless now. It was a fitting backdrop for the demolished house, a hellish reminder of what we'd all just gone through. The grenade that blew apart Vince had caused little collateral damage, the one that had gone off inside was another story entirely. It had blown out what had remained of the living room window, security bars and all, plus a large portion of the wooden wall alongside the front door. Some of the roof had come down, and scattered shingles for dozens of feet in front of the porch. Even the deck was buckled and had collapsed nearest the obliterated wall. There was little left of the door I'd plunged through. The rest of the visible structure was punctured and pocked by bullet holes. Rain had overflowed some of the gutters and caused little waterfalls to splash on the floor.

I sat on my arse in the mud, staring at the house. The latest events in my life had begun with a wrecked house and were ending with another.

'I still think you should give some thought to moving here,' said Rink, 'you might get the place cheaper now that it's a fixer-upper.'

He stood alongside me, cradling the carbine. We were both confident that the threat to our lives had ended with Vince's death, but it paid to be vigilant. It was a pity we hadn't been more astute on our return to the ranch — perhaps even in the days beforehand when Vince's team must first have found us — but then we hadn't been as sharp, thinking our own personal thoughts of how we'd honour Sue's memory.

'Do you think the fridge survived the fight?' I asked. 'I could drink one of those beers now.'

'You might be in need of somethin' a bit stronger, brother,' said Rink. 'You do know there's a lump of metal stickin' outta your back, right?'

I craned over my shoulder for a look, but it was too painful, the deep cut on my jaw stung like hell. 'Pull it out for me, will you?'

'Not yet, or you'll be pissin' blood all over the place.'

I grunted in mirth. My shirt and trousers were so sodden it looked as if I'd taken a communal dip with Countess Elizabeth Báthory. 'Bit late to worry about that now.'

'Seriously, Hunter, I ain't pullin' that out til I know you won't bleed to death.'

'Forget my back for now then. How's my face looking?'

'Ugly as ever.' He tapped the old scar on his chin. 'Don't worry about that on your jaw, I've cut myself worse shavin'. Besides, y'know girls love guys with scars, right?'

'My arse.'

'It's true.'

'No, I mean my arse is killing me. I think I might have some shrapnel stuck in it too.'

The Fourth Option

'I ain't pullin' that out either.'

'I'm not asking you to give it the kiss of life.'

Rink guffawed.

'Help me up?' I extended my hand.

'Gimme the other one,' he said, 'that hand looks cut worse than anywhere. Can you still move your fingers?'

'Only this one,' I said, extending the middle finger and flipping him the bird.

We were both laughing as he helped haul me, grunting and moaning, to my feet. Laughter is not only the best medicine; it can also help you refrain from crying.

'Gee, Hunter, you're a damn wreck.'

'Yeah, well I just got blown out of a house by a frag grenade,' I reminded him. Actually, the wall the grenade came to rest against had taken most of the brunt of the explosion, dispelling some of the blast upwards towards the roof, and also out of the broken window. I'd only been tickled by the explosion as I'd smashed out the door, not been engulfed by it, so had gotten off with a few bits of shrapnel in my flesh rather than having my limbs blown off altogether. My words caused Rink to turn and squint at the mushy red remains of Vince further out in the yard.

'Man,' he wheezed. 'I never liked that frog-gigger, and he needed killing, but I wouldn't've wished that on him.'

I avoided looking. Vince had become an enemy, and I had no option but to shoot him, but blowing him to smithereens was extreme, and not something usually in my playbook.

'Where's Mercer?' I asked.

'No idea,' said Rink, with a nod towards the long grass, 'I was too busy fighting an armed guy back there to look out for him.'

It occurred how the gunman set to shoot me had performed a crazy dance just prior to me blasting him off the porch, and understood who had caused his jig. Mercer must have taken shelter under the deck, and shot the man through the planks, undoubtedly saving my life. He must have been lying close to where the grenade detonated.

'Shit, I think he's buried under there—' I took a step towards the decking and the strength in my knees failed. Rink grabbed me one-handed, helping me to sink down safely.

'Let me check on him,' he said.

As Rink approached, there was a clatter and movement at the front of the deck. Some splintered planks and fallen shingles were shoved aside and a hand extended out. 'Guys, I could do with a hand here?'

Rink crouched, pulling aside more of the wreckage, until he could see Mercer blinking up at him through a layer of brick dust and splinters. Rink appraised him with a flash of teeth.

'Boy, am I pleased to see you,' said Mercer. It was possibly the first time since Rink shot him that he genuinely meant it.

What happened next, I've no idea. I passed clean out from blood loss.

45

Rink tapped the base of his beer bottle against mine.

'Cheers, brother,' he toasted.

'Skol,' I responded, as if we were a couple of Vikings.

We sat companionably on his balcony, overlooking the communal gardens at the rear of his condominium at Temple Terrace, a neighbourhood in Tampa, while we supped our drinks.

With no replacement house of my own sorted yet, I was still calling the couch in Rink's condo home. I'd used it for several days since checking out of the military hospital to where I'd been medevacked by a chopper hailed via Walter when it became apparent I was injured worse than I'd first let on. It wasn't the shrapnel in my back or butt that was my main problem, or the wounds from Vince's garrote; it was the bullet hole in my leg that had severed a vein and drained me of pints of blood. I'd been transfused, stitched up, and given meds to stave off infection and pain, but the forty-eight hours of solid sleep afterwards had equally worked their magic on me.

Jason Mercer had also received attention for his injuries, but there were miraculously few new ones considering he'd been buried beneath the collapsing deck and walls. He checked out of the hospital a day before I did, but did me the courtesy of hanging around to say goodbye, for now, before he planned on disappearing back into the underground network set up by Sue. Only the indomitable brute that was Jared Rington had survived the latest fight without as much as a scratch.

Rink had collected me from the hospital and delivered me back to Tampa, and I hadn't moved beyond the condo's confines since. I sat with my leg elevated on the railing, easing my injury, but ironically it wasn't troubling me. For all I'd been shot at numerous times, survived a car crash, been blown up, beaten and garroted, the only pain bothering me was the throbbing of my ear. It was a hold over from when Sue had punched me when I'd disturbed her flight from the house in Panama City: the pain was probably psychosomatic.

We were holding the wake for her that had been disrupted by Vince's final assault, but we did it lost primarily in our own thoughts. Sometimes it's enough to have your best pal beside you without having to say a single word.

We had reason to celebrate our recent victories. Vince was dead and wouldn't trouble any of our friends or us in the future. Arrowsake was already showing signs of implosion, with Walter reporting how several of the key players had already withdrawn and were eager to distance themselves from the organisation. His prophesy had come true, including how Spencer Booth's sudden disappearance would be explained: the story was that the former ASD(I) and his security detail had reputedly perished when Booth's chauffer-driven limousine broadsided a gas tanker and all three men were immolated in the resulting fire. As for all the other remains left in our wake, including those most recently at the ranch, they disappeared without a trace and without fanfare.

For now we were safe from attack and prosecution, and that would do.

Honouring the truce we'd struck with Arrowsake, Walter kept the evidence dossier he held buried, but those with Harvey and Velasquez were kept safely on stand-by should our agreement ever crumble. Walter had severed his ties with Arrowsake, and he'd also tendered his resignation with the Central Intelligence Agency. He was old now, he said, and wanted to spend at least a few years in retirement enjoying his granddaughter and great grandson without having to worry about any more enemies. He half-jokingly suggested engaging Jason Mercer's services to help him disappear into Sue's network of safe houses to live out his golden years, but the old fart wasn't fooling us, because he could never retire – he was thinking how he could use the network to his benefit, but in another way entirely. See, he wasn't letting on, but I just knew that having withdrawn his funding from Arrowsake, multi-billionaire playboy Wyatt Carling had been tapped by Walter to fund a new enterprise…Arrowsake, under a new guise and new leader might rise again.

Author's Note

In October of 2018 I was sitting at home relaxing in front of the TV when I was struck by the news that Hurricane Michael had made landfall in the Florida panhandle and devastated the city of Mexico Beach. I admit that my first thought was, 'Oh no, where's Joe Hunter going to live now?' For a number of years I've given Hunter a home beside the sea in Mexico Beach, and now his beach house was gone, along with huge portions of the city. Hunter is a fictional character, but being his chronicler, to me he is a living, breathing person that resides not only in my head but also out there on the Gulf coast. I was horrified by the destruction wrought upon Hunter and his friends and neighbours by the hurricane, and that of course extended to the genuine inhabitants whose homes and livelihoods had been devastated. For some years, Hunter has been feeling restless, wondering where he really belongs, and as horrible as the aftermath of the storm was, it gave me a reason to move him forward. Hunter couldn't just walk away though; he had become a part of his community and wished to assist with its recovery. It is a reason why I set a large part of this tale in and around his hometown post Hurricane Michael, as Hunter would be deeply affected by this traumatic event, and would want to help. I hope I have been respectful to its genuine inhabitants in doing so. I have used locations and premises fictionally, and invented others for the purpose of the story, but have tried to show the true ex-

The Fourth Option

tent of suffering the people of Mexico Beach must have endured during the hurricane and in the aftermath. I do not want what I've written to trivialize the disaster and hope the good people of Mexico Beach will grant me the liberties I took to tell what I believe is an important part of Hunter's story. My heart, and my best wishes for a speedy rebuild and recovery, go out to all those affected by Hurricane Michael.

About The Author

Matt Hilton quit his career as a police constable to pursue his love of writing tight, cinematic action thrillers and has now published thirty books. He is best known as the author of the high-octane Joe Hunter thriller series, and the Tess Grey and Nicolas 'Po' Villere thriller series. His first book, Dead Men's Dust, was shortlisted for the International Thriller Writers' Debut Book of 2009 Award, and was a Sunday Times bestseller, also being named as a 'thriller of the year 2009' by The Daily Telegraph, and has been an eBook bestseller on several occasions since. Hilton also writes books in the horror and crime fiction genres.

He is a high-ranking martial artist and has been a detective and private security specialist, all of which lend an authenticity to the action scenes in his books.

He currently resides in Cumbria in northern England, with his wife Denise, and two dogs, Spooky and Akisha.

The Fourth Option

Other books by the author:

Joe Hunter thriller series:

Dead Men's Dust
Judgement and Wrath
Slash and Burn
Cut and Run
Blood and Ashes
Dead Men's Harvest
No Going Back
Rules of Honour
The Lawless Kind
The Devil's Anvil
No Safe Place
Marked For Death
The Fourth Option

Tess Grey and Nicolas "Po" Villere thriller series

Blood Tracks
Painted Skins
Raw Wounds
Worst Fear
False Move
Rough Justice
Collision Course
Blood Kin

Kerry Darke thriller series

Darke

Horror/Sci-Fi/Fantasy novels:

Dominion
Darkest Hour
Preternatural
The Shadows Call
Mark Darrow and the Stealer of Souls
The Phoenix Man
Wildfire

Printed in Great Britain
by Amazon